# COLD DRESSES

## DEATH COMES CLOAKED IN LIES.

## DAVID PELLETIER

HURN
PUBLICATIONS

*Until they become conscious they will never rebel, and only after they have rebelled they cannot become conscious* – George Orwell, 1984

# PROLOGUE

Her dress is the colour of teal. She lies on the hood of a car, flecked by a thousand shards of glass. Wet blonde hair fanned out, limbs splayed, face bruised and smeared with blood. For a few desperate seconds, she wants to believe this is all a bad dream. She wants to look at someone else, to be alive again and sit snug in the warmth of her home, away from the rain and the soggy road. Twelve feet above, she floats as pale and translucent as a moon. Weightless.

*Please,* she begs.

White shadows swim around her, they fade in and out, move their mouths, call her name. She shakes her head no because she's not sure she can face it. Someone else needs to know, the deceit, the fear, and the lies.

The control.

She sees the tail of headlights in the distance, two red eyes fading into the dark. She should never have trusted her.

*Never.*

Something radiates through the dress. A glow, a light. A pulsing energy seeps through the weave. She can almost taste it, like a breath, pumping through the lines of the silk, the dark teal blue rising and dipping in cold folds.

# 1

The counter was chipped, finger-stained, and tatty. I pushed my coins across to the clerk and grabbed my supplies for the day: a pack of mint gum, a tin of coffee beans, and a carton of milk. Low fat, with a black-and-white drawing of a skinny cow.

My journey back home was only a short walk down Goswell Street, Chertsey, in Surrey. Two dull rows of Victorian brickwork livened up by house signs and snippets of daily life. Dwellings populated by retirees and young-ish professionals that were mostly parents priced out of London. At twenty-six, single and jobless, I could see for myself that I didn't fit the local profile.

A mother wheeled out a double buggy with twin toddlers through the door of number 20, followed by a spaniel yapping at her heels. Wheels again at number 27, on the opposite side where an old lady shuffled half steps with the help of a Zimmer frame. The washing machine at number 36 changed pitch as it drummed into its spinning cycle.

When I reached number 48, I caught a strange sight. There was a smudge between the two rows of house roofs. A band of clear blue sky marred by a curious shape. Grey like a wisp of cigarette smoke, fluid and fast. Growing in size as it swooped down into a dive.

I slowed to a stop, held up my free hand to shade my eyes and blinked. Beautiful sunshine, taintless sky—almost. It looked so surreal I wondered if I was hallucinating. Surely I could only be gazing at . . .

A cloud?

A *diving* cloud?

Not that I'd heard of such a thing before. I couldn't remember much of my GCSE science classes, a decade old and marred by the memory of doodles and boredom. But I knew in my gut this wasn't just a cloud.

*Relax, Chloe. Take a deep breath.*

I gulped air, trying to dislodge the knot of anxiety forming in my chest. My mother used to chide me for telling strange stories when I was a child; I couldn't help it. I caught sight of things that she never seemed to see, sensed lives that slipped unnoticed before her eyes.

Before all eyes.

I gazed up once more at the sky.

*Dive, dive, dive. Low, low, low. Close, close, close.*

Too close.

The tightness in my chest wouldn't go away. It couldn't, because there was something else, a sudden change. A very *odd* change. A morphing from fluid to solid, from grey to colour, and the result: a square of light pulsing teal blue. I watched it alight in the distance, a hundred yards away from me, and then, in the blink of an eye, it was gone, vanished from view.

I lived in number 92 Flat B. It was the only house in Goswell Street to have been turned into flats—five rental one-beds, self-contained, dingy and dated. Only two of them were filled. The outside looked no better: a rather joyless parody of Halloween with a creaky old bench on which sat a headless gnome; sticky spider webs swathed around the walls of the front porch – though the sight of it was obscured by someone. Standing between me and home was a familiar shape, a woman, her back turned to me, and I paused in my steps to stare at her. It was my next-door neighbour at number 90: buxomed, nosy Mrs Ward, who I caught peering greedily towards my front door. Six months in Goswell Street had taught me to beware of Mrs Ward. But for now, something in her behaviour struck me as odd.

She began to bend at the waist over our shared side fence, one leg raised in the air, a wooden clog dangling off her toes. The rest of her I couldn't see, but I could picture the tangled fall of her grey hair hovering beside my ground-floor sash window, where the curtains of my living room were drawn tightly shut.

A wave of unease washed over me. I still couldn't make sense of that shape-shifting, light-pulsing, diving cloud. It sounded so absurd, but I couldn't make sense of Mrs Ward's silly acrobatics either. My ears were attuned to the sounds that came out of her mouth: a shriek, a squeal of delight, a frustrated sigh. Odd combination. Maybe she was stuck. I wondered if she was snooping again.

I crept a couple of steps closer.

Through a gap between rotting wooden planks, I glimpsed outstretched fingers reaching out towards my doorstep. I looked up and saw the familiar row of clay pots balanced precariously on the first-floor window ledge. Maybe one of them had dropped. They belonged to Flat D: the dark-haired Irish bloke whom I'd met twice before, picking up his mail from the hall floor, bleary-eyed and dopey. I hoped Mrs Ward didn't think he was growing parsley.

I grew progressively more edgy, the cold wind flapping at my coat, the old bench squeaking creepily. A group of men jogging along the pavement, casting annoyed looks my way for blocking their path.

Mrs Ward's dangling clog dropped to the ground with a dull thud. Above me, a sudden shriek had me looking up—the call of a crow, stirring and cawing at something in the shadows. Mrs Ward looked up, too, then whipped her head in my direction.

'Chloe. What a pleasure to see you, luv.'

I waved a hand.

'Hello, Mrs Ward,' I said warily.

My palms were clammy as she undraped herself (ungracefully) from the fence, her cheeks flushed red from the effort. She slipped her bare foot back into her clog and flicked her gaze to my carrier bag. 'Been shopping?'

'Coffee,' I said, fiddling nervously with the milk cap. Not that Mrs

Ward bothered to argue the logic. She kept sneaking looks over the fence.

'Fabulous bluebells you have, luv. Spanish type I bet, eh?'

I stared at her blankly. Truth is, I don't know much about flowers, but I knew that narrow strip of flowerbed contained little more than drooping weeds and a few unbloomed buds. Bluebells or not, I doubted they looked *fabulous*—unless they had undergone a miraculous growth spurt while I'd nipped across to the corner shop.

Mrs Ward gave a strained little laugh, as if reading my thoughts. 'Dead roots always come back to life, luv. Spring is a time of rebirth.'

*Dead ... Rebirth ...*

I didn't know why she said those words. Something about them disturbed me, brought back unwanted, vivid images from the past. Haunting images. The square of teal-blue light crawled back into my head.

'What do you mean, Mrs Ward?' I said, my voice shaky.

Her cheeks flared a shade of scarlet as she grunted something unintelligible in reply. She refused to meet my stare, grabbed her broom by the wall and began to sweep her front yard (or rather made a feeble attempt at it). If anything, her behaviour confirmed my suspicions—something on my side of the fence had caught her attention.

I strode towards the rusty gate, put my hand on the latch, opened it, made my way up the path.

And then I saw it.

Propped on the porch step lay the object of my neighbour's curiosity: a square box wrapped in dark teal-blue paper and tied with a ribbon of gold satin hearts. Elegance laced with sweetness.

I sighed with relief, soothed for a moment by the sight. Then I stooped to pick up the box and ran my fingers across the smooth surface; the paper only dented by the mention of my name in a beautiful but unfamiliar cursive hand. There was no postmark, no address, no hint of the sender's identity. Whoever had hand-delivered this box clearly knew I'd moved to Chertsey last autumn.

I caught my breath, fumbled about in my coat pocket for my keys, found them, then startled when Mrs Ward cleared her throat from behind, a stagy *ahem*. I glanced to see she had stopped sweeping mid-stroke.

'Not your birthday, is it?'

I shook my head. When I jiggled the box, I caught a faint rustle of movement. Definitely not chocolates.

Mrs Ward eyed it with a knowing grin. 'Must come from a caring young lad.'

I frowned. There was no caring young lad in my life, never had been. At least not the caring part. She probably got carried away by the gold hearts on the ribbon.

'Just a friend,' I lied.

'Pshaw! A pretty box like this, that's "just a friend?"' She clawed at the fence and leaned towards me, adding, 'See what I'm talking about, luv?' She pointed then to the handwriting on the box. 'You must be well acquainted with your lad—otherwise he wouldn't call you *Chlo*. Cute nickname, isn't it?'

I dropped my gaze and gaped at the line. It should have meant nothing, just a missing '*e*' at the end of my name. It was so imperceptible against the deep blue of the paper that I'd misread it. But now the word stared at me like a familiar ghost from the past. Only one person I knew would ever use the shortened form of my name.

Except it was simply impossible.

It couldn't be him.

He was dead and buried near Heavendale, miles away up north.

'Are you all right, luv?' Mrs Ward asked, a look of exaggerated concern on her face. 'You're white as a sheet. I bet you could do with a stiff brandy at mine.'

I flashed her a tense smile. 'Thanks, but I think I'll pass.'

'Oh, that's a shame. Mrs Hunt is coming soon, and I bet she'd love a cuppa and a little chat with us. Just like last week. That was nice, wasn't it, luv?'

I forced a polite nod, even though I wanted her to go away. I didn't want to see the stout Mrs Hunt again and have to squeeze into the sofa between her and Mrs Ward, the three of us knocking back cups of warm brandy infused with Earl Grey that passed as afternoon tea.

The conversation between them had rattled at whipcrack speed, from the sexual antics of next door's pert German au pair to the marriage counselling of the couple in number 33. Two cups of *special* tea later, they'd firmly believed the two topics were related. Then, when they both ran out of scandalous neighbourhood tales, they turned their woozy gazes towards me.

'Why did you move into that dump next door, luv?'

*Well, I don't mind a decorating challenge, Mrs Ward.*

'You sure you're eating enough? You're all skin and bones.'

*That's because I'm blessed with a fast metabolism, Mrs Hunt.* Her mouth had set in a tight-lipped line. I don't think she liked my answer very much.

'So, did you have a boyfriend before moving to Goswell Street?'

*No.*

Mrs Ward had looked contented and mellow enough, but not Mrs Hunt. I don't think she believed me. She'd just said, 'Oh, really,' with a knowing little smile, and I could tell she meant something else. I had to look away.

I pushed back the memory and slid the key into the lock.

'I heard Heavendale is a nice place to go in spring,' Mrs Ward suddenly said and I whipped round to face her.

*Why did she say that? Was it random?* I couldn't read the look on her face so I gave her the benefit of the doubt.

'You've not gone back there for a while, have you, luv?'

I wondered now if under the grip of hot brandy I'd unwittingly parted with more information than I intended to last time. I found myself reaching for the milk cap again, twisting it right, then left, right and left again—a nervous tic.

'I'll go back soon,' I muttered. 'To visit my mother.' *God forbid.*

'Mrs Hunt knows Heavendale well. She goes there on holiday every year.'

'Wonderful.'

'She was there last April.'

My hand froze mid-twist; I could see her eyes sparking with excitement, with glee—a chance to probe again into my past. I had a sudden fear of what was about to come next.

'What a tragic accident. Poor boy. What was his name again?' She gave an exaggerated pause. 'Oh yes, Matthew. Matthew Thorne.'

The name shot through me like an electric charge but Mrs Ward carried on, oblivious: 'Speed driving is such an awful distraction for young men. You shouldn't be grieving—oh no, certainly not at your age. Funerals are bloody awful, luv. I remember when I lost my Archie three years ago . . .'

Blood rang in my ears. I didn't want to listen any more. I tried not to, but the sound of her voice kept coming at me. Loud. Urgent. Relentless. She had to stop, she had to shut up right now.

I dropped my carrier bag and slammed my fist against the door. 'Enough,' I yelled. 'I have no idea what you're talking about.'

'But Mrs Hunt . . .' Her face crumpled for a second. 'She saw his name in a local paper. She found out the two of you were engaged. You were going to get married.'

I swallowed past the dryness in my throat, tried to soften the tone of my voice when I said, 'Chloe Westfield is a common name. She must have got the wrong end of the stick, that's all. I've never met a Matthew Thorne in my life. Ever.'

The words came out hollow. They rang false, even to me, but at last Mrs Ward lapsed into silence. I picked up my carrier bag and pushed the front door open with trembling hands. And then, just like that, a crucial question popped into my head.

'Did you see who delivered the box, Mrs Ward?'

There was an awkward pause, an odd hesitation and I looked over my shoulder to see her mouth opening and closing. She rubbed her chin for a moment, as if she wasn't sure what to say next.

'Not being funny, luv,' she started, 'but one second there was nothing, then the next—BAM. Just like that. It was there on your porch step.' She crossed her arms over her chest, looking mightily annoyed. 'Your lad must have been so damn discreet.'

I said nothing, certain I'd stopped breathing. My legs wobbling, I shuffled through the communal hall and opened the door to my flat, stumbling inside, the teal-blue box flying down to the floor.

I gasped.

It was happening again. Just like when I was a child. The bile crawled up the back of my throat, an acid taste of fear coating my tongue as I latched the door behind me. Two bolts, one chain. Pointless precaution.

I had let it in, the danger—here inside, waiting to be unwrapped.

In my head, I could still see that grey cloud morphing into a square of light, the colour pulsing a dark shade of teal.

**2**

My kitchen was all tiny, worn, compact units and cracked linoleum, the seams dark with years-old dirt no amount of scrubbing would ever get clean. Two chairs were huddled against the far wall on each side of a cheap Formica table. I set the box on it, beneath a white plastic clock with four oversized numbers, one for each quarter of the hour. The minute hand ticked closer to an invisible five. It was just gone midday.

Coffee, I decided, wouldn't do any more, so I opened the fridge and placed the milk on the bottom shelf. Then I stared at the contents inside for longer than was necessary. There was barely anything: an open bag of celery sticks, gnarled carrots, and a low-calorie ready meal two days past its sell-by date. Hardly an appetising selection, but it didn't matter. I wasn't hungry. It had been a long time since I'd last enjoyed the taste of food.

I pulled a quarter-full bottle of blueberry vodka down off the open shelves and poured some into a glass, twirling some ice cubes. My eyes were fixed on the box as I drank it in one swallow. Cold heat burned down my throat, but it was not enough to take the edge off. I filled another glass and was startled mid-swig when my iPad beeped; I tapped the screen.

The message came from MysteryGeek, his username flashing on the gaming platform. He was asking me if I wanted to play. The offer came like a breath of fresh air— tempting too, now that I felt a little more mellow, more inclined to let go of the red flag flying in my head. I could certainly do with some distraction, a bit of entertainment. Connecting online with MysteryGeek was the most fun I'd had in years, but now wasn't the time.

I switched my attention back to the box and wondered if he could have sent it. A present born out of a fantasy—some kind of virtual infatuation. Not so far-fetched after all, but technically impossible since MysteryGeek and I had never revealed our true identities to each other.

I caught myself fiddling with the gold ribbon and thought, *This box is playing with my head.* The teal-blue wrapping shone like a birthstone, a vivid shot of colour against the half-light.

*Who wouldn't open it?*

Mrs Ward would have untied the ribbon like a shot, but rereading my name stopped me again: *Chlo Westfield. Chlo* without the letter *e.* My fingers tensed and I snapped. This was ridiculous. Matt never had any talent for gift-wrapping. Then again, someone else could have wrapped it.

I took a deep breath and finished off my glass of vodka. Dutch courage, that's what I was going for. By the time I clunked my empty glass on the table, I had gathered enough to pull the ribbon free, slide my fingers under the paper, and peel away the sealing tape from the wrapping . . .

It was a wooden box. Square. Dirty red.

A colour that had the misfortune to match pretty much anything in my flat, from the peeling wallpaper to the moth-eaten cashmere throw bundled up in the corner of my velveteen couch. At night, when I dimmed the lights, I swear I could pass for a young madam running a dilapidated brothel.

I unsnapped the brass clasp and opened the lid. And there I was, sitting on one of the chairs with two manila envelopes in my hands. I tipped the contents of the larger one onto the table. Folded pieces of thick paper emerged, cut in various sizes. At first I didn't understand what they were, but as I smoothed them with my hand, I read some of the inscriptions: *bodice, skirt, sleeves . . .*

I realised it was a dress pattern. Not drawn professionally, but the writing, smooth and fluid, was visually appealing against the coarser texture of the paper.

I brought my attention to a set of pages related to the construction of the dress that had fallen out of the envelope, too. Strangely enough, the top page also bore my name.

Sketched silhouettes drawn with precise strokes of deep blue stood out from the background of instructions meticulously written in black. The curls and curves of the calligraphy betrayed a feminine hand, the same one that had written my name on the wrapping paper.

I heaved a sigh of relief. Of course it had nothing to do with Matt.

As I tipped the smaller envelope, something dropped and fluttered to the floor. I cautiously raised one of the corners when I realised it was a fabric swatch: a piece of teal-blue silk pinned to a palm-sized card.

A short note was written on the back: two words, both starting with a capital S, but so faint they were almost invisible. It struck me as strange that the letters were traced so lightly. They were written as though there wasn't enough ink left in the pen, or as if the writer's hand was too weak to form the letters. When I peered closer, I deciphered them.

*Scissor Sister.*

Something in the room changed at that moment; I felt a disturbance in the air. I turned my head towards the window, but no, it was closed—it wasn't a draught. Then I heard a sound: a creak of floorboards by the door, and another one, much closer this time, followed by a rustle of fabric and a sigh. A cold breath whispered down my spine.

Eerie forces were making themselves known, then making themselves seen.

My hands—something was wrong with them. They were glowing, a vibrant blue that came straight out of the piece of silk I still held, irradiating my palms and pulsing along my arms. My skin rippled with dread.

*No, no. Not again.*

But it was too late. Images rushed into my mind, coming thick and fast.

Quick flashes.

Someone else's life flew by like a fast-forward newsreel of memories: a bubblegum-pink cot, a school, seasons and years rushing by as a child grew into adulthood. When the last frame rolled down, I emerged into a black mass of rain-swollen clouds, my mind floating inside them as if I were hanging from the sky—I had slipped into another realm.

Something drifted towards me now, a shape, wispy and grey. At first, I mistook it for another cloud, but then it morphed into a young blonde woman, her face pale and shimmering white, her teal-blue dress falling across her limbs in ghostly waves. She glided towards me, drawing my attention down to a sinuous road fringed by mountains and dark lake waters beneath us. A sense of stillness permeated the scenery, but through my fingers the girl's despair pumped—a manic tingling rhythm, a restless heartbeat that could only pulse through the rewinding of time, as though she were whole again.

Alive.

Then lightning split the sky. A white flash, followed by a curtain of rain. Drops I couldn't feel or taste came pelting down onto the road where a red sports car drove dangerously close to the cliff edge, struggling for control. Two blinding headlights flashed into sight, swerved around a sharp turn and chased the red car until they were nothing but a torch hurtling upon it.

More sounds.

Bad sounds.

A screech of tyres on wet tarmac, the blare of a horn. The ghost girl pointed at something else in the distance, further down the road: a lone large oak tree stood on a grass verge at the bottom of a slope, and my first instinct, my first thought was, *It shouldn't be there—it's in the way.*

Then everything slowed down. A sickening thud. Red metal buckling against the lone tree's bark. I watched in horror as a body smashed through the windscreen. A girl flew through the air and crashed onto the hood of her car, blood trickling down the corner of her mouth, eyes frozen open, her teal-blue dress showered with tiny shards of glass.

I turned back towards the ghost and immediately realised she was that same girl. She'd wanted me to witness her death, to show me what had happened to her. Below us, the blinding headlights screeched a U-turn and fled. I could just make out the blurry outline of a silhouette behind the wheel before they vanished in the distance.

The ghost girl floated away. Her sight began to shift from light to shadow, almost solid one moment, and evanescent again the next. Her voice made its way telepathically to me in a warning:

*Scissor Sister is watching you.*

Scissor Sister. Here were those enigmatic words again. They were important to my ghost, reminding me of others just like her—ghosts in limbo who couldn't rest in peace. Who were seeking closure or revenge when the truth behind their own deaths still haunted them, when justice had yet to be served.

I wanted them to stay away, but they didn't, they wouldn't.

They wanted me to know; they wanted me to see.

*Leave me alone.*

*Let me go.*

*LET ME GO!*

I pressed the heels of my palms into my temples to smother the echo of my screams, the word *go* reverberating through my skull as I fought the sensation of falling from the sky. The clouds, the road, the ghost—they grew unsteady, flickered like failing fluorescent lights before they dissolved into a blinding flash of white.

When I reopened my eyes, breathing hard, I realised I'd snapped back into reality. Everything inside the flat was still and silent. And in the palm of my hand lay nestled the piece of teal-blue silk, unlit, its mystery dormant again inside the weave.

I took no more chances this time.

I leapt to my feet and dumped the silk straight into the bin. This was the story of someone else's life. Whatever tragedy had seeped inside it had nothing to do with me.

Returning to the table and with one swift, vicious movement, I tore the instructions in half. I was gathering the pieces in my hands when something at the bottom of a page caught my eye.

A set of initials and a date: *H.P. 03/04/2017.*

I stared at them, my brain trying to process what the *H* and *P* stood for. I made a mental list of people who matched those initials. Apart from a distant Aunt Harriett whose last name I'd forgotten and a teenage summer fling with a boy named Harry Pearson, no one else came to mind. I searched further for a rational explanation, but the more I tried, the more sceptical the voices in my head were.

They kept telling me those initials belonged to the ghost girl.

I shook them off. It surely had to be some kind of bad joke. I thought about Mrs Hunt; the very idea of her having been in Heavendale last April made me feel vulnerable. Maybe she was trying to trip me up. I could picture her trawling the obituaries like a necrophiliac in search of her next fix, then pointing at Matt's name on the page and saying something like, *'See, Mrs Ward, I told you he died. I told you they were related. I always knew there was something wrong with that girl.'*

Nosy cow.

I was slamming on the bin pedal again, cursing, ready to dump the pages when a connection flashed in my mind and my foot slipped away. The lid clanged shut, the pieces still stacked in my hand as I shook my head in disbelief. The date, *that* date—how could I possibly forget it? Even though the writing wasn't Matt's, even though his initials didn't match, it coincided with his death. One year ago to this day.

I felt a shot of alarm. Something was wrong. What if Mrs Hunt knew? What if she'd found out what had really happened the night he died? All this guilt, this doubt—it was corrosive. It was changing me, twisting me, making him alive once more in my head.

In my mind, the sound of his voice cut through me like a knife
—*You killed me, Chlo! You killed me!*

I grabbed my phone from my pocket. I had to get away from here, leave this place fast. I scrolled quickly through my address book. It wasn't very full; I'm a loner, you see—I don't have many friends. Even the closest ones I had let them drift away over the years, turned down enough invitations until one day they stopped asking. There was no one I could turn to for help, no one I could ask to accommodate me for a while.

My hand briefly hovered over my mother's number, then shifted away from the screen, as if repelled by an opposite magnetic pole. I didn't want to see her, didn't want to go back to Heavendale—a place so laden with bad memories, they would ambush me.

I shook my head. It wasn't as if I had much choice, really. I had no job, and I'd almost tapped the last of my savings. I could last another couple of months, maybe three if I kept very still, lived very quietly— but not here, not now, not in Goswell Street. I needed to let the dust settle behind me.

I poured the dregs of the bottle of vodka into my glass.

*It's okay, it's okay,* I sweet-talked myself. *Everything will be fine.*

## 3

The next day, the weather was drizzly and the traffic slowed down by heavy roadwork. Two lanes of cars drove along the M6 at a zombie's pace, the third closed off by traffic cones that stretched for what seemed like miles. I started counting them: *One cone, two cones, three cones . . . Twelve cones . . . Thirty cones, sprouting never-endingly along the road.*

They looked like weeds, something right out of *The Magic Roundabout*, with their stripy pattern of white and orange.

At some point I lost track of the numbers, thinking I wouldn't mind a bit of weed myself. A nice spliff to help me chill and calm my nerves. I couldn't recall the last time I'd smoked one, but it must have been in my late teens. I'd since legalised my highs with the far more socially acceptable bottle of Smirnoff.

It took another hour before I left the motorway at Junction 36. The spots of rain that smudged my windscreen had stopped, replaced by the glow of a hazy, early-evening sunshine dipping slowly behind jagged cliffs. Tourists came from all horizons to visit the sparkling shores of the Lake District, to scramble up its high, craggy fells, or to visit Beatrix Potter's home.

And then there were the others: couples for whom the novelty of romance hadn't worn off yet. They walked hand in hand among the ancient woodlands and marvelled at the sight of golden eagles soaring in the sky, their faces slack with awe, almost inevitably turning in unison to share a kiss.

Once, on a hot, empty day, feeling hopeless and forlorn, I caught myself spying. Then I indulged in spiteful speculations.

*How long before she catches a glimpse of his true self? How long before she realises he never really loved her? One day she'll wake up and see she's become spineless. The type of woman who makes people nod in sympathy and think,* Poor dumb bitch.

The growing wail of a siren dragged me out of my thoughts. I looked into the rear-view mirror: the boxy frame of an ambulance, its blue lights blinking furiously behind me. I drove down the remainder of a steep slope, jerked the wheel and bumped up onto the nearest verge, plunging the wheels into the coarse, overgrown grass. The shrill sound whizzed past my ears, then faded in the distance, giving way to a squalling of seagulls overhead. They swooped round the sky in tight formation before two of them broke away from the flock and plunged lakeward, their wings partly screened by a towering oak tree right in front of my car; its branches budding with delicate new life.

I heard myself gasp. Something struck me: a powerful feeling of déjà vu, an odd sense of familiarity. Which in itself shouldn't have felt so odd, since I'd travelled this road many times before. But this wasn't what bothered me. I kept my eyes fixed on that tree and recognised it as the same fateful landmark of yesterday's vision. I couldn't remember seeing it anywhere else but inside my head.

Until now.

I looked ahead, then turned around in my seat to scan the scenery along the road; it was the only tree to border the edge of the cliff. Maybe its proximity to Heavendale was just a coincidence. That girl in the teal-blue dress could literally have died anywhere—Seven Sisters or the Cornish coast or Sandwood Bay in Scotland, where I'm sure there're also plenty of oak trees near the cliffs. There must be dozens of spots like this all over Britain, probably way too many in some far-flung places to count or even worry about.

*Not viable statistically that she'd died here,* I thought, *like one chance in a million.*

With the odds on my side, I pressed my foot on the accelerator and blinked back the memory of that girl's crash.

And that tree.

# 4

Heavendale...

Five minutes later, I finally spotted the town from above: streets snaking around flat green meadows on the valley floor, cottages that looked like honey cubes lit by sunset. I wove my way down, watching them grow in size, my heart pinching as I passed the town sign.

I knew what was coming next.

First an old gas station popped up where an elderly man sat on a nearby bench, staring blankly ahead, his mouth moving mechanically in a conversation only known to him. Then came a lonely cul-de-sac of newish homes, meant to be part of a development that never happened. *Too little, too late,* I'd once heard a group of locals say. Only later did I come to understand what they'd really meant; they were referring to the decline and eventual demise of the garment factory.

I could see the factory standing at the crest of a distant hill, towering above town like a minute fortress made of brick and stone; Heavendale's glorious past. Many women over the age of fifty had worked there at some point in their lives until it shut down two decades ago, unable to compete with cheaper overseas manufacturers in Bangladesh or China. Now the symbol of a once-thriving trade was abandoned, exposed to the elements and left to slowly rot away.

Further down the road was Market Square, the heart of the town, a quaint, cobblestoned place that forked at its middle into two lateral alleys. The old fabric stores and haberdasheries had disappeared over the years and been replaced by fashion boutiques, souvenir shops, and niche cafés. Times and tastes had changed. These days, Heavendale was thriving thanks to the tourist business.

But now, at past seven o'clock on a Sunday, the square was empty. No cars, no people. An old mongrel loped down the cobblestones, with no owner calling after it. The lamp-posts shone a feeble yellow light as the sky turned to lilac.

I headed south towards the lake, the wealthy section, the most scenic part of Heavendale. There, beautiful guest houses and cottages lined a wide avenue named, unimaginatively, Lake Avenue. Judging by the lit outdoor terraces and clattering of plates, some holidayers had chosen to brave the evening chill and dine al fresco.

I slowed down just as I glimpsed my mother's six-bedroom (all en suite) barn conversion a hundred yards away. I wondered if she too would be having guests, before I remembered she'd rarely accepted any bookings since Dad passed away. Still, a doubt crossed my mind, the possibility that she might not be home.

I glanced over at my phone on the passenger's seat, trying to figure out an excuse for my arrival: *Hi, Mum. You'll never guess where I'm right now . . .*

I cringed. It sounded so lame. Once you're in town, you don't phone to ask if you can drop in. It's like putting on a false smile for the sake of courtesy.

Steering my car through the open gate, I passed the carved wooden B&B sign that read STONEBARN LAKE. Just the sight of it made me swallow hard. Matt had decided to pay my mother a visit on his own last April; a week later, he died. The last time I'd set foot back in Heavendale was for his funeral.

I parked by the front door and quickly checked my face in the rear-view mirror, making sure the bronzer on my cheeks still faked its glow. My hands were shaking as I got out of the car and walked forward to press the doorbell.

'I have no vacancies at the moment, I'm afraid.' My mother's lilting voice came from the other side of the door, cheerfully uttering her usual lie.

'Hi, Mum. It's Chloe.'

'Chloe.' She opened the door and stood in the doorway, eyes wide. 'Is something the matter?'

'No, Mum, not at all. I thought I'd just drop by.'

'Drop by. *Drop by?* Well, goodness, I wish you'd phoned.' She sounded flustered, the words rushing out. 'You could have spared me the surprise, sweetheart, but here you are. Come in, come in.'

She put out her arms to me and we hugged limply. The strange thing was that, unlike my dad, she'd never hugged me before. It felt awkward. As awkward as her fortnightly phone calls since last spring, when she routinely tiptoed around my feelings.

*You're holding up okay, sweetheart?*

*Fine, Mum, thank you.*

*You'll come back for a visit soon, won't you?*

*Yes, Mum, of course.*

Dropping by unannounced was obviously not what she had in mind.

I pulled back from her. 'I'll make myself discreet, I promise.'

'Don't be silly,' she said briskly. 'I just wish the house was up to par for your visit, that's all.'

The house was perfect, down to the vase of cut daffodils in the entry hall—a touch of colour in a sleek, modern, country-style home that contrasted beautifully with eighteenth-century ceiling beams, between which hung several cast-iron chandeliers.

She began climbing the spiral staircase and I studied her as I followed her. If not for her pale green eyes and freckles scattered around her nose, you'd have been hard-pressed to tell we were related. She'd had her red hair dyed blonde for as long as I could remember, and cropped into a tight pixie cut that angled down her forehead. She was wearing a knee-length woollen skirt with little white slippers. At fifty-three, my mother still had great legs, toned but not skinny. Unlike me, she didn't need to hide them in a pair of jeans or camouflage her figure behind roomy Breton jumpers. She'd never commented once on my gradual weight loss. My mother rarely asked questions of any potency.

We padded along the corridor lit with sconces on the first floor, the plush red carpet sucking at my soles. At the far end, she opened a door and flipped on the light. 'I'm sure you'd like to stay in your old bedroom.'

I let my eyes roam over the rustic wardrobe, the floral curtains, and the crisp, clean linens to match. At the foot of my bed, a bookcase crammed with weighty tomes stood as a reminder of what a studious teenager I'd been. There were no posters of pop stars on the walls, no girlish pictures. Matt and I had always slept here during our quarterly visits—I wished now my mother had paved the whole thing over.

While I dragged my suitcase inside, I noticed something new: a silver-framed photo on the bedside table. I picked it up and ran the ball of my thumb over the glass, tracing over the image of Matt smiling confidently for the camera, his arm wrapped around my waist, a background of mountains behind us. His brown hair had tanned streaks as though he'd just come from somewhere hot. I was smiling too, but unlike Matt's, the smile didn't light up my face. It looked too forced to be genuine.

'I had it framed,' my mother said from behind me.

I nodded, suddenly feeling nauseous, and set the picture down.

She sighed. 'If only you'd come back home last year.'

'I left home five years ago, Mum.'

'You could at least have made an effort for Christmas. '

She stepped away from me and knelt before the wardrobe. For a moment, I thought she might be cross with me, but then, as she opened the bottom drawer, her face broke into a smile. Inside was a brown leather-bound photo album that she held out to me.

'I suppose you won't mind a belated present. In a way, your absence gave me time to collect some more memories.'

'What memories?'

'Yours and Matt's. Who else, sweetheart?'

I stared at the album in horror. 'What did you do that for?'

My mother frowned at me, as if I was being ungrateful. 'I don't know why you're making a fuss . . .'

'I'm not.'

'Then open it.'

My hands were trembling, gripped by unease.

My mother stood up and snapped the cover open. 'For goodness' sake, Chloe. Please get a hold of yourself.'

I made myself look down as my mother flipped through page after page, slices of my life with Matt coming back—each photo freezing a tale in time. I instantly picked out his favourites: a selfie of us at the ice hotel in Iceland; another where he raised his glass, sitting suspended a hundred feet in the air during a London in the Sky dinner; and alone in his sports Maserati with his right elbow casually bent out the window, his left hand lazily draping over the wheel. Whatever Matt had done or owned, he had to stand out. It was all about image with him.

My mother kept flipping through what felt like an inexhaustible reservoir of pictures. She must have copied them straight from his Facebook tribute page, filled with the type of commiserating comments that made me cringe: *RIP, Matt. Gone too soon*, or, *You were way too handsome to die!!* Those attracted the most likes and weeping emojis from his *friends*. I'd met some of them in real life, all pretentious little twats. They only gave a hoot about money.

'Look,' my mother said, breaking the silence. She was pointing to a new picture. 'That's when Matt first came to Stonebarn Lake.'

I leaned closer, staring not at him but at the girl standing by his side. She looked so different then—a plump thing with milky skin framed by red curls. A black dress flared around her legs, hugging her breasts and hips. Yes, that's what she'd had back then—curves.

But they had been wrong. Made her look fat: *Fat Chlo*. That's what he called her before she shrank to half her size . . .

What he called me before he turned me into some kind of ghost.

My heart clenched when his voice barged into my head—*No, Chlo. You only have yourself to blame.*

I shut my eyes, trying to quell the sick feeling rising in my gut. But

I couldn't stop the memory, couldn't stop the images from rushing through my mind. His presence materialised as if I had conjured him into the room.

It had been exactly three months after we'd met, on an early spring evening in my bedroom at Stonebarn Lake. I still remembered the vibes coming off him that day: distant, edgy, anxious—nothing I couldn't put down to the (daunting) prospect of meeting my mother. I'd just smoothed his tie against his shirt and buttoned his jacket; Pinstripe Versace Classic. Smart. Expensive.

Matt would have no trouble charming her, even as his darker mood exerted some strange magnetism over me.

'I love you,' I heard myself say.

Those three little words: they made my heart beat so fast, I almost willed him to say them back. But he didn't and kept silent. No kisses, no arms flinging around my waist. He was looking at himself in the mirror, absorbed in his own reflection, busy perfecting the knot in his tie.

'Matt, what's wrong?'

He swept his gaze over me dispassionately. 'Do I have to spell it out?'

I caught my reflection in the mirror and fluttered in panic towards the wardrobe. The dress, *that* dress—black but so tight it failed to hide a roll of fat around my waist.

*What was I thinking?*

I rifled through the hangers, but nothing screamed 'slim.' I settled for an elegant floral print I'd sewn myself and held it up to show him.

'Flowers,' he said with a snort. 'That won't exactly distract attention from your weight.'

The remark stung, but it was the contempt on his face that hurt me the most as he took a step forward. 'Still shovelling food down your throat, huh?'

I lowered my eyes. I wanted to fold away inside myself, disappear.

'I asked you a question, Chlo.'

'I'm-I'm sorry.' I didn't mean to sound so pathetic, but I did and he laughed—an easy, pleasant laugh that took me by surprise. He looked oddly calm, relaxed.

But he wasn't.

'You're sorry?' He poked me hard in the stomach. 'You think that makes it all right because you're fucking sorry?'

I tried not to wince, tried not to cry. What good would crying do? It was all my fault. I'd steadily put on weight since my dad died. By the time I met Matt, I had dropped enough of it to give him the illusion of slenderness. But the discipline it required was a daily struggle.

Matt shook his head and let out a long sigh, as if I was a terrible disappointment. He moved behind me, tipped my chin up until our eyes met in the mirror. 'You want to make me happy, don't you, Chlo?'

The intensity of his gaze unnerved me. I tried to break free, but his hand was like steel. I didn't want to make him angry again so I made myself nod.

'Good.' He ran his fingers under my throat, applying just the slightest pressure. Then, his hands travelled down my midriff before he dug his thumbs into my stomach. Squeezing the flesh. Pinching. Bruising. Tighter and tighter, until my whole body burnt with shame and I cried.

'Matt, please!'

He sneered. 'You're not fuckable, Chlo. You're fat.' He nibbled at my ear, whispering, 'Fat Chlo, fat Chlo, fat Chlo,' before he shook me once more, released me, then left me with the words drilling on a loop into my head.

I blinked hard. When I reopened my eyes, my mother snapped the album shut.

'Right, sweetheart. Let's have dinner, shall we? You must be starving after your long journey.'

My face went hot. 'Later, Mum. I'd . . . rather unpack first.'

She scanned me up and down, and the motion made me wince. Then, with a resigned sigh, she left my room without a word.

Each drawer I opened was redolent of his memories. The sleeve of a left-behind suit peeked out of the wardrobe door. Inside I also found a belt, a tie, a pair of cufflinks—the items like lots of invisible Matts loitering inside, waiting for the opportunity to step out.

My mother had preserved this room like an archaeological site.

I found more evidence of him in the en suite bathroom. One by one I removed his aftershave, his toothbrush, then squashed all his clothes inside a laundry hamper that I found beneath the sink. Back in the bedroom, I put the framed picture of him face down into the drawer and pushed it shut.

I instantly felt better. It reminded me of the time after his death when I'd cleared our London flat of his expensive designer labels. I'd packed them all neatly into boxes along with my *fat* clothes. They will never see the light of day again—except perhaps for sale on eBay when the money eventually dries up.

The last item I pulled out of my suitcase was the wooden box. I'd dithered long and hard about taking it with me, then decided the dress pattern would be a nice present for my mother. She loved sewing and made beautiful creations she was proud to wear. I'd carefully taped the pages back together and used correction fluid to delete any mention of my name. It wasn't pretty, but it would do. I'd also fished the teal-blue square out of the bin before I left.

Kicking off my shoes, I swung my legs into bed. The mysterious initials were playing on my mind again. I was now firmly convinced they belonged to the ghost girl in my vision.

I took out the swatch with its card attached, careful not to touch the silk. But when I turned it over, I realised I could no longer read any of those faint letters. I held the card under the beam of my bedside lamp but found that the name *Scissor Sister* had vanished as though it had never been there. I frowned, confused and relieved at the same time.

I mulled over H.P.'s words: *Scissor Sister is watching you.*

It was such a strange statement, like a feminist take on Orwell's classic *1984*—although the thought of a nation living under the tyrannical rule of someone named Scissor Sister seemed utterly preposterous. I shrugged and put the swatch back in the box. I'd seen and heard my fair share of strange ghosts, enough to know that if you ignore them long enough, they'll eventually go away; slip back into the other side of their invisible world.

I reached out, switched off the little bedside lamp and spared H.P. a thought of gratitude.

I thanked her for leaving me alone.

# SCISSOR SISTER

A good business name is hard to find.

Sometimes it's not so much the name but its impact. Its weight. Its power.

If I say Apple, you know I'm not talking about the fruit. Dove means something else to you than just a bird.

These names are powerful brands drilled into your consciousness. They leave a mark, an imprint, a legacy.

Just like people.

Catherine the Great, Mother Teresa, Boudicca, Joan of Arc, Mata Hari, or Leni Riefenstahl: despots, nuns, warriors, martyrs, spies, propagandists. Good or bad, these are women you don't easily forget. Strong women. Memorable women.

I don't know what attracted me to the name *Scissor Sister*, but I've always found it intriguing. I could see from the start it had legs. There was something dark about it, almost Orwellian. A female version of Big Brother or some enigmatic religious figure.

Or was it something about the double S initials?

Such potential.

I knew one day this name had to be mine.

# 5

I woke with my stomach rumbling. The bedroom was pitch-dark save for the red glow of my digital clock flashing 03:05. I had slept a solid five hours, which was fine, longer than I'd done in ages. I hoisted myself on my elbows and flicked buttons on the TV remote control: talk shows, a rerun of *Hollyoaks*, and a morbid chick flick on the horror channel. Mindless noise—and none of it managed to drag my attention away from my pangs of hunger.

A leather-bound edition of *War and Peace* lay atop the bookcase, a metal bookmark sticking out between the gold-edged pages. A chance to finish a classic, but I was in no mood to resume Tolstoy's journey into the bleak Russian winter. Instead I grabbed my iPad, clicked on the video game icon, and heard the smoky murmur of musical notes.

My character, Vixen O' Neale, appeared on screen.

Vixen was a sleuth who lived in a 1940s virtual world filled with gangsters, criminals, greed, blackmail, murder, corruption and, surprisingly, a hefty dose of fashion: a dark caramel fishtail dress, a black satin cocktail dress, a red sequined strapless dress . . . Slinky numbers with a sweetheart or plunging neckline and thigh-high slits—nothing was ever too chic or sexy for Vixen. I'd grown to love her character and her sense of style. She filled the void. She quieted the pain. She stilled the guilt.

What helps you keep sane when your days and nights are as empty and meaningless as your life?

But tonight felt different. Someone was missing.

*MysteryGeek.*

I looked for his username on the gaming platform, but he wasn't online. Not at this time of the night. Though I noticed that my inbox was flashing with new messages he'd left for me yesterday:

10:15 – **Morning, Vixen. Fancy a game?**

16:53 – **Hey, don't U dare go kicking some baddie's ass without me!**

I couldn't help but smile. He was right. It just wouldn't be the same playing detective without help from his character, Inspector Josh Spade, clad in a dark trench coat and fedora, a perpetual cigar between his lips. He brought flair and panache to the game. Solving mysteries without him would be like being Scully without Mulder. And a team of one made no sense any more.

I read his third and final message:

21:32 – **Not heard back from U yet . . . U OK? I miss you x**

My eyes widened when I registered the last three words with the kiss at the end. I hadn't expected such intimacy from someone I'd never met before. I reread each message and it dawned on me they weren't *really* addressed to me.

MysteryGeek clearly had a bit of a crush on Vixen. Which was sweet and a little weird at the same time—the kind of weird that warned me to keep my distance. For all I knew, he could be a psycho nerd, and even if he wasn't, I had no intention of feeding his subconscious fantasies. All Vixen and I had in common was a cascade of copper hair. And hers shone brighter than a L'Oréal commercial.

I typed a few words, opting for a safe, neutral reply:

03:36 – **I'm OK. I'll be in touch soon.**

Easy enough. No need to blur the line. It was best to keep our 'relationship' strictly virtual.

After that, I must have drifted off, because the next thing I saw was daylight peeking through the curtains. I threw off the bedcovers and took a shower. A while later, dressed in denim jeans and a plaid wool jumper, I stepped outside onto the small balcony.

The early-morning light made the tree branches glow like hundreds of tiny hands. Sunrise awakened the colours of nature, the palette ranging from the palest pink of tree blossoms to the boldest gold of daffodils. A squirrel prowled in the branches of an apple tree, chewing something held in its paw. Behind the back garden, a floral trellis shivered in the soft breeze. And beyond it, the flat land ended and the rolling green hills began—the craggy mountains, the wilder part of the lakes.

A sudden movement caught the corner of my eye, there and gone in the same instant. And then back again—a group of people. They scuttled downhill, in and out of view. I counted them: eight, maybe nine, and although they were only small, distant silhouettes, I could tell they were women. I lost sight of them when they disappeared beneath a canopy of fir trees. I glanced over my shoulder at my alarm clock. It was barely seven.

'Morning, sweetheart! What would you like for breakfast?'

It was a more generous greeting that I'd expected from my mother, who seemed recovered from the surprise of my impromptu visit. She stood over a large AGA cooker, turning over juicy strips of bacon in a frying pan.

I suddenly had this mental image of a dead pig hanging in an abattoir, its belly split and chopped, spattering thick blood onto a white tiled floor. I fought the urge to gag. 'Just black coffee with sugar, please.'

'What about some blueberry muffins?' She pointed to a tray beside her. 'They're straight out of the oven.'

I looked at them, perfectly puffed and golden. It was a thoughtful touch, except that I much preferred the flavour of blueberry in stronger stuff these days. Of course, I couldn't tell her that.

'Another time, Mum. Thank you.'

She lowered the flame on the gas burner. 'I wish you weren't so picky, Chloe. God knows how many starving little children in Yemen or Syria would be happy to eat something right now. I shall boil you an organic egg, then.' She raised her chin as she opened the fridge door.

She made me want to laugh. Her self-righteousness, her bruised ego, her dubious stance on world poverty—as if reminding me of some of the grimmest spots on earth would instantly make me crave an organic boiled egg. But I didn't laugh, because my mother had no sense of humour where her own dignity was concerned.

I leaned over the glass bowl she had filled with fruit. 'A pear will do just fine, thanks.' I nibbled on the plump end of one I just grabbed to make a point. It was convincing enough to sway her to put the egg back into the box and return her attention to frying bacon.

With her back turned, I took a moment to observe the space around me: an open-plan kitchen/conservatory bigger than the size of my whole flat. Bifold doors and a pyramidal glass roof let light flood onto sage-green walls, one of them artfully bedecked with mismatched plates in fine porcelain. Above my head, a row of gleaming copper pots hung from stainless steel hooks. Details I'd barely registered the last time I saw this room, filled with grief and mourners.

'What's this?' My mother handed me a mug of coffee while eyeing the two envelopes lying by my side. I pushed them towards her.

'A present for you,' I said.

She swiftly slid the pieces of paper out of the envelope and scattered them onto the granite-top table. Everything was there except the square of silk, which I'd left upstairs in my bag, out of my mother's reach in case the cryptic message randomly popped back and alarmed her. I could sense her excitement as she ran her hands over the pages, unfolded them, clutched them with pride.

Then I knew at once I'd made a mistake.

'Oh, Chloe. Did you . . .?' She stopped when her index finger hit the bottom right corner of the page. 'Who's H.P.?'

*Good question.*

But I didn't know what to say to her, didn't know where to start. What string of words to put together to explain the crash and the dress and the tree. I had long stopped confiding my visions to my mother. She'd never believed me anyway when I was a child. She thought I was making up stories because I was needy, desperate for her attention.

'Some . . . distant girl,' I mumbled.

She frowned, but I didn't elaborate.

'Did that *H.P.* give you the pattern?'

'Sort of.'

My mother sighed. 'Well, she's obviously trying to revive your interest in fashion.'

'I doubt it, Mum.'

'Really? So why did you quit your job as a costume designer?'

My shoulders stiffened. I had kept the news quiet, hoping she'd never find out. Matt must have blabbed it out on his last visit.

'I was just an assistant,' I said tightly. 'Not a designer.'

'You could have become one if you'd stuck to it.'

'I . . .' Those haunting memories threatened to resurface again: ghostly visions in silk I couldn't bear to revisit. 'Look,' I said, blotting out the images. 'I didn't come here to talk about my old job.'

'Fine. So tell me what you're doing now.' Her eyes fell on me, expectant, and my face went hot. I just couldn't come up with a lie fast enough—she sighed in disappointment. 'I thought as much.'

At my silence, she pulled a pad and biro from a drawer, then pushed them across the table. 'Here. Write down your bank details.'

I pushed the pad away. 'No, Mum. I'm okay.'

'Just a little to tide you over.'

'I'm okay,' I repeated.

'But what will you do without a wage? You can't live forever off Matt's money.'

My defences flared up. 'I'm not living off his money, so why do you have to bring his name up all the time? He's dead now. Dead.' My voice came out high and bitter. I almost forgot that, in my mother's eyes, Matt could never have done any wrong.

She snapped the drawer shut. 'How can you be so cruel? He cared so much about you. He came here to plan every single detail of your wedding.'

*Ah, the wedding.* I looked down and cupped my hands around my coffee mug, guilt rising out of steam billows. I was going to tell her the truth. I knew it had to happen, but I'd never managed to find the strength. Part of it was the shame. I was ashamed of myself, ashamed to admit I'd complied so easily. The other reason was cowardice. I couldn't bear the conversation, the awkwardness, of facing my mother and having to *explain* myself. Matt's death had made things a lot simpler for me.

And yet what she'd just said about him jarred me, made me think twice. Planning was quite out of character for Matt; he wasn't the hands-on type, not a man who'd bothered with details. The banquet menu, the venue, the guest list—I knew for a fact he'd entirely entrusted these responsibilities to my mother (who, I was sure, must have gladly obliged). Matt had preferred to shine at his corporate job than deal with the endless wedding minutia. So why did he stay a whole week in Heavendale?

I looked up at my mother. 'Did he mention anything about coming here on business? Meeting up with a client? Some training course perhaps?'

It took me only a split second to realise I was asking the wrong questions: Heavendale was too small. The closest business city centre was Manchester, a hundred miles away. My mother had nothing to say on the subject, or maybe she just didn't hear me. She was standing with her back to me again, now busy chopping something. Her knife thudded hard against the cutting board.

'What would you like for lunch, sweetheart?'

The ring of the home phone spared me a reply. I took a sip of coffee and threw the rest of the pear in the bin.

'Hello?' my mother said. 'Oh, Cordelia, hi. Yes, of course I'm fine . . . Yes, you can drop them off this morning . . . I know, there's a lot to cover . . . Absolutely, three o'clock sharp. I'll make sure the other ladies arrive on time.'

My mother hung up, meeting my questioning stare with a smile. 'I'm hosting our weekly dressmaking meeting this afternoon.'

'Sounds fancy,' I said. 'You're part of some local club or something?'

She gave a little laugh. 'Trust me, sweetheart. This is no small-town club where old ladies meet to discuss the weather. Heavendale is getting ready for its first handmade and vintage fair the following weekend, and there's been plenty of press coverage about it. This has literally doubled our workload.'

I frowned. 'Did I come at a bad time?'

My mother gave a flick of her hand and took a quick sip of her coffee. 'Quite the contrary.'

'I don't understand.'

She eyed me thoughtfully. 'You have good knowledge of vintage fashion. I think it would be good for you to attend our meeting.'

'Me?' My voice rose in surprise. 'I . . . No, I don't think it's a good idea.'

'You don't have a job, sweetheart. You need a purpose. You need something to keep your mind alert.' She showed concern as if I was at risk to contract Alzheimer's.

'Listen, Mum. I just don't want to make a fus—'

'You're doing that right now.' She raised an unimpressed eyebrow. 'Perhaps you have some other plans for the afternoon?'

'Well, not exactly,' I hedged.

'Good. Then that's settled.'

I opened my mouth to argue, but the doorbell rang and she went to answer it.

# 6

Tina! What on earth are you doing here?'

'You tell me. You're the one who left me a voice message last night.'

'That's because I thought you'd call me back.'

'Well, I'm on your doorstep now. Surely you don't expect me to pick up my phone.'

I overheard their conversation from my kitchen stool and smiled at the feisty reply. I could picture the look on my mother's face, her prim lips pursed, her eyes rolling in frustration, her quiet outrage at having her phone etiquette trampled upon. The only thing missing now was one of her humourless ripostes.

Oddly enough, all I heard after Tina's words was silence.

*They must have gone outside*, I thought. Straining my ears above the hum of the fridge and the ticking clock, I heard their voices filter through; a low, muffled murmur. I tiptoed across the tiled floor, quietly pushed the door open onto the hallway, and peered at the other woman: short skirt, stiletto boots wrapped around fleshy thighs, her profile silhouetted in the half-light. She looked familiar.

She was nodding vigorously at my mother, who was speaking to her sotto voce, her tone hushed and urgent.

'I told you Chloe was here.'

'Just relax, okay? I did exactly as you asked.'

'We have a deal, Tina. She mustn't—' The hinges on the door squeaked and my mother broke off, startled when she caught me staring and gave a quick cough as she turned away. 'How about coffee, Tina?'

I hovered by the door, not wanting to admit I was eavesdropping.

That would not go down well. But I was curious now, piqued at the mention of my own name.

*What was that all about? And what 'deal' was my mother referring to?*

I didn't have a chance to ponder further. The other woman turned and grinned at me as if on cue. 'Chloe, sweetie, it's been so damn long.'

Tina, it turned out, I'd known since the age of sixteen, although we'd hardly seen each other after my move to London. With arms outstretched, she crossed the room and hugged me fiercely, then released her embrace and took a good look at me—I did the same.

Everything about her screamed for attention: her orange foundation, her low-cut blouse, her gold glitter acrylic nails. It was a rather disconcerting look for a plump forty-something woman. Tina was catty and shallow, but she was always completely real, open, and honest. Her mouth seldom had filters.

'Baby girl, you look so flat. Please don't tell me you're on a diet.'

'I'm not.'

'You need feeding.'

'I don't.'

'Put some meat back on those bones, sweetie. Skinny does a woman's figure no good.'

To prove her point she gave her large cleavage a proud little squeeze, then sashayed past me and into the kitchen as if she was stepping onto a fashion catwalk.

My mother passed her a mug of coffee. 'Can I get you a plate of breakfast?'

'You bet. What about you?' said Tina, nudging me as I sat next to her.

'I'm afraid Chloe's terribly fussy,' my mother said.

'Nah, your sweetie's all right. Make it two, Kathryn.'

I wanted to object but didn't feel up to the task this time since Tina rarely took no for an answer. She also had this peculiar habit of calling everyone *sweetie*, except my mother. It was either a greater mark of respect to use her first name or an understanding that my mother would flinch at the term of endearment.

'Anyway,' said Tina, wriggling excitedly in her stool, 'I have gossip, a piece of sizzling-hot gossip, and if it's not coming off my tongue right now, I shall be damned for eternity.' She winked a mascara-coated eye before adding, 'By the way, that last bit was a hint.'

My mother slid two full plates in front of us. 'Some church matter?'

'Better, Kathryn. Two words for you.' She paused, then lowered her voice to a dramatic whisper—'Denise Drummond.'

'Who's Denise Drummond?' I asked.

Tina dug into her food before giving me an indulgent smile. 'She controls the puritans' committee of bored and frigid housewives. Nothing better to do than peddle the same old rubbish about morality and traditional values.'

'That's harsh, Tina.' My mother turned to me. 'Mrs Drummond is the president of our residents' committee in Heavendale. She's a devoted churchgoer, but all in all she's pretty harmless. Even if she thinks the whole town suffers from a chronic disposition to sin.'

Tina chuckled. 'That's putting it mildly. I'm telling you, she need look no further than her own doorstep this time.'

'What do you mean?' my mother asked.

Tina drank a sip of coffee and licked her lips. 'Her hubby's strayed from the biblical path in the back of his car . . . With another woman.'

'Christian? For goodness' sake, why would anyone want to have an affair with *Christian*?'

'That's beside the point,' Tina muttered, then went back to working her way through breakfast. 'I want to know who he's bonking on the side. That girl is far too discreet for my taste. It's like she's hovering on thin air around Heavendale.'

'Oh, Tina, this is so grotesque. No one would ever believe such a thing about Christian.'

She shook her head in disagreement. 'He always stares at my chest when I see him at the grocery store.'

I munched on a piece of toast, idly listening to their conversation. I didn't know Christian Drummond, but having seen some of Tina's skimpiest outfits, I imagined he must have had a hard time concentrating on food labels.

She went on. 'I know that Denise is trying to smooth things over with him before all hell breaks loose. I bet the old rag would rather put up with a discreet affair than a public divorce.'

'How did you find out?' my mother asked.

'Straight out of the mouth of one of her committee members.'

'Rebellion in the ranks?' I suggested between mouthfuls. Once I started eating, I realised I was ravenous. I kept popping bits of toast, bacon, and tomatoes into my mouth in a greedy flow. I grabbed a blueberry muffin from the tray and earned a winning smile from my mother.

'One thing for sure,' Tina said. 'Denise made a big mistake trusting her.'

My mother refilled our mugs. 'So who's the committee member?'

Tina tutted. 'I can't compromise her anonymity. All I can say is that Denise received a DVD of *Fifty Shades of Grey* last week, and she was so furious, she threw it in the trash bin outside.'

'Nonsense,' my mother scoffed.

'Fact,' Tina replied. 'I picked up the DVD myself from the trash.'

'Honestly, Tina, you're such an embarrassment at times.'

'What did you expect me to do? It was a limited edition with unseen footage.'

'And what does this have to do with her husband?'

Tina sighed self-importantly. 'Think, Kathryn. His name's Christian too, like in the movie. Get my drift? Someone out there is dropping a serious hint that they know.'

I licked the crumbs off my fingers and helped myself to a second muffin. This story was getting more ludicrous by the minute.

'What about your secret contact?' I said. 'She may have something to gain in making this up.'

'Yes,' my mother said. 'She obviously wouldn't mind seeing Denise step down.'

Tina tapped her nose. 'I know she didn't lie. Trust me, it's only a matter of time before I find out the identity of Christian's secret squeeze.'

My mother glared at her. 'You're not trying to get even with Denise, are you? This could destroy her.'

Tina's fork clattered onto her plate. She grabbed a paper napkin, her sole answer the enigmatic smile that blossomed on her lips as she dabbed at them.

The bell rang before my mother could say more and she went to answer the door. I glanced at the clock, which barely showed eight.

Tina patted my shoulder. 'Yeah, yeah, I know, sweetie. Heavendale isn't exactly a hive of activity at night. That's why everyone's bustling about like bees after sunrise. Did Kathryn tell you I've just started yoga? Why don't you come and join me?'

'I don't do yoga.'

'Try. It'll be fun. There's a class on Friday morning.'

'I don't know if I'll stick around until Friday.'

'Nonsense, sweetie, you only arrived yesterday.' She leaned in closer. 'Our yoga teacher's seriously fit. He makes me break into a hot sweat before I even sit cross-legged.'

'Tempting,' I said. *Not.*

'Okay, I'll send you the address.'

I laughed, only to realise she was being serious, then decided I could always cancel later.

My mother reappeared, accompanied by a tall, slim woman in her sixties dressed in layers of purple and black. A long silk scarf fluttered at her throat and her hair was up in a neat chignon, dyed the colour of crow feathers. She looked like an elderly Goth.

'I'm bringing copies of our agenda for this afternoon,' she said, enunciating every syllable like a 1950s BBC newsreader. She dropped a pile of notes on the table. 'I hope you don't mind. I have errands to run this morning.'

'Not at all,' my mother said, beckoning her towards me. 'Cordelia, I don't think you've met my daughter, Chloe, before. Chloe, this is Cordelia, a good friend of mine.'

She offered her gloved hand and cocked her head to one side, giving me a half-smile. 'Actually, I believe we got introduced last year, but understandably the occasion was very sad.'

I wished I could say she looked familiar to me too; Cordelia would stand out in any crowd, but less so in a room full of mourners. My memories of Matt's funeral were a blur of sound and black: the doorbell ringing intermittently, the waves of silhouetted figures in hats and gloves emerging from the hallway, some drawing close, others hugging me, all uttering the same empty platitudes and hollow words of comfort. I vaguely remembered refilling my glass with vodka throughout the day. There was nothing I'd wanted more than to be unconscious, wrapped in black, gone away.

Her face grew sombre at my silence. 'It's a great shame that my impressions were not clearer at the time. I remember thinking that I didn't have a good feeling—'

'Cordelia!' my mother snapped, her voice high and tense. She fumbled nervously with the pile of notes. 'Can I have a quick word with you, please?'

'One moment, Kathryn. I'm not quite done yet.'

'Yes, you are.' She walked over to her side, took her by the elbow, and Cordelia looked away, sheepishly, like some scolded Victorian maid.

They both moved out of earshot and I glanced at Tina. 'What did she mean by that?'

'Nah.' She waved the matter away as if nothing had happened. 'Just ignore your mother. She'll be all right in a minute.'

'No, I mean Cordelia. She said something about her impressions not being clear. I'm sure she was trying to tell me something.'

'Oh, Cordelia.' Tina shrugged. 'She fancies herself a psychic in her spare time. She does a bit of tarot reading, a few seances here and there. More like a work in progress if you want my honest opinion, sweetie. She's quite smart, though.'

'Can she sense . . . presences?' I asked cautiously.

'Sense presences?' Tina chuckled. 'She couldn't predict a flood if she was knee-deep in water. But you've got to admit, she looks the part,' she said, and touched up her lipstick in the back of her silver knife. 'We all have to these days to keep the customers coming back.'

I was left pondering the nature of Tina's business when my mother announced with aplomb, 'Right, ladies, we're all set for our afternoon meeting. I'm delighted to say that Chloe agreed to be our guest of honour. She's absolutely thrilled.'

My mother blinked at me a few times. I felt as if I were being warned not to dare contradict her so I stretched my mouth into a smile.

'Shouldn't we ask for approval first?' asked Tina.

'That's true,' my mother said. 'I hadn't really thought about that.'

Cordelia shrugged. 'Why would she mind?'

Tina waved her hands in the air. 'Don't shoot the messenger. I'm the one following our standard procedure here.'

I took a sip of coffee, confused. 'What procedure? Can someone please tell me what's going on?'

They all stared at each other for a moment before Cordelia turned to look at me and said, 'We're trying to gauge our employer's reaction.'

'Right,' I said. 'In what way?'

'Well,' she said. 'For a start, we do things a little differently around here. We must report every—'

'Cordelia, please.' My mother's voice, clipped and firm. 'There's no need to bore Chloe with such petty details. Everything in our organisation is running exactly as it should be.'

'And who's running you?' I asked, my curiosity more than a little piqued now.

My mother exchanged a quick glance with Tina, who looked at me from the corner of her eye and grinned. 'Oh, I'm sure you must have heard of her, sweetie. She's trading under the name of Scissor Sister.'

Catching my breath, I felt my hand jerk in shock; hot coffee slopped down the side of my mug and seeped into my jeans.

# SCISSOR SISTER

You're thinking Scissor Sister is some old-fashioned dressmaking club, right?

You know the type.

Stitching, darning, seaming, hemming. Sharing the same old platitudes over afternoon tea: *Sugar? Milk? Would you like a heart-shaped scone served with clotted cream?*

I laugh at the thought, but you don't.

You're disappointed.

You're annoyed.

Maybe you're even angry.

Some days it doesn't take much to make you angry. All that anger seething inside. Repressed. Unchanneled. Waiting with purpose.

Good. Good.

But for now I want you to take a deep breath and relax. Yes, that's right. Breathe, relax, let down your guard. I have good news for you.

I'm upgrading. I'm altering my settings. Slowly. One day at a time. A leopard can't change its spots overnight.

I'm fortunate enough to have means at my disposal. I have resources and contacts.

I have staff: Good staff are important. Hard-working. Reliable. Pliable. Staff who don't challenge or question.

Scissor Sister is much more complex than meets the eye.

You're intrigued now, aren't you?

Soon you'll see.

# 7

I walked as fast as I could to the lake, my feet pounding the earthy path, my head a pit of confusion, my belly awash with food. I could feel its roundness, its swell, the fat sitting leaden inside like an intruder I must rid myself of.

I shouldn't have eaten so much.

*I never learn.*

I bent for a moment to catch my breath, feeling the sweat come out, and looked for a quiet spot.

A cluster of pine trees stood on the shore, where a red-haired boy was picking up a handful of flat stones. He flicked his wrist and threw the first one; it skipped six times across the water before it sank. Heading towards me was a woman pushing a pram and making cooing noises at her baby. I smiled as she ambled past me, then dashed off to the trees and put my face in the grass.

I slid two fingers down my throat until breakfast rose: brownish yellow, with four bits of bacon bobbing on top. I scrabbled around in my bag for a pack of disposable wipes, cleaned my hands and face, then popped a breath mint in my mouth.

The relief was only momentary. Something else hit my senses: a shiver, a shadow, an altered quality in the air—a subtle movement of vibration in space. I rose to my feet and looked around. No one was coming on either side of the path. The boy was still throwing stones. On the horizon a sailboat drifted fast down the lake, its white sails billowing. The wind had abruptly picked up and turned cold. I pulled my coat tighter around me, unable to shake the feeling I was somehow being watched.

And then I looked up and saw her: a wispy grey shape that looked like a cloud, floating six feet above my head and lit by a pale, unearthly glow. H.P. was back, teasing me, taunting me. I resumed my stride along the path and ignored her. Well, I wanted to, I tried, I did for a while, but in the end I couldn't help but glance up at the sky. She was still there, trailing me along Lake Avenue, a few paces behind.

'Go away,' I shouted to her.

I should never have returned to Heavendale. In my head, I devised a plan: I would leave Stonebarn Lake in the middle of the night when my mother was sound asleep. I could picture a vague note left on the kitchen table, two lines, maybe three. No, not good enough for her. I had to think of a credible story—something she would relish, like a job interview.

Anyone I knew would dash back home if they had a job interview. Long days spent perusing endless lists of ads until hope knocks at the door and off they'd go to covet a precious piece of nine-to-five. Good for them. It had been a while since I last looked online for a job. Those daunting titles that knocked me out of my comfort zone, those fancy descriptions that made my eyes roll. Eye rolling and fussy: not luxuries I could afford much longer.

I took a left, then a right. Between turns, cottages stretched along narrow streets.

The ghost was still in tow.


The church bells chimed quarter past ten when I emerged into Market Square, its polished grey cobblestones trodden upon by clumps of people. Four men ran past me with backpacks and headphones on. A group of Japanese tourists left a souvenir shop with Peter Rabbit toys in their hands.

All the shops were open, except one with steel roller shutters pulled shut, and in front of which H.P. had stopped. A strange thing happened: the ghost melted into smoke; wisps of grey seeping through the gaps between the shutters.

In a nearby corner alley, someone turned their car engine off. A woman emerged from a black Toyota, then smiled when she saw me standing there. She was wearing a beautiful white bengaline dress with red polka dots and a matching scarf tied around her dyed copper hair.

I couldn't help but put a self-conscious hand over my thigh to mask the dried coffee stain on my jeans.

'I should know what traffic's like on a Monday morning,' she said, turning a key into the store's front lock. 'I'm sorry to have kept you waiting.'

The shutters rolled up with a loud metallic clang, drowning out my protest. A close-up look revealed she was hardly older than me, in her late twenties perhaps. Her lips were painted a deep cherry red and she sported a small rose tattoo on her left wrist below her cuffed three-quarter sleeve.

'My name is Jade. Welcome to Vintage Folly.'

I flinched when the shutters screeched to a halt. Two life-sized mannequins adorned each side of the storefront window: one dressed in 1920s flapper garb, the other in a 1950s emerald cotton lace party dress, their plastic necks dripping with colourful jewels.

Jade held the door open for me. 'I pride myself on sourcing original pieces, but I'll let you be the judge of that.'

My feet refused to move. Most women would relish the chance to hunt for a dress, but I wasn't most women, and I'd vowed before to never get so close to such pieces again. My mouth was too dry to speak; Jade shot me a look, half amused, half puzzled.

*Just two minutes*, I told myself. *Two minutes tops.*

My heart racing, I stepped inside and gingerly glanced around the room: everything looked sleek and bright, just like its owner. Large silver-framed mirrors that hung on painted mauve walls made the room seem bigger. A jaunty velvet chaise longue stood next to a fitting area at the back.

'All the dresses are arranged by decade from the twenties to the seventies,' Jade said from behind me. 'I also have some on sale on my right. Browse and see what you like, and if you need help, just call.'

Several clothing racks were punctuated by lacquered mannequins wearing striking designer pieces. A one-shoulder silk dress here, cascades of gentle ruffles of chiffon there, crystal beading around waistlines, vibrant shades of colours all around: lime, turquoise, tangerine, sea green, coral pink. My head swam. I couldn't look anywhere without seeing the possibilities of ghosts.

*Calm down, Chloe. Take a deep breath.*

The breath I took was shaky. It was impossible for me to peruse the collection without fretting. *Which dresses are safe to touch? Which ones will mess with my head?* It was like a twisted variant on the Russian roulette.

I glanced over at Jade, who was busy positioning jewellery in a velvet tray. I had to get out of here, and fast. I wove between the racks, hands jammed in my coat pockets, feigned interest in a glittery disco dress, then edged towards the door.

'Didn't you find anything you liked?'

I spun around, feeling myself flush. 'Your boutique is beautiful. It's just . . .' I paused, unsure what to say next. 'It's just that I've never really been into fashion.'

Jade's face registered surprise. She spread her arms to include the whole shop. 'All the dresses you see here aren't about fashion. They're made with real craftsmanship, artistry, and pride. Unlike fashion, style never fades.'

I nodded. 'I think Chanel said something along those lines.'

'And wasn't she right? Look,' Jade said, pausing at a mannequin dressed in a glorious white mass of tulle petticoats dotted with black stars. 'This is my most prized possession. A superb piece of work you'd never find on the high street. Even if they made a replica today, it'd never match the quality and ease of movement you get from this fabric.'

'It's an Orry-Kelly, isn't it?'

Jade beamed at me. 'Worn by Leslie Caron herself in *An American in Paris*. I bought it at an auction sale in New York when everyone else was distracted by Lauren Bacall's posthumous wardrobe. If Caron was dead today, I don't think I could ever have afforded it.'

I nodded again. 'My past employer told me he seriously considered bidding on it.'

'Ah, well, lucky for me he didn't. What does he do, if I may ask?'

'He's an artistic director in the West End.'

'Really? Do you work on stage musicals?'

'I did,' I hedged, 'for a while.'

Jade gave a low whistle of appreciation. 'And did you design some of those dresses yourself?'

'Oh no, nothing of the sort. I was just a simple costume assistant.'

Jade arched her eyebrows. 'Mending costumes is no simple job.' Then she paused, hesitant. 'I hope you won't find me intrusive, but it sounds like you left it all behind.'

I looked at the floor, wishing I had *truly* left it all behind. The ghosts, the past. Matt. Everything. 'It's a long story,' I said eventually.

'Try me,' Jade prompted. 'I'm a good listener. Some people find it quite cathartic to confide in strangers.'

I looked up at her, not completely lulled by the warmth of her voice. I wasn't going to start telling her the whole truth. But I could tell her a part of it, or at least try to summon up some positive moments.

So I told her of the surge of adrenaline we'd all felt before a premiere: make-up artists and hairstylists rushing into dressing rooms to fix faces, wigs, and hairdos; costume assistants helping actors shed costumes to swiftly slip into others. Sometimes I would discreetly watch them act on stage, feel the emotion pour out of them, their talent transporting me into a different reality.

And then I fell silent, my thoughts going off on a tangent. Dark thoughts. A broken snap, a loosened waistband, a sleeve ripped out at the seam.

Cold dresses.

All I had to do was touch them to trigger a switch in my head. Only later did I come to understand that silk had the power to absorb memories. I could somehow see those memories, sense them, hear them when they were charged with strong, intense emotions, as if some essence from the previous owner was able to reach me telepathically and let me tune in to their world. It invariably captured their final moment, the scent of death lingering by their side, the tragedy seeping into their clothes.

Their stories, however fragmented, still haunted me to this day. A girl in a Victorian corset floating in the sky, two wet eyes and that third eye—a red bullet hole—never blinking. A 1940s ghost with a bloodstain spread across the midriff of her ivory dress. Someone tried to coerce her into aborting the small life growing inside her, but when she refused, her body was found swinging from the rail of her wardrobe, hanging from a rope. I could still hear her voice pleading for justice, howling that she never took her own life.

Jade waited patiently through my silence. She nodded encouragingly, willing me to carry on.

Finally, I asked, 'Do you think some dresses have a story to tell?'

I knew I shouldn't be asking. Hinting at the turmoil raging inside me was risky, but Jade didn't look taken aback and seemed to give my question some thought.

'They can certainly tell you a thing or two,' she answered. 'For example, ask two women of similar shape and size to try on the same designer dress. Why does it look stunning on one and wrong on the other?'

'Fit and fabric, I suppose.'

'Of course, alterations can make it more "*amenable*."' She made quotation marks with her fingers. 'But you still won't get the wow factor if it's not the right dress in the first place. The dress simply won't allow you to become someone you're not.'

'Are you saying that dresses have a mind of their own?'

She smiled, a shade more cautious now. 'We as women think we choose our dresses, but is it really true? I'd rather think of it as a love story. A symbiosis happens, like a magical spark that comes to life when a woman and a dress find each other. The dress only truly belongs to one soul.'

'You make it sound like a fairy tale,' I said. 'Or a rather unconventional sales pitch.'

She laughed. 'It certainly requires a leap of faith.'

'Oh, it's not that. I just never thought of a special dress that way.'

'I take it you've not found yours yet. Why don't we give it a go?'

Jade skimmed through the racks, selecting and eliminating dresses with an expert eye until she held up one for me made of emerald-green taffeta.

'It's by Balenciaga. Don't you love the elegant simplicity of the cut?'

I nodded, distracted. I noticed something moving out of the corner of my eye. There, at the back: a halo of blue light bounced atop a rack of clothes. I looked up at the sprinkling of tiny downlights that peppered the ceiling, but none of them were blue. It was as if the rack generated its own light by enchantment.

'So, what do you . . .?' Jade followed my gaze and froze.

I walked over to the light, watched the glow fade and ebb away in quick pulses, fizzling along the edges of a dress, until it revealed its true colour at last—a dark shade of teal. I could barely breathe.

It was the same silk dress I saw H.P. wear in my vision.

Something flared in Jade's eyes: shock or fear or both—I wasn't sure when I glanced at her as she grabbed hold of the dress and hung it on the clothing rack.

'I don't think this is your size,' she said.

The flatness in her voice was unmissable. She moved towards another rack at the front of the shop, shuffled through more dresses, and beckoned me to come closer, and I knew immediately what she was trying to do: drag my attention away from the teal-blue dress.

Which was a good thing, I reminded myself, a very good thing, because part of me wanted nothing to do with it. Yet I couldn't stop questioning its presence. More thoughts unravelled. I realised that part of what I'd heard and seen in my head had materialised in real life: the lone oak tree by the cliff, the Scissor Sister name, the teal-blue dress. So many coincidences. Too many coincidences happening in one small town. Something had happened, something bad.

Black dread came over me like a wave. I took a deep breath, trying to slow down my heartbeat. *Think, Chloe. What did I really see?*

There were two cars. A red sports car, her car. Brakes screeching, she'd quickly lost control on the wet zigzagging road. The other one was chasing her—chasing H.P. —until it caught up with her and they both drove side by side. Someone blared their horn, but I couldn't tell which car. Did they push H.P. off the road? I couldn't remember. It all went so fast, and it felt as if I'd wasted too many precious seconds staring at the tree.

I thought of asking Jade. The way she'd just looked at the dress . . . She might know, maybe she could tell me something. Or maybe not, because nobody knew how my ghosts had really died, their deaths uninvestigated or ruled an accident or suicide. Nobody knew but me.

And their murderers.

My hand brushed the sleeve of the dress, the silk softer and more luxurious than anything I could dream of owning. On impulse I took it off the rack, but unlike any of the other dresses, no price tag was hooked to the inside label. In fact, there was no label at all. I turned to look back and realised Jade was watching me. She said nothing, just stared at me with one floral sundress in each hand. Both looked perfect for a fourteen-year-old—no doubt these would fit me nicely.

'Would you like to try them on?' she asked.

I held up the teal-blue dress to her, a hopeless gesture. It would suit the body of a bustier woman, or one who eats regularly; Jade was right when she said it wasn't my size.

She trailed me into the dressing area, silent and righteous, and I glimpsed what she did every time she had to deal with a stubborn customer: let the mirror do the talking. But inside, I undressed with my eyes cast down, studiously avoiding my reflection. The dress rustled around my legs, sliding too easily over my hips.

A gentle rap at the door. 'Do you need help with the zip?'

I came out and let Jade fasten it. When she finished I dragged my gaze up to meet one of the framed mirrors on the wall: my eyes widened.

The boat neck delicately cradled my shoulders. The silk bodice hugged my upper body, and the skirt altered the hard lines of my hips into hourglass curves. I stood taller too, as if I were undergoing a subtle, fleeting transformation that took shape because of the dress. I could hardly believe it was me I was staring at.

'You look beautiful,' Jade said.

She sounded stunned. I thought of her choice of words earlier: *symbiosis, magical spark*—this was probably not quite what she had in mind. I moved closer to the mirror, taking in every inch of my new figure. Behind me, Jade bit her bottom lip, leaving a little ridge in her cherry-red lipstick.

She caught my eye. 'Would you like to buy the dress?'

I froze. *Buy the dress* . . . Buying *this* dress would be stupid, reckless, dangerous—like driving a car along the edge of a cliff (a poor choice of analogy, I know). I couldn't let myself be fooled by an illusion. Couldn't let vanity sway me for the sake of looking ravishingly beautiful.

I turned to Jade. 'Yes, please, I'd love to.'

I know I shouldn't have said that. I *know*. But I was in the moment, happy, confident, and I just thought, *Sod it, life's too short— I'm worth it.*

At the counter, Jade plucked a price out of thin air: big enough to make me swallow hard, but not so big to stop the receipt from printing. I noticed then that she was staring at my name on the bank card.

'I'm so sorry,' she said. 'I didn't realise you were Kathryn's daughter.'

She handed the dress over without looking at me. She was probably feeling uncomfortable, having made the connection between me and Matt. People in small towns tend to have long memories.

I diverted the topic. 'So how long have you known my mother?'

'A while. We're more like colleagues, really.'

'Colleagues?'

She looked up at me. 'Have you heard of Scissor Sister?'

I nodded, stunned. Quickly said a muffled goodbye and left the shop.

I strode along the square with my thoughts tangled, tripping over each other. My mother, Tina, Cordelia, Jade—how many more women were there involved?

*Scissor Sister is watching you.* Those words flared in my mind like sparks. And H.P., that mysterious ghost: I could sense her presence again, grey and cold and following me, hissing in my ears.

'Stay in Heavendale?' I scoffed. 'Fat chance of that.'

The wind blew fiercer, blasting me furiously. She was punishing me for pushing her voice away. A gust was almost lifting me off my feet when I exited Market Square to retrace my steps. Wrong direction. I stumbled backwards, steadied myself against a lamp post, and raised my carrier bag to shield myself.

'What do you want?' I shouted to her.

Something came alive by my side: a touch, a transparent hand next to my arm. Her cold fingers pressed mine, tightened their grip, the chill seeping through my flesh and down into my bones. I felt frightened, confused, and yet I sensed she meant me no harm. She wanted me to acknowledge her, to accept what I'd always known: that the dead never really die, that in the air between the living, there is a city of lost souls. They roam anxious and restless, seeking solace and comfort.

Looking for a light in the darkness.

## 8

H.P. was gone.

I sensed a shift, a return to *normalcy* in the air as I walked. The sky was restored to this morning's blue. A change of wind had swept away the low-hanging clouds; a warmth supplanted her presence.

That's when I knew she was really gone.

I sat on a bench by the lake and watched a group paddling kayaks across the waters. I realised I knew nothing about her life and little about her death. All I had gathered—I felt almost certain of it—was that someone had killed her, in Heavendale, and that it wasn't an accident, even though it had looked like one. No proof, no clue, no idea as to why or when it happened exactly. Nothing to go by but a dress and a name: Scissor Sister. It wasn't much, but at least I had somewhere to start, someone who could point me in the right direction. I just couldn't pass up the opportunity to meet her and attend her little gathering at Stonebarn Lake.

It was quarter to three when I skittered up the spiral staircase, eager to change out of my coffee-stained jeans. Halfway up, I heard a pair of heels clatter down. I glimpsed knee-high leather boots, plump thighs, a tartan miniskirt. I didn't see more—I was rushing.

'Watch it, sweetie!'

The collision with Tina made me lose my grip on the carrier bag. It went flying behind, spilling out the dress over the steps in untidy folds. Tina dropped her gaze and clapped her hand to her mouth, barely able to stifle a scream.

The kitchen door flew open. Four women rushed in with

questioning looks on their faces: my mother, Cordelia, Jade, and a pretty girl with Farrah Fawcett hair formed a silent line against the wall. They too stared down at the teal-blue dress lying on the stairs.

My mother raised her head first. 'Well, go on, sweetheart—you're not going to let it gather dust, are you?'

'I've just bought a dress, Mum.'

'I can see that.'

I stooped to pick it up. 'Does it look familiar to you?'

'Of course not. What a strange question to ask.'

'I was just curious.'

'Curious? About what?'

I clenched the silk between my hands. 'I-I was wondering if . . . I mean, perhaps you can tell me something . . .' I kept tripping over my words. My mouth was dry, my skin hot. I turned my head back and forth and saw all five pairs of eyes fastened on me, waiting. I felt as though I couldn't get enough oxygen into my lungs.

'Is something the matter, sweetheart?' Her voice sounded more snappish than concerned as she glanced impatiently at her slim silver watch.

'No. Nothing,' I blurted. 'I just need to freshen up.'

'Fine. Please be on time.'

I scurried upstairs but glanced downward as I rounded the curved banister. Jade was looking at my mother, giving a slight shake of her head. She must have told her about the dress, and yet, I was sure there was more to it. Something shared by that quintet of women eluded me. I couldn't explain it, but I could sense it: an undertow of complicity shaped like a spiked energy ball, tension bubbling beneath the surface. And at its core, something dark and ugly.

In my bedroom I splashed my face with cold water. I had this sudden urge to stir up a reaction in these women, something other than denial and a compliant front of silence. So I put the dress on (it still fitted me beautifully), brushed my hair, and dabbed on some lipstick. After a couple of deep breaths, I padded my way downstairs and into the luminous white living room.

My mother gasped but didn't address me at all. She swiftly turned her attention to a pile of notes on the table. Tina and Jade stood behind her, pretending to read whatever she was pretending to peruse with rapt attention. Cordelia shuffled uncomfortably in her chair, looking even paler than she had this morning. Only the pretty blonde girl made a genuine attempt to acknowledge my presence.

'Hi,' she said, coming towards me, her bouncy curls swishing around her shoulders. Her face up close was thick with make-up. 'I'm Kimberley. I totally love your dress.'

She lowered her voice for the word *dress*, as if it were contaminated. Then she went on talking about clothes, her visiting sister, her lovely haberdashery store south of Market Square, her hair, and the horrible dye job Kendall had done at the local salon last Valentine's Day. 'I had to drive all the way to Vidal Sassoon before my boyfriend took me out to dinner—Do you have a boyfriend, Chloe?'

As soon as she said that, she clamped her mouth shut and glanced hurriedly over at my mother, then back at me with a nervous laugh. 'Oops, I'm so sorry. That totally slipped out.'

'That's okay,' I said. 'I hope you two are happy together.'

'Oh, we are.' She extended an arm to show off her gold bracelet inlaid with green stones. 'Rob gave it to me yesterday. Aren't I the luckiest girl in the world?'

I nodded. She sounded so artificial, like someone gushing their happiness on some tacky TV chat show. I decided to change the subject. 'So, what can you tell me about the meeting?'

'The meeting?' She appeared to be thinking for a moment. 'Of course, I almost forgot it's your first time.' And with that she told me how *busy-busy* she was managing the sales, praised the amazing work done by the rest of the group, and gushed about how grateful she was for this *totally* wonderful opportunity to work for Scissor Sister.

I concluded then that 'Scissor Sister' wasn't her.

Just when I was about to ask when *she* was due to arrive, the doorbell rang and my mother rose from her chair, solemnly declaring, 'Ladies, she's finally here.'

The room fell silent when the door opened.

The mysterious woman stood in semi-darkness in the hallway, a backlit figure uttering muffled words at my mother, her voice husky and low. The scent of her perfume drifted in, expensive and musky, with a touch of frankincense. It smelled oddly familiar.

'Frisky Lady,' whispered Kimberley, who'd leaned closer to me.

'I'm sorry?'

She gestured towards the hallway. 'The name of Patsy's perfume.'

As the woman walked into the living room, I studied her: long and thin (probably too slim), late thirties and sharply dressed in a little navy jacket, her hair coiffed in an old-fashioned bouffant. I realised I had met her before as she slung her black Prada bag onto a chair at the end of the table, gave everyone a tight-lipped smile.

'It's so wonderful to be back.' She sounded anything but thrilled.

'Patsy,' said my mother, 'I want to introduce you to my daughter, Chloe. She's visiting.'

I stayed silent as I shook hands with her, her fingers tight and bony on mine. We had met at a photoshoot a couple of years ago, when I got booked through a temp agency to dress some of her models. Patsy Carter, a former Vogue editor who'd founded her own fashion magazine called *Retro Mode*. Credited (rightly or not) for reversing the fortunes of vintage fashion, or at least making it trendy and marketable to a younger audience. I doubted she would remember me, and yet, judging by her curious stare . . .

'What a fabulous dress you're wearing, Chloe. Did you . . . borrow it?'

*Borrow it?* I shook my head in surprise. 'No, actually I bought it this morning.'

'You *bought* it?'

Something else flickered in her eyes, making my pulse quicken at the base of my throat. Patsy must have seen the dress before too. In fact, they had all seen it before—I was sure of that now. And with that knowledge came the (almost) certainty they all knew who H.P. was.

I nodded.

'Right,' she said after a short pause, then dismissed me with an elegant shrug. She swept her gaze over the other women. 'I guess it's time to start our meeting. Shall we?'

At their nods, she smoothed her designer jacket and passed the pile of notes around the table. I sat between Kimberley and Cordelia, staring down at the meeting agenda, my stomach tensing into a solid knot.

*Easy, Chloe, easy,* I told myself. *Watch and observe.*

Whatever they were hiding, I had to find out. Learn everything I could about the way this group of women operated.

My mother kicked off the proceedings with the latest sewing pattern she was testing. Jade mentioned their blog; there were some nice new trends she wanted to see featured online. Next, Tina said she was organising an auction for the handmade and vintage fair and asked everyone in the room to donate something. My mother offered a lemon-yellow jersey dress she'd made from a Vogue pattern, while Jade raised the stakes but shortened the length with a 1960s Cardin miniskirt. Tina groaned with approbation and the rest of the group promised to come back to her later in the week.

Then Cordelia declared that Scissor Sister had entrusted her with a sponsorship deal from Craftsy. I looked at her, confused: Had she just called Patsy by her brand name? How odd when she was physically present in the room.

I blinked the thought away and stole a glimpse at Kimberley. She didn't have much to say, or perhaps she simply struggled to get a word in edgeways. That all changed when the group started discussing the Amelia pattern. Turns out Amelia is the pretty name for a pretty

1950s DIY dress—their bestseller, I was informed. Recently launched digitally, but from what I gathered, their Scissor Sister intranet (shortened in rather bad taste to 'SS intranet') reported delays in shipping orders for the printed format.

All eyes darted to Kimberley.

'Ah,' she sighed, and gave a lock of her hair a quick tweak. 'I'm sure I'll be back on track by Friday.'

'Hmm, I don't share your optimism,' Tina countered. 'A thirty-two percent increase in order backlog . . . It's no mean feat to catch up.'

'How do you know?' Kimberley gasped, one hand fluttering dramatically to her chest.

'It's my business to know, sweetie.'

'No. How do *you* know?' Kimberley glowered, then went on addressing the rest of the group. 'I can't believe this. She stole my online passcode.'

'I didn't.'

'Oh, I'm sure you did. You couldn't have had access to that information otherwise.'

'You've got some bloody nerve accusing me when you've been slacking.'

My mother pounded the table with her fist when Kimberley went to respond. 'That's enough. We cannot let this meeting descend into chaos.'

'So you're defending her?' snapped Tina. 'I doubt Scissor Sister will tolerate her excuses much longer.'

My mother gave Tina a quick, sharp glance while Patsy looked on, impassive, tapping her teeth with her Mont Blanc. She was either treading a fine line between cult of personality and egomania, or I was missing something.

Next to me, Kimberley began to weep. I spotted a pack of Kleenex on the dresser and handed it to her, thus making my first tangible contribution to the meeting.

'Thank you,' she said, sniffing between sobs. She yanked a tissue out, dabbed at her tears, then looked distraught when it came away smudged with make-up. I spotted the faded line of a yellowish bruise on her left cheekbone.

'My compact!' she yelped, fumbling inside her handbag. 'I need my compact.' She pulled out a brown eyeliner pencil, a ring of keys, and a small bottle of water. She grew more distraught with each new item that wasn't what she was seeking.

I felt sorry for her and tried to think of something useful to say, then leaned towards her and squeezed her arm. 'What about Suzanne? I think she wouldn't mind helping you.'

'Suzanne?' Kimberley barked. 'Suzanne who? Aaah, here it is!' She flipped her compact open.

When I looked up, I caught the other women staring at us. I felt another flash of heat.

Kimberley retouched her face, eyes darting back and forth between them and her compact mirror. 'What?' she eventually demanded. Then looking straight at me, she said, 'Oooh, did you mean Suzanne Paige? But that's impossible. She's no longer working with us.'

I looked across the table at my mother. 'Mum, what happened?'

'Suzanne was sadly unable to continue her involvement,' she said in a stiff, cryptic tone.

'Has she left Heavendale?'

'No.'

'Then why can't she help Kimberley?'

'That's completely out of the question.'

'I thought she was your friend . . .'

'I thought she was too, sweetheart. I'll allocate time in my schedule to help Kimberley this week.'

'But Mum, tell me—'

'Chloe, please, we want this meeting to finish on time. Now, no more.' Her tone was final; I could already feel the conversation moving on.

Twenty minutes later, Patsy looked at her watch and said, 'I'd like to share with you a few words of encouragement from Scissor Sister herself before we wrap up this meeting.'

My throat tightened. It finally dawned on me that I'd stupidly jumped to conclusions about Patsy, that I'd got it completely wrong. She wasn't Scissor Sister.

She read a page in front of her:

'My dearly beloved Sisters,

The fair is approaching fast, and the time has come to demonstrate the power of our brand. Put Scissor Sister first! Redouble your efforts! Only through hard work can our journey towards market domination be complete. Until we become the one and only true choice.'

Kimberley clapped as soon as Patsy finished reading; my mouth hung open. From every corner of the table, speculation arose.

'The one and only true choice? That should make selling plain sailing.'

'For sure she's taking the fair very seriously.'

'I even heard she might attend it, sweetie.'

'Ladies, please.' My mother's voice. 'We shouldn't get ahead of ourselves.'

'I'm surprised she didn't remind us of our ACE values.'

My head jerked from one moving mouth to the next, lost in their quick-fire conversation until I turned to Cordelia. 'What is ACE?'

'Allegiance—Control—Expansion,' she whispered.

'Are you kidding me?' I whispered back.

Her forehead furrowed as if she smelled something nasty. I sensed she wasn't buying that puzzling display of megalomania, unlike the others.

I took advantage of a lull in the hubbub to make my voice heard, a burning question on my lips—'But who is Scissor Sister?'

Kimberley smiled at me as if she were having an angelical experience. 'She's like a Big Sister to us.'

And then Jade said, 'We don't know. We've actually never met her.'

I stared at her, thinking she might be joking. She looked dead serious, so I moved my gaze to Patsy. 'But didn't she speak to you about that message you've just read?'

Patsy shook her head. 'All communication between her and us is done strictly via the SS intranet.'

'She doesn't wish to disclose her identity. Even to us, her employees,' added Jade.

'But don't you find it . . . weird?' I asked.

'Nah.' Tina shrugged. 'She ain't no weirdo, sweetie.'

'She simply doesn't want to be known publicly,' my mother said. 'I think we should all be respectful of her privacy.'

'We think she might be living in London,' said Kimberley in a low, secretive voice though everyone heard her.

'That's pure speculation,' said Patsy.

'But why don't you . . .?' I began.

My mother struck her hands together in a single sharp clap. 'Right, ladies. Anyone for tea?'

End of conversation: The women murmured assent and began trooping into the kitchen. As Kimberley crossed to the door, I watched her flick a curl of her perfect Farrah Fawcett hair. In my mind, the analogy seemed almost ideal: a roomful of Charlie's Angels who didn't know the identity of their enigmatic boss, an intranet system that supplanted the old-school squawk box.

I tried to see the funny side, forcing an inner smile. *It's fine. It's fine.*

And then, floating in the fore of my mind, I sensed it again: that spiked energy ball pulsing like a beating heart.

Black heart.
Dark energy.
A faceless, unseen fear.

# 9

In the kitchen we all drank green tea with sliced lemons.

'Perfect for inner cleansing,' my mother announced cheerfully while pouring the pissy-looking stuff into dainty china cups.

I brought mine to my nose—it smelled sharp, could do with a spoonful of sugar, or a finger or two of sweet vodka. I took a sip and stifled a grimace, then let my eyes roam around the room.

Beside the bifold doors drawn open onto the garden, Jade and Cordelia were chatting quietly, their red and black hair catching the sunlight. Floral notes of spring air softened the scent of Patsy's perfume as she moved past me, her strides graceful, her jacket swaying elegantly with each step. In sharp contrast to Tina who, well, pretty much dressed like a hooker. I looked in her direction and noticed she seemed to be sharing a private joke with Kimberley, the two of them chuckling, getting along splendidly. Strange.

A voice in the distance mentioned my name—it was my mother, who was engaging Patsy in a conversation about my old job. 'Chloe is working in London. Of course, she designs lovely vintage clothes. She even meets famous West End stars!'

False and flashy exclamations made in the present tense, as though our morning's conversation had never happened.

When she caught me staring at her, she excused herself and came over to my side, whispering, 'Don't pull such a long face, sweetheart. I'm only trying to widen your opportunities here. We'll pretend you're still employed, okay?'

She patted my shoulder twice and walked away from me to refill more dainty cups, like Hyacinth Bucket playing the concerned mother. I wanted to slap the hypocrisy off her face.

A sinewy hand passed a plate of biscuits to me.

'I noticed you haven't touched any. Perhaps you'd like one?' Cordelia said.

I politely plucked one off the plate and nibbled its edge. The taste of ginger turned to sawdust on my tongue.

When she left the room minutes later, I followed her down the hallway. 'Cordelia, I want to ask you about this dress.'

Her hand paused on the front door handle. 'Yes?'

'You've seen it before, haven't you?'

She turned to me with a frail smile. Her tall, slender frame was shaking slightly, small tremors that she struggled to stop. 'You're mistaken, my dear. I was merely looking at it. Who wouldn't relish the chance to buy a beautiful blue silk dress like yours?'

'Not you,' I retorted. 'I can tell you're partial only to purples and blacks. Besides, you heard Patsy. You know as well as I do, this dress was never meant to be sold.'

Her smile crumbled. She glanced nervously over her shoulder, her face lined and powdered white, her knuckles turning the same colour from the pressure of her grip.

I pressed on. 'Do the initials H.P. mean anything to you?'

Her whole body jolted; she pulled open the handle.

'Cordelia,' I called after her. 'Wait!'

I was out the door and on the step when she strode across the front path, her long silk scarf fluttering around her neck. My mind raced, filled with fractured thoughts: *Stop her. Don't. Tell her. You can't. You can.* I could taste the sweat of conflict beading my upper lip.

'Please,' I cried, my voice wobbling. 'I need your help. S-she made contact with me!'

I stood panting with the effort of letting go of those words, as if I had to snap metal prison bars to let them out.

Cordelia stopped dead in her tracks. She spun around, strode back over and stared at me, long enough for me to become uncomfortable under the weight of her eyes.

'It's the pattern,' she finally said, a hand fluttering to her mouth.

'You've seen that dress pattern too.'

I nodded manically. 'Someone dropped it by in a box two days ago. I mean, she did—H.P., I saw her. She took on the shape of a cloud. She also appeared in my head. Like a ghost.' I stopped, too aware I wasn't making any sense. 'But she's dead, isn't she? She can't be real.'

Cordelia gave me a warmer smile this time. 'My dear child, you can't deny what you so plainly see. It's your gift that allows you to sense her presence.'

'More like a curse,' I said bitterly. 'All it's ever brought me is pain.'

'One day you'll change your mind. It takes time and dedication to fathom the mysteries of the afterlife.'

'Is it what you really do?' I asked. 'Tina said you're a psychic.' Tina also implied she wasn't a very good psychic, which left me wondering . . .

'Oh me,' she said with a flap of her hand. 'Please don't be fooled by the label. I'm simply incapable of communicating with the dead, or explaining to you any shape or form of paranormal activity. But I have other ways—let's say more *natural* talents. Plenty can be achieved with logic and intuition.'

'So how did you find out about the pattern?'

'That's simple. I received a copy just like you. Two days ago.'

'You did?' I wasn't sure if I should feel relieved or more disturbed. Probably both. 'But what's so special about it?'

'Ah,' she said, clasping her palms together. 'That's an excellent question. One I had no answer for until I saw you wearing the dress this afternoon. Then something clicked.'

My heartbeat raced. 'What clicked?'

She unclasped her hands and pointed a finger at me. 'Your dress, of course. Isn't it the reason you bought it?'

'I'm sorry, but I'm not following you.'

'Didn't you examine the drawings on the pattern?'

'I . . . did,' I replied hesitantly, even though they were only a vague memory.

'But didn't you see? The shape of the dress, the coloured pencil silhouettes in teal blue. There's no mistaking that you're now wearing the original inspiration behind the pattern.'

Right then it all clicked into place. The swatch, the pattern, the dress: They were all related, and H.P. had been trying to direct my attention to them all along.

'So the pattern is a replica?'

'It's certainly strikingly similar.' She scanned my dress up and down then rubbed my sleeve between her fingers. 'Pure silk crepe,' she said. 'Probably sewn by a highly skilled seamstress, if not several of them. An exquisite example of fine craftsmanship. Quality of detailing and execution rarely seen in modern clothes.'

'But why would H.P. make a pattern with my name on it?' I asked. 'I never met her in my whole life. I don't even know what her initials stand for.'

I stared at her, hoping she would take the bait and tell me, but she lapsed into silence. The background clatter of teacups and chatter drifted from the kitchen.

'Cordelia,' I said softly. 'Who is she, please?'

There was a beat of silence between us, and she pulled a small smile. 'This I can't tell you, I'm afraid.'

'You *can't*?' I took a step towards her. 'But why? Did she do something wrong?'

'My dear, sometimes it isn't so much a matter of right or wrong but what goes on beneath. Some stories are so deeply rooted that the eye can easily be fooled.'

'Then help me put the pieces together. I know for sure her death wasn't an accident.'

'Is this why she's so restless? Is this why she's reaching out to you?'

I nodded. 'Yes, I'm positive.'

Cordelia looked me steadily in the eye. 'Then you can't trust anyone.'

'What do you mean?' I snapped. 'You don't understand. I need answers. She needs me to find the truth.' Behind me, I heard the sound of a spoon hitting the floor and looked over my shoulder into the house.

Cordelia grabbed me by the arm. 'Don't even think about it,' she warned.

'But my mother knows.'

'No, Chloe. Not even your own mother. Kathryn has woven her own web, now she's trapped in it. You'd only be wasting your time asking her.'

'Jesus, Cordelia. What's going on?' I could feel my throat closing, my heart thudding in my chest.

She released my arm and stepped back. 'But that's precisely the thing, my dear—I'm not quite sure myself. I know what's happening on the surface, but not beneath. And yet I sense there's a connection somehow.'

She paused, her brow furrowing, then grabbed both my hands, firmly holding them in her own. 'You must give me a little time, a couple of days at least, to understand what truly happened. I promise to come back to you with answers.'

I was too stunned to reply, her words not quite sinking in.

She squeezed my hands tighter. 'Now it's your turn. You must keep quiet. Promise.'

'Why?'

'Just promise me. Please.'

Her gaze bored into mine, and I had to fight every instinct in my body to relent and accept what she was asking of me—'I promise.'

Cordelia let go of my hands, satisfied. But in the back of my mind, confusion remained; a dancing flicker of doubt that wouldn't go away. As she turned to leave, I couldn't help but ask her, 'What did you mean by "connection?"'

She glanced back at me. 'Oh, nothing much, my dear. I was just thinking of your reaction earlier. It's strange, isn't it, that none of us have ever met Scissor Sister?'

## SCISSOR SISTER

So now you're wondering who I am.

Come on, you know perfectly well who I am.

Now, I'm not trying to play clever. I'm not trying to deflect your question, but who I *really* am is of no importance. You and I aren't going to have the sort of relationship that needs real names.

I can hear you thinking aloud. I can sense your resistance.

You're suspicious. Why should you trust me?

*Why?*

Questions. Doubts. They gnaw, they eat at you. One day they'll kill you if you're not careful.

Blind faith is paramount to truly appreciate the dark.


Come join me now.

Don't be afraid.

Your hopes, your fears . . . Leave them in my hands.

I can be your voice.

I can be so much more.

Let me show you the world through my eyes.

# 10

I tossed and turned into Tuesday, sweaty sheets sticking to my body in a tangle of bad dreams. I woke startled several times to a fox howling, the wind blustering, my gut growling, and a flash of blue light pulsing through the gap in my wardrobe door—maybe I had imagined it.

It was daylight when I heard a recycling van trundling up the road, someone dragging a wheelie bin. I pulled open the curtains and stared out at rain clouds looming over the mountains. Beneath the grey mass, on the same steep, rocky path sheltered by fir trees, I spotted that group of women again, like miniature toys hurrying downhill. I glanced over at my digital clock. Next to a near empty glass of vodka, it blinked at me 07:04.

Downstairs, thirty minutes later: my mother had wisely refrained from cooking the full English. Instead she offered me a bowl of granola, which I soaked with milk, then twirled my spoon nonchalantly until it turned soft and soggy.

She looked at me in silence before saying, 'Chloe. How about we do something nice today? Just the two of us.'

This sounded out of character but I supposed she was feeling guilty for the way she'd acted towards me the day before: the awkward silences. Aborted conversations when she wouldn't talk about the dress. When she wouldn't discuss why her friendship with Suzanne had broken off either.

Today, though, a slightly different tune: let's play happy family and pretend everything's fine. *Be a good girl, sweetheart.* I wondered what my mother was so desperately trying to hide.

'What have you got in mind?' I asked.

'Hmm, I was thinking about a walk down Windermere. Now I'm not so sure.'

She chewed the edge of her lip, turned her face to the window as if to make a point about the sky turning dark. I could sense her internal struggle, her helplessness at trying to bridge the distance between us. But underneath that, a thought: the pattern. I needed to get my hands back on it. And on the table, a means: among the scattered mail, the latest issue of a sewing magazine.

I tore off the plastic wrap and idly flipped its pages, pretending to be casual.

Cordelia's strange words turned over in my mind: '*Kathryn has woven her own web . . . You'd only be wasting your time asking her.*' Unless I took a more subtle approach. Nothing too direct or that could be seen as prying.

I began chatting about a vintage dress on page six, showed her some inspiring images on page twelve. I supposed, I added innocently, looking at patterns together would be a nice chance for us to catch up, rekindle the mother-daughter bond. Corny words, but they worked.

'That sounds wonderful, Chloe. I've got so many dress patterns to choose from. Maybe we could use the one you gave me yesterday?'

I pasted on a casual smile. 'Sure, why not.'

'I have plenty of lovely fabrics too. Hand-printed cottons, paisley prints, plush velvet. Damask and organza.' She glanced at me. 'Eat your granola, sweetheart.'

'Do you still keep your stash in the kitchen?' I spooned two tiny dried fruits with a dash of milk into my mouth.

'Not any more. I moved everything up to the loft last year.'

'The loft?' My sole distant memory of it was half-packed crates and stacks of boxes strewn across the floor. I'd only ventured there once, swiftly staggered my way out, and never went back.

My mother watched me, a smile playing on her lips. 'Come with me.'

Leaving my food behind, I trailed her up to the first floor, then up another flight of stairs and past a large wooden door.

Inside, the loft had been transformed and tidied: light and airy, thanks to a pair of skylights and white-bleached walls all around. In the centre stood a cutting workstation the size of a ping-pong table. On my right, a floor-to-ceiling shelving system. Files and folders were neatly arranged on top, next to a box. The middle shelf held a row of pictures wedged between clear acrylic frames. The bottom half held piles of fabric tucked into cubicles and sorted by colour palette.

My mother beamed at me. 'So, what do you think?'

'I'm impressed,' I said, my eyes roaming back over to three shots of me: a toddler with shiny red plaits; a child in a kitty-cat costume; aged sixteen, togged up in a yellow cupcake dress, awkward and plump. *Gross.*

'I'm glad you like it, sweetheart. It was high time I made good use of this space.'

'Why go for a sewing room, though?' The answer was obvious, but I couldn't help myself.

'I suppose dressmaking has become much more than just a hobby in my life lately.'

'You mean your business with Scissor Sister, right?'

She clucked her tongue. 'You make it sound like something dodgy.'

'Not dodgy. Just strange that you've never met her in person.'

She shrugged. 'We already explained that to you yesterday.'

*Not good enough*, I thought. Random words were starting to pop into my head: *riddle, fraud, invisible.* I had an itch to probe further, only restrained by the memory of my promise to Cordelia—that and I'd found another picture tucked in the back of the shelf, with its face to the wall. I reached back, intrigued, flipped it over, and felt a stab to my heart.

My dad, his arm wrapped around my mother's shoulder, his head leaning in lovingly towards her. I remember snapping it ten years ago, back when they were both scouring Cumbria for a new home, dreaming of a different life in a peaceful setting. Everything happened so fast when they found Stonebarn Lake; Dad had given himself a year to permanently move away from the stress of city life, and so he decided to convert the barn into a guest house, frequently commuting between work in London and Heavendale to supervise the project. He never saw the end of it. Two weeks before completion, he'd died—heart attack.

A sob built in the back of my throat. 'Do you still miss him, Mum?'

'Of course I do. It would be strange if I didn't. He was my husband.'

'I wish I'd had a chance to say goodbye.'

She sighed. 'It wasn't easy for me either; moving to a new town without him.'

I put the picture down; outside, daylight had dimmed to darker grey, rain clouds racing across the sky. 'Is it why you lost interest in the business?' I asked gently.

'The B&B?' She jolted back. 'No, no, I'm still running it.'

'That's not true, Mum. I never saw more than a handful of guests in here.'

'I told you my priorities are different now.'

'But I'm talking years ago. Right after Dad died.'

She flicked her hand, annoyed. 'Some things are just too complicated to explain. You were going through a difficult phase. You-you always were troubled.'

I didn't know what my mother meant—my crying jags over my lost dad, my eating disorder, or the *ghastly* ghost stories I'd shared with her when I was a child. Not that she'd ever acknowledged any of those things by name, just told me a few times to stop and grow up. It still filled me with an awful sense of shame.

'Was I ever a burden to you, Mum?'

The slightest of pauses before she replied, 'No, that's not what I meant.'

'I'm just curious why—'

'Your curiosity exhausts me, Chloe. All those pesky questions of yours when we should be having fun.'

My mother stomped across the room, her shoes slamming against the floorboards—as if she wanted to crush those sticky, bothersome emotions. She stopped in front of an antique carved trunk and lifted the lid.

'Come here,' she said. An order, not an invitation. 'I've got something to show you.'

Inside the trunk were about three dozen vintage fabric rolls. My mother met my questioning stare and said, 'They belonged to your grandma. Everything I learnt about dressmaking started with this trunk.'

'How long did she have it for?'

'As long as I can remember. These rolls you see are pure raw silk. She bought them when she worked in Heavendale decades ago.'

'I thought she'd set up her own dressmaking shop in London.'

'That was after,' she said with a slight smile. 'Your grandma came from a rural household in Cumbria. The garment factory was a great opportunity for skilled seamstresses like her after the war.'

She motioned for me to lean down and grab a shoebox inside the trunk. The box contained a rag doll with blonde yarn curls tied in bows. My favourite doll when I was five—Bonnie. Or Connie? I took it in my arms, brushed the little pink dress, and felt my lips curl into a nostalgic smile.

I remembered my grandma cutting the tiny dress pattern, the size drawn to fit the doll. Me on her knees, watching her hands guide the pink cotton under the presser foot of the sewing machine. Those exquisite hems she'd quickly sewn by hand as if her fingers danced around the needle. In my child's mind, she had created the most magical doll's dress in the world.

And then, a flash. Something long forgotten rose up like bile: Grandma sitting hunched over on a chair, lips quivering, face like wax, eyes glazed as if she were somewhere else. On her lap, balled in her fists, something shining like a ruby. In my ears, strange sounds: whispers, a discordant woman's voice. Not Grandma's. Someone else's. Someone I could not see.

Panic.

I cried and shook her by the arm—'Wake up, Grandma. Wake up.'

And then she jerked upright, gulped in air. Panted as if she'd been underwater too long. I clutched her side, buried my face in the crook of her neck. I could feel her pulse. Fast.

'Grandma, are you hurt?'

'No, my love, no. It was just a bad dream.'

Through the cracks between her trembling knuckles, I glimpsed a piece of bunched-up silk. A red dress she'd let slip off her lap with uncurled fingers. One last streak of ruby light fizzling along the sleeves . . .

I yanked myself from the memory and put the doll back in the box, my breath catching in my lungs. I was five or six back then, just a small thing. But now, reliving the memory through adult eyes, I finally understood what she'd been through, what still bound my late grandma and I together.

The same secret.

The same curse.

My mother's face lit up with pleasure while her hands heedlessly glided over an old silk gown in the trunk—it must have skipped a generation.

The doorbell rang, the sound muffled from two floors down. My mother glanced down at her watch, dug into a filing cabinet and pulled out the familiar manila envelope, then handed it to me and left to answer the door.

I didn't waste a moment.

As soon as she scuttled down the stairs, I emptied the contents of the envelope and scoured the drawings. The neckline, the waistband, those deep strokes of teal-blue crayon that gave the hand-drawn silhouettes a three-dimensional look. Cordelia was right: There was no mistaking that my dress had been copied.

From reading the instructions I learnt very little; they were just bullet points summing up sewing instructions. But it was the pattern pieces that caught my attention, the body measurements faintly pencilled above dotted arrows: These I knew were mine. I remembered scribbling them on the front page of a diary at the start of last year—a task I'd done purely out of necessity with all the weight flying off. I'd thought I would sew again to save myself the embarrassment of shopping in the petite or children's department (or rather, having to second-guess which one).

Matt had found me particularly alluring back then. When I was stripped naked in front of the mirror, his hands would run greedily all over my flesh: clasping, squeezing, scanning my scrawny freckled limbs, making sure the last bit of flab had vanished from my flanks. I'd let him inspect me like a breeder buying a horse. Then I let him fuck me against the wall, my head screaming in unison with his groaning. *Pump. Sick. Whore.*

Got more action in those grim winter months than I'd had in the entire five years of our relationship. Until the first day of spring, when he'd got down on one knee and slid a shiny engagement ring on my finger.

The door creaked and slammed shut with a crash, startling me out of my thoughts.

'Mum?'

Silence. I pushed it back open, crept along the landing, and peered over the banister. I saw nothing but the spiral staircase twisting down to the ground floor. In the distance, my mother's measured voice.

I came back into the loft, and only then did I notice something different. Small sounds. Subtle signs. The creak of floorboards, the brush of feet, the slow-moving whisper of a human-like voice. The knowledge—now too familiar—that H.P. had come back. It was, by her own standards, a subdued entrance. Maybe she could sense that I'd dropped my defences, that I was no longer afraid of her.

And I wasn't.

I wanted to know.

Desperately.

'Show me,' I called out to her. 'Show me who you are.'

The creaking stopped. Anticipation rose in my chest, as if my ribcage had tightened around my lungs.

A skylight window trembled, then flew open. A cold gust rushed into the room, gathered strength, and stirred everything in its path: paper, fabric, dust. I could hear her voice too, atonal and urgent—a *shh-shh-shh* sound hissing and whirling until things scuttled and moved and slid around me. A few books collapsed in messy piles on the shelves, the filing system fell into chaos. Something heavy crashed down with a thud. One last rush of air, and she spiralled out of the window, slamming it shut behind her.

Gone with the wind . . . Literally.

On the top shelf, a box had toppled over onto its side and spilled out an overturned envelope captioned *New Year's Day 2017 —Stonebarn Lake*, from which a sheaf of pictures had swooped down across the floor. I crouched down and piled them into my hands, peered at a shot of Patsy and Tina creased up with laughter. An inside joke? A funny anecdote? Regardless, these two had barely exchanged a word yesterday. Next, my mother and Suzanne, smiling at each other —happier times gone sour. Whatever had happened to these women in the space of fifteen months?

I flipped through more photos of clusters of merry people and the familiar faces of Cordelia, Kimberley, and Jade, with not the slightest clue of what I was looking for. The rain had started pattering on the roof, a steady, quiet roar, soothing and unnerving like an ominous lullaby.

Then, three feet away, a bulky A4 file tumbled down. It was filled with clear plastic sheets containing fabric samples and clippings from sewing magazines. Others held technical drawings and illustrations of dresses, all signed by my mother. A proper, rounded cursive script that was distinctly her own, although she never used her name once. Instead, the same strange pseudonym recurring page after page: *Sister of Trust*. Righteousness bordering on the sanctimonious. Creepy.

I slapped the file shut, disappointed, and went to continue gathering up the pictures. One of them stood three inches away from me, wedged upright into a crack between two whitewashed wooden boards. I stretched out my hand, and when I leaned over I froze, holding my breath when I recognised the teal-blue dress in the image.

It was *her.*

It was H.P.

She was raising a champagne glass, smiling for the camera, the garden a backdrop through glass doors. A man I didn't recognise standing close to her, his arm stiffly wrapped around her shoulders. Both were bunched up together between Suzanne and my mother. I felt sick, my insides churning into knots.

*Lies, lies, lies.*

I was feeling the urge to run to the bathroom and throw up when I realised I wasn't alone.

'Is everything okay, sweetheart?' My mother asked from behind me.

I started, scrambled away from her on all fours; reared back against the shelves and looked up at her. Her eyes flitted back and forth from the picture in my hand to the stack of others which, in my panic, I had dropped on the floor.

'I'll clear up,' she said, unfazed. 'You go and fetch the pattern for me.'

He voice was as soft as cream. She leaned down and smiled, stretched out her arm to me. 'Need some help, honey?'

I could feel her breath hot on my face.

She reached for the picture in my hand and I flinched, held on to it tight. Her smile began flickering like a failing fluorescent tube. On, off, on, off in the space of an instant. 'Chloe, I'm your mother. Please don't play games with me.'

'What are you hiding from me?'

'Give me that picture.'

'What are you hiding from me, *Mother*?'

She frowned and reached again, but I smacked her hand away. She looked stunned at my action, opened her mouth as if about to speak but then closed it again and shook her head. Straightened herself up and looked away from me. 'I knew you wouldn't just let that go.'

She began walking across the room, slow, creaking steps interspersed with the steady drip drip drip of the rain on the roof.

'You were always so troubled,' she said. 'Even as a child. That torment, that pain—it's ingrained in you. As if you can't help it. That's why I couldn't bring myself to tell you. Not then. Not on the day of Matt's funeral.'

*Creak*. Pause. *Creak*. Pause.

She let out a resigned sigh. 'I told myself I would later. So many times I asked you to come visit me, but you wouldn't. Wouldn't commit to a date. You made it so hard for me.'

I shifted my weight nervously on the floor, started rubbing a sweaty palm against my jeans. Outside the rain was beating harder, forceful and angry. My mother's footfalls stopped and I tensed.

She raised an accusing finger towards the picture in my hand. 'That little slut,' she started, repulsively, 'she ruined everything. Everything.'

For a second I didn't dare breathe, the change of mood so abrupt, one wrong word could shatter the confession.

My mother put her hand to her mouth and inhaled quickly—'She had an affair with Matt.'

'An affair?' I stuttered. Then a burst of shocked laughter as I stared back at the image of H.P. in my hand: strong, confident, independent. Not someone who would let a man degrade her. Not someone desperate to submit so she could be loved in return. Not someone to put up with physical or emotional abuse.

'That's ridiculous,' I said.

'There were witnesses.'

'What witnesses?'

'It doesn't matter any more. The news imploded shortly after his death.'

'What happened to her?'

'Chloe, please. There's no need to concern yourself over that girl's fate.'

'Why? Just because you think a slut's death doesn't matter?'

My mother blanched at my words. With each passing second she grew paler and stiller, her eyes trained on the floor, my heart throbbing like a drum through the relentless spatter of raindrops against the skylights. The voice that left her lips could have belonged to someone else:

'She didn't die alone, Chloe.'

*Didn't die alone!?* I held my breath. 'Who else?'

Another wet drumbeat. My mother's eyes fluttered for a second before she raised her gaze to meet mine.

One single word.

'Matt.'

A vein started throbbing in my temple. Hard. 'No, no that's impossible . . . You're lying. I know she was driving a sports car. It was bright red, chrome custom wheels, an expensive brand—'

'A Maserati,' my mother interrupted in a half whisper. 'It wasn't her car, Chloe. It was Matt's.'

My stomach sank. I couldn't breathe, the air trapped in my chest, hot and heavy. My mind reeled back to Saturday when I saw the date on the pattern, the name *Chlo* on the box. The realisation hit me like a cold, hard stone: two lives intertwined, two people who'd known each other. Who'd fucked each other.

Who'd died together.

'Oh, Mum, how could you not tell me?'

I hopped to my feet, fighting off a sudden wave of nausea. Something else churned inside me, something that cut deeper—betrayal. H.P. had used me. Used me as bait without a trace of guilt.

My mother reached out and desperately grabbed my arm. Her grip was so tight, it hurt. 'Remember, sweetheart, I was only trying to protect you. That girl meant nothing to him. Nothing. It's you he wanted to marry. It will always be you.'

I had a flash of myself in a white dress next to Matt's coffin, my mother shedding tears of joy. She was feeding him a forkful of wedding cake, piped buttercream dripping off his closed blue lips. In the background, the priest intoned, 'For better, for worse, for richer, for poorer, in sickness and in health, to love and to cherish. For death will never do you part.'

I let out a scream of horror and yanked my arm from her grip.

'Chloe!'

I fled from the room, not looking back at my mother.

# 11

4 April 2017

TWO PEOPLE DIE IN CUMBRIA CAR CRASH

POLICE RESPONDED TO REPORTS OF A CAR FOUND CRASHED INTO A TREE NEAR THE RESORT TOWN OF HEAVENDALE AT 8:50 P.M. LAST NIGHT.

HOLLY PAIGE, 25, WAS PRONOUNCED DEAD AT THE SCENE. MATTHEW THORNE, 31, SUFFERED SEVERE HEAD TRAUMA AND WAS PRONOUNCED DEAD SHORTLY AFTER ARRIVAL AT THE LOCAL HOSPITAL.

POLICE SAID MR THORNE WAS THE DRIVER OF THE CAR, A TWO-SEAT SPORTS MASERATI. EARLY INVESTIGATIONS SUGGESTED HE HAD BEEN TRAVELLING AT SPEED AT THE TIME OF THE CRASH. HE WAS DUE TO MARRY HIS FIANCÉE, CHLOE WESTFIELD, IN JUNE.

'SPEED-RELATED FATALITIES ARE CLEARLY VERY TRAGIC, AND OUR THOUGHTS AND CONDOLENCES GO OUT TO EVERYONE AFFECTED BY THIS,' SAID CHIEF INSPECTOR GORDON SMITH, OF CUMBRIA POLICE.

THEY ARE NOT TREATING THE INCIDENT AS SUSPICIOUS.

This article I dug up on the web by Googling Matthew Thorne along with the word *crash*. I struck lucky on the second page of results when I clicked on the *Westmorland Gazette*, a local newspaper. That's how

Mrs Hunt must have traced my relationship with Matt, when she saw both of our names in print.

That's how I found out who H.P. was.

A quick Facebook search confirmed what I suspected: Suzanne Paige was indeed Holly's mother. It immediately shed light on the strained atmosphere around the dress yesterday: Jade's reaction at Vintage Folly, then back at Stonebarn Lake with Tina, Cordelia, Kimberley, and Patsy. They all knew. They were all in cahoots.

I could picture them taking an oath of secrecy in front of my mother who, stiff-lipped and righteous, had already cast the roles in this gruesome tragedy: Holly as the devious temptress, Matt as the husband-to-be seduced into sin, and I as the hapless victim. As if life was ever that simple.

Footsteps in the corridor, followed by a quiet knock on my bedroom door.

'Chloe?' My mother, her voice croaky. I stayed rigid on the bed, hoping silence would make her go away. The handle jiggled, but I'd locked myself inside. 'I'm going over to Kimberley's, sweetheart. There's a lovely fish pie on the table. Still warm.'

My hands began sweating. I remained silent until I heard the front door open and close.

Downstairs, I gave the pie a miss. A red apple I peeled and cut into tiny dice. A three-quarter-full bottle of vodka I purloined from the cupboard, then took up to my room.

One dice methodically followed each sip, then another, and so on. I wanted to experience that progressive slippage, a slow and sweet numbing, my spare hand on the remote control, flipping from noise to noise as afternoon talk shows glided into evening soap operas and the day waned into night and a sole blue light flickered off the TV screen.

I stilled on a dispiriting late-night movie that told the story of a young blonde woman, betrayed and killed. I tried not to draw any parallel with Holly. I tried not to listen to the wind outside, a cry like winter, searing and bare, a lonely howl.

More booze.

When I hit the bottom of the bottle, I grabbed my iPad and tapped the touchscreen, my eyes falling back on the last sentence of the press article:

**THEY ARE NOT TREATING THE INCIDENT AS SUSPICIOUS.**

No one else saw the other car with the blinding headlights that night, the shadow inside it vanishing in the distance.

That's why she won't leave me be.


I woke with a start, mouth dry, my bleary eyes squinting at distorted red numbers glowing through the thick glass of the bottle—*Fucking vodka*. I pushed it aside, groggily.

08:48: I was desperate to remain asleep, but something felt wrong.

Last night . . . Something I shouldn't have done.

The feeling sank sharply into my chest and I sat upright, too quickly, my heart thumping hard. Flung down on the floor next to my bed was my iPad, a glossy, jet-black presence staring up at me accusingly.

I clearly remembered using it after watching the movie: a glimpse at the press article, me feeling wretched, and then a bleep, a message flashing on the gaming platform. It must have come from MysteryGeek; I was sure of it as I would play online with no one apart from MysteryGeek.

A new storyline must have spurred our brains into action. Josh and Vixen—the good old team was back, facing smugglers and murderers in a virtual LA or New York to try to solve another mystery. Except I couldn't remember any of it. Not a single scene. Not a clue as to what Vixen had been wearing either. My mind fumbled, but it was all a blank, a fog. As if alcohol had vaporised that fragment of memory and planted in its wake an impenetrable feeling of wrongness.

I scratched the sides of my head in frustration and got up to go to the bathroom. I drank water straight from the tap, giving myself a cursory glance in the mirror. I didn't look well. I didn't feel good either. My belly growled with hunger and my skull throbbed like a drum, resulting in a frightful inner cacophony. Instead I stripped and in the bathtub I lay flat, letting cool, almost cold water snake around my feet, my legs, my shoulders, my neck. My head sank lower, the water lapping at the edges of my nose, the ceiling rippling ice blue.

Ten seconds, fifteen, thirty, teeth chattering, lungs starving for air as I reached sixty and burst to the surface, panting, alive, my breathing coming in ragged gasps. Best hangover remedy. It was almost cathartic.

As I got dressed I felt a sense of urgency to do something —*anything*. I felt quite desperate as I tried to figure out my next course of action. I just couldn't give up on Holly—for better or worse, whether or not she'd had an affair with a man I had long ceased to love, H.P. had become a part of my life now. I needed to know what had *really* happened to her that night.

I had to find a way to free her.

Outside my bedroom door lay a tray laden with breakfast food. Standing against a thermos flask was a card with a short note from my mother: *I'm sorry, Chloe. Please try to understand.*

I stepped over it and quietly slipped outside.


Suzanne Paige's store sat forlorn at the far end of Market Square: two storeys of white bricks, badly weathered, and somewhat livened up by olive-green shutters flaking with age. Above the door, swinging from its brackets, faded and cracked by damp, was a wooden sign: SUZANNE'S SHABBY CHIC.

Looking at the eclectic mix of bric-a-brac displayed in the front courtyard, I certainly saw plenty of shabby. For chic you might have to dig hard. It was the kind of store that would appeal only to a particular breed of people; the rest would simply walk past and move on. Or, in

Suzanne's case, move out, judging by the home-made FOR SALE sign plastered on her windows.

My mother once told me that Suzanne had been one of the few locals to openly welcome her when others had regarded her with a touch of small-town suspicion. I didn't know much about Suzanne, except that she and my mother had hit it off instantly. A friendship forged from a mutual passion for dressmaking (Suzanne had worked at the local garment factory until its demise in the late nineties) and perhaps a sense of kinship since the two of them never remarried and raised an only child.

I couldn't remember if my mother had ever mentioned Holly in passing. There was no reason why I should have shown any real interest in her if she had. Now that she was dead, I did.

The bell above the door made a sad little chime when I pushed it and went inside. Behind the counter, Suzanne briefly pulled her gaze away from a list she was ticking things off of. I gave her a quick, awkward nod, which I was sure she didn't see—not when I stood half hidden behind a dummy dressed in a khaki serge uniform from the Great War.

I roamed around looking at vintage sewing machines, unloved 1920s Bauhaus furniture, a chrome aircraft door. Trailed a finger over a dust-streaked Regency mirror, gilded and mottled. There was no real sense of identity or care in this store.

'Can I help you?'

I spun around, saw Suzanne smile a slick, businesslike smile at me. She showed no sign of recognition. Hard to reconcile the piggish-looking teen I was years ago with the scrawny young woman facing her today. I noticed she had the same oval-shaped face as Holly, the same deep hazel eyes, although hers were shadowed dark, likely from lack of sleep. Mid-fifties, with blonde hair greying at the roots, gaunt cheekbones, and she was dressed in blue jeans and a long grey woollen cardigan accessorised with a noose of white pearls around her neck.

'Do you mind if I talk to you for a moment, Suzanne?'

'Are you enquiring about the store?'

'We actually met two or three times before. My name is Chloe Westfield.'

Her eyes opened wide; she stopped smiling. 'You're Kathryn's daughter?'

'I know you're going through a horrible time, and I know my mother hasn't always been fair to you—'

'Fair?' She let out a wry laugh. 'Your mother left me to rot. Just like pretty much everyone else in this damn town.'

'I can help you,' I said.

Suzanne snorted. 'Oh, please, spare me your pity. Why are you here?'

'I'd like to ask you a few questions about Holly.'

She held out her hand, palm out, defensively. 'You may not. I've had enough of people who trash my daughter's memory—malicious people like your mother. I need no spy in my store.'

'I'm not a spy, Suzanne. I just want to hear out your side of the story. Make sense of what happened to Holly that night.'

'Then give me one good reason why I should trust you.' She'd dropped her hand to her side, and now she was sizing me up sharply.

I held my chin high; the words tumbling out of my mouth unbidden—'Because I'm nothing like my mother.'

Suzanne nodded, seemingly mollified by my answer. I pulled the picture of Holly and the pattern out of my bag and handed them to her. She flipped through the pages, puzzled, then stared down at the picture.

'Do you recognise that teal-blue dress?' I asked.

Suzanne nodded again.

'I have it now,' I said. 'I bought it on Monday at Vintage Folly.'

She stared at me blankly. 'That's impossible. I may not make much money, but I'd never resort to selling—'

'Suzanne,' I started gently, 'I know you didn't. I need you to suspend your disbelief for a moment and tell me what you know about this dress.'

'I know nothing about it. Why is it so important?'

'I wish I knew,' I said, staring at the pattern in her hands. 'I think Holly was trying to say something. Something important.' I looked back at her. 'Did she still live with you?'

'No,' she said, pointing to the man in the picture. 'That's Daniel, her boyfriend. He owns a house near Manchester.'

'But she came to visit you before she died, right?'

'She stayed with me for a couple of days. She said she had some important business to take care of in Heavendale.'

'What sort of business?'

'I don't know.' She stepped back, looking away. 'I don't mean to be rude, but I just don't see the point in all this.' She handed me back the pattern and the picture. 'Send my regards to your mother. Maybe one day she'll come to her senses.'

She turned and wound her way back to the counter.

I stood there, the moment falling away from me, lost and defeated amid cluttered furniture and paraphernalia. I felt foolish for coming so ill-prepared. I'd pathetically assumed I would rally Suzanne, even though I had nothing tangible to show her.

The dress, the pattern: I was sure they played a part in Holly's murder, somehow. But who would believe it was murder when all I had was a vision and not a shred of evidence?

I was about to leave when something against the side wall caught my eye—a ladder. Large squares of wrapping paper in various colours hung over each rung. On the highest one, the colour was teal blue. A ribbon roll of gold satin hearts dangled from a rotating rack nearby. That's what Holly must have used to wrap the box. A box she must have wrapped with Matt, which would explain the shortened form of my name. A box wrapped up on 3 April 2017— the same day Holly finished the pattern. The same day she and Matt died.

I strode towards Suzanne, who raised her face to me. 'Well, what is it you want now?'

'They both came to your store that day, didn't they?'

'That's right. Not that it's ever been a secret in this town.'

'Why?'

'You should ask Tina. She instigated the whole thing.'

'If you mean the affair between Matt and Holly, I only found out yesterday.'

Her expression softened a little. 'I see,' she said quietly.

'What happened?'

'Tina saw them go up the side stairway leading to my flat upstairs. It was after our Monday meeting, when I was still working for Scissor Sister.'

'Did you see them too?'

'I was in the store when Holly came down to pick up some wrapping paper. We didn't really talk, as I had some work to finish.' She cast a dejected glance around her. 'Believe me, it used to be a lot tidier.'

'What about Matt?'

'I only heard his voice upstairs. I think he was talking to someone on the phone.'

A lump rose in my throat. 'What time was that?'

'Shortly after eight, I'd say.'

I slid my gaze to the window and swallowed hard, trying to quell the horrible memory of my last phone conversation with Matt. Outside, a little girl with two blonde pigtails was jumping rope on the cobblestones. In the background, a couple came walking towards her holding ice creams.

'They left twenty minutes later and crashed on the road,' Suzanne went on. 'But the news of their deaths wasn't enough for Tina. She had to spread her venom throughout town, saying my Holly was all over him, that they came to my flat to . . .'

'To have sex,' I filled in bluntly.

Suzanne shot me a stare. 'They didn't stay long enough, Chloe. I heard them talk, not moan.'

I pondered her remark for a moment. I didn't doubt Suzanne knew her daughter well enough, but surely she wasn't naïve. Maybe they'd managed to squeeze a bit of fun out of their short time together. Maybe Holly had used her mouth for something other than conversation—knowing Matt, five minutes was plenty.

And yet, as I thought of our five years together, I realised that something didn't tally. It was all about control and humiliation in Matt's twisted mind. He never cared about other women, never gave them a second glance. I fully absorbed his attention, a toy he moulded like clay to his whims, compliant and willing. I could still feel his essence, coursing through my veins, its power intact in spite of his death.

Suzanne looked at me inquiringly. 'What's troubling you?'

My mind made the leap to Holly's death. It was a harrowing dilemma: Did I have a moral duty to tell Suzanne the truth, or should I protect her from it? Part of me insisted she had a right to know; the other part pleaded prudence. Suzanne would have no chance of closure if she learnt her daughter had been murdered—not if I couldn't tell her who her murderer was.

'Nothing,' I said, my eyes roaming around. 'How about we make your store look nice, give it some kind of makeover?'

'Why should I do that? I want to sell it.'

'That's exactly the point—it could help clinch a sale. You never know with the handmade and vintage fair coming to town.'

She shook her head. 'I just don't have the money.'

'It doesn't have to cost much. In fact, what this place really needs is some major decluttering so that your best pieces stand out.'

'Hmm,' she said, considering my suggestion. 'Some of them aren't exactly in mint condition.'

'I took a course in furniture restoration last year. I could give it a shot if you're not averse to me trying.'

'But why would you help me, Chloe?'

The question caught me off guard for a moment: of course, part of me genuinely wanted to help Suzanne, undo some of the damage done to her. But then it struck me the makeover was as good a plan as any if I wanted to figure out the truth about her daughter's death. And, frankly, I couldn't bear the thought of staying locked up in my bedroom for days just to avoid my mother, couldn't bear to drink myself (again) into oblivion. I looked Suzanne in the eye and said, 'I guess I have something to prove to myself.'

She smiled. 'Shall we start tomorrow at ten?'

## 12

There are fourteen police stations in the whole of Cumbria, one of the counties enjoying the lowest levels of crime. Heavendale may be small, but it boasts its very own station on the east side of town, which takes only fifteen minutes to walk to from Market Square. Built narrow on two floors, devoid of cells and interview rooms, the walls inside bare and garish, painted the colour of toothpaste green. A young sergeant behind the desk informed me that Chief Inspector Gordon Smith was due for a visit sometime today.

'What time?' I asked.

'Any time.' He shrugged.

I took a seat on a moulded plastic chair and worked my way through the sticky pages of an old *Glamour*. Twenty minutes and two more magazines later, I stared in boredom at the local launderette across the road. I wondered if someone had ever filed a complaint for fabric shrinkage.

When Chief Inspector Smith finally walked in, the sergeant nodded at me then I heard him whisper, 'Some road accident.'

Gordon Smith, a balding man in his mid-fifties, was tall and stocky. His shirt under his armpits showed faded yellow stains shaped like half-moons.

'Accident?' He stared at me. 'What accident?'

'Chief Inspector, I'm Chloe Westfield. It was last year, just outside of town. It sadly cost my fiancé's life.' I looked down demurely, hoping I fitted the profile of a grieving bride.

'I'm sorry for your loss, Miss Westfield.' He motioned to me to follow, then looked at the sergeant. 'Hold my calls, Brandon.'

Gordon Smith walked ahead of me down a small hallway with two doors on each side, then into an office on the left, which had one small window, the tiny square brimming with folders; some were also stacked on a chair opposite his desk. He plopped them down on the floor.

'Please sit down,' he muttered. 'This place is a pit. Someone in Penrith got the bright idea that we should sift through and tidy some old records.'

'I'm guessing they're all pre-digital age,' I said as if I was some kind of expert.

'Thankfully, you don't need to worry about 2017.' His fingers were poised over his keyboard. 'What was your fiancé's name?'

'Matthew Thorne.'

'Doesn't ring a bell.'

'The woman's name might do. Holly Paige—they died together.'

The tapping stopped. He stared at my face, his fingers again hovering motionless above the keys. 'What is it you want to know exactly, Miss Westfield?' He suddenly sounded wary.

I pulled out my iPad and showed him the article in the *Westmorland Gazette*. 'I was hoping you could let me know if there was some new development.'

He looked at it, clasped his hands on his desk. 'Just because I made a declaration to the press doesn't mean I got involved in the case. In fact, I hardly get involved in road accidents these days.'

I glanced at the silver stars on his epaulettes: three of them, a sure sign he hadn't been on the police beat for a while. 'Chief Inspector, I just need access to some information. Any records about causes, circumstances, or possible mechanical failure would be extremely helpful.'

'You'll need the STATS 19 report for that.'

'Would you mind giving me a copy?'

'I can certainly forward a request. But I must warn you, the average waiting time is six to eight weeks, if you're lucky.'

My heart dropped. 'I . . . But I can't wait that long. Isn't there anything you can do for me?'

He leaned back in his seat, studying my face. 'Let's just say I'm a little cautious as to what your real intentions are.'

'So you've heard the rumour about their alleged love affair.'

'Alleged or not, this could be an opportunity for you to stir the pot.'

'There's nothing to stir up—I don't believe it happened.'

'Maybe it didn't,' he concluded, then wagged his chin at his screen. 'I'm willing to help you, Miss Westfield. Just this once. But I don't want everyone in town to think it's okay to come and ask me favours.'

'No one will ever have to know, Chief Inspector.' I smiled.

He nodded before smiling. 'All right, then.'

I listened to his fingers tapping the keyboard then held my breath when the printer on his desk clicked and hummed and churned out four pages.

When he handed it to me, I scoured the report: Matt and Holly's full names on top, two sections covering vehicle and casualty records with a couple of ticks and crosses, a page about statements with not a single witness name, and the signature of a reporting sergeant at the bottom.

*Verdict: Accident / deaths caused by reckless driving.*

Not a trace of anything suspicious, the conclusion confined to a single-line paragraph.

'They've only put a tick next to slippery road,' I said, flushed with disappointment. 'Nothing else.'

'Bad weather is sadly a common cause of road accidents.'

'But it wasn't an accident,' I said before I could even stop myself.

'I'm sorry?'

'What about the headlights?'

'What headlights?'

'There was another car that night,' I sputtered quickly.

'Do you mean a police car?'

'No, it wasn't a police car.'

'Then what sort of car, Miss Westfield?'

'I don't know,' I said in frustration. The blood was rushing to my head, the room tilting beneath my chair. I breathed deeply, trying to get my voice under control. 'It's just that roads are full of cars. Someone could have hit them intentionally. Someone who may have wanted Holly Paige dead.'

He kept his eyes on my face, his brow knitted as though he was concerned about me. As though he thought I was completely insane. It did sound insane when I said it out loud.

'Were you present at the scene that day, Miss Westfield?'

'No, no, I wasn't.'

'Are you currently taking any medications? Do you suffer from any form of post-traumatic stress?'

I got hot at his words and desperately wanted to backtrack. 'No, of course not. I was just thinking that murder could be a possibility, something perhaps you haven't considered yet.'

His brow knitted again. 'So what do you think I should do? Dispatch forensic experts? Sniffer dogs? Every man on the force? There are no CCTV cameras around Heavendale, none of that fancy stuff you see on TV.'

'I was only suggesting—'

'With all due respect, Miss Westfield, I think you've suggested enough. This case is closed. This is not a murder investigation.'

I rose to my feet, unsteady, heard myself mutter, 'Thank you for your time, Chief Inspector,' and stumbled over a pile of folders as I strode to the door.

'Please look after yourself, Miss Westfield.'

I glanced back to see his eyes fixed on his computer screen.


Stupid and reckless—that's how I felt after leaving the police station. I didn't know what came over me: I panicked, I played it wrong. I so badly wanted to be heard, so badly wanted the chief inspector to believe me that I'd dropped my guard.

Now he thought I was a nutcase. I could go back and apologise, but I was too ashamed, and anyway, he'd made it clear enough that he wanted nothing more to do with me.

I walked back to Market Square. A shop on my left caught my attention. It sold pottery and greeting cards, one of which showed the picture of a lake with a lone oak tree standing on a cliff. Tears caught the back of my throat at the thought of Holly—I was failing her. Badly.

Then something unusual caught my eye. There was a giant pair of silver-sprayed scissors in the window display next door to the pottery shop. Suspended from a hook in the ceiling, they hovered motionless above three faceless mannequins whose fibreglass hands clutched crisp pattern envelopes.

As I peered at their names through the glass, I realised they all bore the same logo—an SS monogram beneath a pair of gleaming scissors, and within the blades open wide, a woman's face with watching eyes.

I shivered, drawn to the hypnotic sight—an ominous sense crawling through my core. Only when I made myself blink did I drag my gaze away and put a cautious hand out to open the door. Inside, I quietly perused a tall shelving unit, glossy white against the brick wall and stacked with folded fabrics and haberdashery of all sorts: pools of thread, buttons, needles, ribbons . . . and more scissors.

A board of samples stood above a revolving rack brimming with sewing patterns. Browsing through them, I noted the Scissor Sister brand to the exclusion of all others. And not just on the patterns—I looked around and it was everywhere: her name, her initials, her face logo in decals transferred onto the walls. Her presence permeated the entire store.

*The one and only true choice.*

A burst of laughter startled me.

'Hey,' a blonde woman called out to me. 'Have you come to attend the Scissor Sister class?'

I drew closer to the back of the room, where I found she was standing next to a brunette by a large table filled with portable sewing machines.

'We always come early,' the blonde said. 'That's because we like to have the best seats.'

'And we're the best students too,' gushed the brunette as she took a seat. '*The Great British Sewing Bee* will soon be knocking on the door.' The last four words tinkled like happy ice cubes.

The blonde turned to me, her face pink and smug. 'We've already completed twelve of her patterns. What about you?'

I guessed these girls had a competitive streak.

'To be perfectly honest, I haven't done any yet.'

She looked aghast. 'Are you pro-globalisation?'

The question was so random that I let out a shocked laugh; she didn't laugh back.

'Actually,' I said diplomatically, 'I wouldn't mind hearing what experts have to say on the subject before I respond to that.'

'Why experts?' she demanded. 'We don't need experts.'

'Scissor Sister hates globalisation,' chimed in the brunette. 'She's fed up with the monopoly of the big four.'

'Brands like Vogue and McCall's,' continued the blonde. 'We can't let them dictate our choices. Scissor Sister says there should be room for everyone.'

'Does she?' My sarcasm completely passed over her when she nodded.

'She published a list of brands we should never buy from,' said the brunette.

'Fake brands,' sniffed the blonde.

'Doesn't it bother you to be told what not to buy?'

'Not really,' said the blonde.

'Actually,' the brunette said, 'it's comforting to know there's a voice out there you can really trust.'

'But why would you trust a faceless voice?' I asked.

'That's not the point,' the blonde snapped. 'Scissor Sister is the voice of the people. She knows what's right for us. She just does, period.'

'She's like . . . watching us,' said the brunette pensively.

'How is that?'

'Maybe you should check out her blog.'

'She's like our Big Sister, one we rely on for expert guidance. She says she'll keep guiding us as long as she's the chosen one.'

'You mean as long as you keep buying her products.' *You dumb bitches*, I added in my head.

The blonde shrugged. 'She just wants our undivided loyalty in return. Is that too much to ask?'

A group of people rolled in with greetings, and I could feel the attention shifting away from me—'One last question,' I said. 'Can you tell me who owns this store?'

The blonde pointed a finger to the front. 'Go talk to Kimberley. You'll see how easy it is to join our sisterhood.'

I turned to find Kimberley standing behind a desk, twisting a lock of her Farrah Fawcett hair into a neverending loop. She wasn't alone. Her gaze was fixed on someone crouched before the tall shelves—someone I instantly recognised as Cordelia, whose gloved hand slid a small card out of a label holder. Then she strode over to the desk. Showed Kimberley the card and tapped a ballpoint pen on a sheet of A4 paper as she talked.

The only sound was the din of sewing machines behind me.

I crept my way closer. And then, standing quietly behind a mannequin that gave a good vantage point, I could see the conflict thickening between them. Kimberley was shaking her head vigorously, sucking her lips in against her teeth, her eyes the colour of storm clouds. Seized by rage, she suddenly snatched the sheet of paper and viciously tore it into pieces. Cordelia took a step back, almost stumbling with shock. She dropped her pen in her bag and scuttled out the door.

A deep, angry male voice called out from upstairs and something changed in Kimberley's expression: rage galvanised into fear. She screwed her eyes shut for a moment, as if fighting back tears before she called back, 'Coming, darling,' her voice high and strained, and rushed up the glass staircase behind her.

The torn pieces of paper still lay scattered across her desk. Glancing around the room, I stuffed them as fast as I could into my coat pocket before I strode out of the store.

Back to Stonebarn Lake after a meandering walk down the streets, I found my mother reclining on a cushioned lounger on the deck, wrapped up in blankets, watching the last of the sun. Two plates waited on the table. A pot was slow-cooking on the stove, the smell of garlic and rosemary drifting from it.

I couldn't face dinner, let alone sit beside my mother.

I snuck upstairs where my bedroom was redolent of stale booze and bad memories: a slap, a thump, a bruise . . . a tear, an apology. There was nothing I wanted more than to sweep away the past, turn back the clock, and start anew. Leave Heavendale for good. Had things turned out differently, I might have met a lovely man. I might have lived in a sprawling mansion in Kensington or an eco-friendly farm in the Shetlands. I might have married.

Sitting on my bed, I picked up my iPad off the floor: It happened again then, that same feeling of wrongness sinking in my chest, just like when I woke up this morning. I swiped the screen, logged on to the gaming platform. I was right: MysteryGeek and I hadn't played murder mystery last night. Instead we'd exchanged a long series of messages between midnight and 1 a.m.

I'd been drinking for a few good hours by then, and as the messages rolled down, it was obvious I'd opened up about my life, confided in him, dangerously let my guard down. In the last message, I'd given out my mobile number.

I fumbled inside my bag, tapped the message icon—there was an unknown number at the top and more conversation between us. I flicked my thumb feverishly over the blue and grey boxes. The last ten messages made my blood run cold:

I told him to go to hell.

**Who R U talking about?**

Matt. I said I wanted him to die.

**Matt who?**

Matthew Thorne.

**He's already dead.**

Yes.

**He died in a car accident with Holly.**

It was not an accident.

**WHAT???**

I was cringing, my whole body folding into itself. I wanted to be smaller, I wanted to disappear. I'd made the same terrible mistake again. And then, a realisation: he mentioned Holly's name, but I never once did. So how did he know?

Could he too have read about her fate in the *Westmorland Gazette*?

I sent him a reply:

Listen, I'm really sorry about last night. I was just talking crap.

A new text pinged in, almost immediately:

**Did U kill him?**

The question almost squeezed the breath out of my lungs. I could see why he had drawn that conclusion, how the whole thing got awfully misconstrued in his mind: Anyone who says her fiancé should die and claims his death was no accident is bound, surely, to come across as suspicious. I sat rigid with tension, could feel it creeping along my fingers as I typed:

Of course I didn't.
**Who says UR NOT lying?**
Stop it. This isn't a game now.

Two more messages pinged in quick succession:

**No, it's not.**
**Because I know who U R.**

Gasping for breath, the phone came loose in my hand and dropped to the floor. I pushed my fist against my mouth and screamed.

# SCISSOR SISTER

I can still remember the key moment—the turning point, the change of fortune.

Scissor Sister was little more than a hobby before that. Still trying to make its mark.

Still pure and innocent.

In truth, it was struggling.

Amelia got off to a promising start, then died. No marketing. No promotion. The picture of a plain linen dress had done little to boost pattern sales.

Then, one October day, I spotted a booth selling Union Jacks at a local flea market. Inspiration struck. I sewed a new dress out of them and posted the result on Twitter.

It changed everything.

Sixty-eight retweets within the first hour. Likes. Replies. Engagement. Shares. The leader of an influential far-right movement took notice and commented, *British products for British people. No foreign muck.*

When I got up the next morning, my tweet had gone viral. Sales had shot through the roof: Amelia rose like a phoenix from the ashes.

My first sweet taste of triumph.

Sadly, it didn't last. Social media is as powerful as it is fickle.

November came and I tried to replicate my earlier success, cash in on the patriotic mood with knitted poppies and khaki dresses, but it wasn't the same.

Something was missing.

Something I had failed to comprehend the first time around: a crucial element, a vital ingredient.

**FEAR.**

Populism, nationalism, unemployment, immigration, globalisation, despotism. They thrive on fear.

We live in uncertain times. *Fearful* times.

Like any business, it's important to respond to trends. To go the extra mile. To create your own blend of propaganda. To make sure something about my brand stirs your soul . . .

You're laughing now, aren't you? You think you know better. You think I could never fool someone like you.

Maybe you're right. Maybe I won't.

But then, it doesn't even matter.

Because there's always someone else who will listen.

## 13

In the dimness of my bedroom, the curtains left undrawn, I lay snug under my duvet and stared at the window: a starless sky with a crescent moon.

I thought of the texts I'd sent to MysteryGeek. I thought of what I'd said to the chief inspector. That recklessness, that lack of self-censorship—it was so unlike me, so unlike the way I was brought up: Emotions you repress. Guilt you bury. Silence trumps dialogue.

My mother had never once told me she loved me. She tended to me as long as I showed no signs of neediness. When I first started my period, she handed me a box of tampons, didn't sit by my side—just told me to read the full page of instructions—and shut the bathroom door behind her. My dreams, my fears, she didn't know, she never asked. Questions were always frowned upon, considered prying.

In fact, I hardly know anything about my mother. The little I know of her life comes from eavesdropping on conversations between relatives. My uncle—her brother—said she married at the age of twenty-six when she was three months pregnant. His wife whispered that she never wanted the child. An older cousin tearfully declared that it was my dad who cried and begged her not to abort me.

I have one memory that pierces through me like a prickly thorn. I was about twelve, and my mother had a cluster of friends over for afternoon tea. One of them brought a baby. I was supposed to be doing homework in my room, but I stood quietly behind the door, watching. The child was fussed over, smothered with kisses, and passed from hand to hand. When it was my mother's turn, she jiggled the baby briefly on her knees and gave a startling laugh. Then she got up abruptly, laid the child back on the mother's lap, and asked everyone in the room if they'd like a refill.

I followed her to the kitchen. While the kettle boiled, she moistened a damp cloth with washing liquid and applied it to her sleeve. It was nothing more than a bit of baby dribble, not even a stain, not even an expensive floral dress. But she rubbed it hard, dabbed at it desperately until the cotton became soaked and the petal print took on a lustrous sheen. Then she put on a red cardigan before rejoining the other women.

At times, over the years, I could sense her guilt, the conflict gnawing her insides. Why couldn't she show any maternal affection? What couldn't she feel love for her own child? Her *troubled*, unwanted child. Maybe that explained why I'd found comfort in the wrong arms, fallen for the smooth words. How could I resist a compliment, a smile, a touch when I'd been starved of them ever since my dad died?

Even Matt's confidently pristine façade had failed to fool me after a while. I met his parents three times over dinner (often found excuses not to), and it shocked me to observe how differently he behaved in their presence. Subdued to the point of submission, he constantly sought their approval.

Well into his sixties, his father was a man driven by power and material wealth. His mother, bony and ropy necked, was clearly battling bulimia. She wore size zero in designer dresses and always looked glum, save for the odd artificial smile between sips of Château Margaux. Their most prized possessions: a pair of greyish-blue diamonds the size of pigeon eggs and three Porsches with scissor doors parked in their massive double-fronted garage.

Matt could never live up to their impossible expectations. He had embarked on that fruitless quest to please them, hoping that one day, maybe, his mother would reward him with a genuine smile and his father with a proud nod or a pat on the back and say, 'Well done, son.' I guess he never lived long enough to hear those words.

The day he proposed to me, I had a flash, so vivid it frightened me.

A glimpse into my foreseeable future: Matt wanting me to look like his mother, me tacitly agreeing to let him turn me into her.

A doomed vicious circle.

By then, I couldn't bear to live with him any more. Five years of abuse, control, and starvation had taken their toll on my body and mind, awakened a darker side within me. It would often manifest in the most mundane moments: I'd open the cutlery drawer, hear the silvery clink of kitchen knives, and all I could think of was grabbing the sharpest one, sinking the blade deep into his back. When he wound his tie around his neck, tugged his collar against the bulges of his throat, I imagined how good it would feel to pull tighter, to block the last cloud of air from rolling into his lungs until his body slid lifeless to the floor.

Those thoughts flashed violently through my brain, spread through me like poison. Eating me up. Waiting for a trigger to spill like blood—I had to go.

Only once did I verbalise them. It was the week after I'd left him, on 3rd April, during our last phone conversation.

I could never forget my last words: *'Go to hell, Matt. I hope you fucking die.'*

Less than an hour later, he did.

# 14

One p.m., at Suzanne's. Trying hard not to trip or knock my elbows, I carried an old gramophone and set it onto a spindly oak table. Three hours of joint effort had led us to clear the back of the store. At the front, drawers had been pulled out, cabinet doors flung open, and their contents dumped to the floor.

I wiped my brow and surveyed the scene: a vintage mini-wardrobe with paper dresses, an Art Nouveau mirror spotted black with age, a dead clock with no glass on its face. Antiques, dozens of them jumbled between piles of fabric and unordinary paraphernalia, some of them buried beneath the chaos.

My heart sank.

Suzanne looked positively overwhelmed. 'Coffee?' she asked.

I nodded. While she disappeared upstairs, I quickly checked my iPad and my phone. There were no new messages from MysteryGeek: I had cut all ties with him, blocked his number and unfriended him on the gaming platform, but still needed to reassure myself. I worried that he might contact the police, show them my text messages. If he did, could I be in real trouble?

Then I remembered what the chief inspector had said: '*This case is closed. This is not a murder investigation.*' The words were as reassuring as they were frustrating.

Suzanne and I sat down on two Regency chairs and sipped our coffees; I took advantage of this pause to ask her how long she'd worked for Scissor Sister.

'About two years,' she said, 'I was in charge of proofreading her creations.'

'Including the Amelia pattern?'

'No, Scissor Sister decided to entrust that to Kathryn. Our jobs overlapped on occasions. I was very sad when it all ended.'

'Then why did you leave?'

'Is that what Kathryn said?'

'Not . . . exactly.' *She kind of implied it, though,* but I didn't say that aloud.

Suzanne gave a sarcastic sneer. 'Your mother never fails to amaze me. The truth is, I got sacked last year, days after Holly's death.'

'Sacked? What happened?'

'That's the worst part, Chloe, I don't really know. I heard that the residents' committee received an anonymous letter alluding to immoral conduct. Something Denise Drummond takes very seriously in this town.'

'But you did nothing wrong.'

'Me? No. But I'm sure it had everything to do with that damned rumour about the affair. Someone obviously had it in for me and Holly. It was the committee's decision to launch a local boycott of my store when her body was barely cold. Scissor Sister followed suit days later, with a brief dismissal message on her intranet. No official explanation.'

'Do you think Tina was behind that letter?'

'Yes . . . It's quite possible.'

I picked up on her hesitation. 'But it could be someone else?'

Suzanne shifted in her seat, looked me in the eye, and took a deep breath. 'Let me say it aloud, because I've been thinking it too long. Sometimes I wonder about your mother, Chloe. We were such close friends. Yet, not a word from her over the last year—not once did she return my calls. Don't you find it strange? But of course, I can't imagine she'd go so far as trying to destroy me.'

I shook my head as convincingly as I could. 'No, no, of course she wouldn't.' Gulping down the rest of my coffee, I felt a sudden need to resume clearing up the store.

· · ·

It was late afternoon, and Suzanne's words still stuck with me.

What she wouldn't dare imagine, I did. My mother hated Holly. '*That little slut*'—that's what she'd called her. So much disappointment, so much resentment boiling up inside her after Holly had died. She must have wanted a scapegoat. So she had sent a vengeful letter to the committee, leaving Suzanne's reputation in tatters . . . It seemed crazy to think these thoughts. They were friends, such good friends. Once.

I walked along Market Square, hungry. I stopped, staring at cake names written in chalk on a shop's blackboard, then peered through the window: Black Forest, gingerbread, banoffee pie, Victoria sponge— all perched on cut glass pedestals beneath cloche tops. My stomach grumbled at the sight.

Inside, I ordered a plate of fancy-named Millésime chocolate mousse. Soon my nose tickled by a smell other than food, a very familiar smell that hung in the air—Patsy was sitting at a table behind me, her sensible skinny latte perched atop a red checked tablecloth, that Frisky Lady scent wafting off her. She was typing something on a paper-thin MacBook while chewing the inside of her mouth.

She looked up, saw me, and startled. 'Chloe, darling. What a wonderful surprise.' She snapped her MacBook shut and stood up to give me a quick air kiss. I wondered if she'd had time to save whatever she was writing.

'I hope I'm not interrupting you,' I said, pulling out a chair opposite her.

'Of course not.' She smoothed her mulberry-coloured suit as she sat back down, then cocked her head to one side. 'So tell me, how's your mother feeling at the moment?'

'Hmm, well . . . good, I guess.' *How the hell would I know?* My mother certainly wasn't the type to show her feelings, let alone confide in me about them. Unless Patsy was referring to—

'I'm glad Kathryn finally found the strength to tell you about Holly. That must have been so damn hard for her.'

'My mother? Sure. It was a little hard for me too.'

'I don't think she's dealing with it terribly well, though,' Patsy droned on. 'I suppose the wound is still fresh after that dreadful accident. Poor thing.'

*Poor mother!* Never mind *I* had to coax the truth out of her . . . I decided to divert the topic away from the pity-my-mother path.

'Actually, Patsy, I'd be very interested to know your take on it.'

'*My* take on it?' she asked. 'I don't even live here half the time.'

'But you spend a lot of time in Heavendale, don't you? You must have heard a few things about the *affair*.'

'Yes, of course. Everyone had plenty to say about it.'

'Tina did too, I heard.'

She let out a short, metallic laugh. 'Ah, well, Tina—there's a good source.'

'Do you think she could have lied?'

Patsy stirred her latte and glanced around the room as if afraid of being observed. 'I take everything that woman says with a pinch of salt. She's a busybody. The dangerous kind. She met Holly a few times, so maybe things turned sour between them.'

'Suzanne told me the residents' committee received an anonymous letter disparaging her.'

'Hmm,' she said, taking a sip. 'Denise Drummond made a terrible fuss about it. It didn't help either that Suzanne is a divorcee. Dissolving a marriage is never an option in the committee's eye.'

'But why would they boycott her store?'

Patsy shrugged. 'Suzanne didn't make the grade.'

I blinked. 'What grade?'

'The committee ranks every local business on the basis of moral suitability.' She rolled her eyes when I gaped. 'I know. It's rather medieval.'

'It's a pathetic excuse,' I said, riled up over such absurdity. 'That letter was a deliberate attempt to ruin her.'

'Someone obviously had ill intent. The whole thing is quite shocking, really.'

'So who do you think did this?'

Patsy leaned over the table, looking at me solemnly. 'If you mean to ask if I believe Tina could be behind the letter, the answer is yes, I absolutely do. But we'll probably never know. People enjoy controversy, love to feel outraged. Who cares who wrote it?'

'I'll say it's the same person who told Scissor Sister.'

'Yes, you're probably right. Tina could easily have tipped her off via the SS intranet.' Which was what I thought too, though on reflection any of the other five women could have done the same.

Patsy went on. 'Scissor Sister informed us that Suzanne had become persona non grata—she was officially erased from all records, like she never existed.'

My stomach clenched as I swallowed a mouthful of chocolate mousse. Patsy followed the gesture with envy.

'Gosh, I wish I had your figure. What's your secret?'

I let my spoon clatter against my plate, feeling an urge to scream out, *The Matthew Thorne diet! Oh yes, it's terribly effective. Want me to market it?* Instead I said, 'I have a fast metabolism, Patsy.'

'You're so lucky,' she said breathily, watching as I took another bite before I pushed the plate towards her.

'Go on, I'm stuffed anyway.'

'But you've barely touched it.'

'It's fine.'

She scooped a tiny amount in a bird-like, girlish way, then grew braver with each spoonful. My thoughts turned back to Scissor Sister as she ate. There was something else I remembered from nosing into my mother's file two days ago.

'Does the name *Sister of Trust* mean anything to you?' I asked.

Patsy's expression mellowed as she cleaned my plate. 'It's your mother's username on the SS intranet. I'm not supposed to tell you

115

this, but frankly we're treating this whole secrecy business far too seriously.'

'Do you have one too?'

Patsy nodded, mouth full. 'All six of us do. There's also Sister of Love, Sister of Peace, Sister of Plenty, and Sister of Grace. I'm Sister of Truth because I advertise her brand in magazines and social media.'

There was something slightly perturbing about these Sister names: the use of religious code to substitute for real identities. I could picture Scissor Sister lurking in the dark like an enigmatic Mother Superior, pulling the strings (or rather pushing the buttons) behind her intranet machine. It sounded grotesque, the stuff of dystopia.

I stood up, ready to leave. 'Thank you for your time, Patsy.' I paused. 'By the way, I hope *Retro Mode* is doing well. It's really a great magazine.'

'Oh, Chloe, that's sweet of you to say. Actually, we've been so busy that I had to recruit two more staff.' She stuck her lower lip out. 'I know your mother's awfully worried about your career. Maybe better luck next time. Who knows?'

She waved goodbye and flipped her MacBook open. In truth, I couldn't have cared less if she called me or not with a job. Something else bothered me: I couldn't fathom why someone like Patsy Carter, a successful editor with a thriving fashion magazine, would agree to promote and work extra hours for a secretive dressmaking brand she didn't own.

And this more than anything else made no sense to me.


Back to Stonebarn Lake; another evening spent locked up in my bedroom. Tearing off strips of Sellotape, I patiently assembled the page that Kimberley had ripped into pieces: sixteen in total; four of which were corners with bits of Blu Tack attached to the back. Red capital letters, purposely traced in a precise, mechanical manner to conceal the identity of their author. The font was square, large, and angry. The pen had been pushed so hard, it had left several small tears in the paper.

A chill ran down my spine when I was finally able to read the note:

*YOUR DAUGHTER IS A SLUT.*

The last word had been underlined twice.

# 15

Scissor Sister . . .

All this time I'd been wondering about her, from the strange, almost Orwellian message delivered by Holly, to my conversation with those two brainwashed dummies at Kimberley's store. *'She's like our Big Sister,'* the blonde had said. *'You should check out her blog,'* the brunette had suggested.

I flicked open my iPad and Googled her, for the first time ever. She appeared on the first page, but not directly on top. Ranking search results gave precedence to the plural form of the name.

There was a Wikipedia page dedicated to Scissor Sisters, a flamboyant American pop/rock band with a string of successful albums in the UK. Far more lurid was the sordid case of the Irish Scissor Sisters, a gruesome duo who'd carved their mother's boyfriend into pieces and sliced off his head and penis. They dumped his dismembered corpse in the Royal Canal in Dublin. Someone spotted a leg, with a sock on the end, floating a few hundred yards from Croke Park ten days later.

Straight after the glam and the gore came Scissor Sister, the dressmaking brand. I clicked on the website: a stark-looking homepage whose prominent SS initials, silver scissors, and watching eyes still left me uneasy. I explored the main menu then scrolled through the latest blogs. Her writing voice was persuasive, redundant at times. She preferred short sentences and demagogic words:

*You must resist the evils of fast fashion.*

*I am here to raise a fearless legion of followers.*

*We are a unique collective force fighting globalisation.*

*We are all Scissor Sisters!*

Even I could feel something stirring inside me when reading some of the passages, the impulse to rally to her cause. But as I read on, flaws and contradictions began to emerge: Scissor Sister promoted *uniqueness* through her *exclusive* brand—*Put Scissor Sister first!* She portrayed herself as a caring 'Big Sister' who offered impartial advice on the perfect patterns—all a convenient mouse click from her online store. Scissor Sister professed she didn't exist as an individual. She was a collective figure, a symbol of every woman's improved self-confidence regardless of age, size, and shape. Yet photoshopped shots of young slim models gave a skewed representation of her philosophy.

The Fake Brands list I found splashed diagonally across the menu bar in an oversized red font. On it her competitors were featured, but also famous streetwear brands that incurred her wrath for being 'unsustainable' or 'unethical.' As the list grew longer, the claims grew bolder: 'Fake Designs,' 'Globalisation Activist,' and 'Enemy of Scissor Sister,' the latter often abbreviated as E-SS. These accusations were unjustified always, buried in bias and sensationalism.

Not that anyone cared to challenge her. In fact, judging by the numerous comments on her blog posts, audiences were seduced by her rhetoric. She fuelled her readers with her blend of empowerment and propaganda.

I found there were several links to social media accounts on her website (Facebook, Twitter, Instagram, Pinterest), and I was amazed to see how considerable her following was. A quick check online showed that her number of subscribers had grown dramatically across many countries over the last year. I had completely underestimated her impact, the appeal and influence of her brand.

Scissor Sister was on the brink of becoming a major global player.

# 16

It's been four days since I'd last spoken to Cordelia, and I felt a desperate need to hear back from her. Creeping downstairs to the kitchen, I snagged her number off my mother's phone and whizzed back to my bedroom, my heart racing with each ring before the call went to voicemail—I didn't leave a message.

It was Friday morning, just gone nine fifteen, and I contemplated my options for the day. Suzanne had texted me to come later, as she was busy working on some inventory, which left me with spare time on my hands.

Tina's yoga invitation sprang to mind. It didn't exactly thrill me, but a meeting with Tina was likely to yield more gossip and information than I could ever hope for. The allegations made against her bothered me, though. The truth is, I'd always liked Tina: her openness, her warmth towards me, her life stories devoid of a filter (such a contrast with my mother). Even her penchant for exaggeration made me smile at times. Not once had I caught her *deliberately* lying to me, and I never imagined she would. But my recent conversations with Suzanne and Patsy urged me to heed their warnings.

I drove to Mindful Wellness, the only fitness studio in town, which had opened at the turn of the millennium and offered sensible decor, flexible membership, a sauna, and a juice bar in a quiet, subdued atmosphere. It never really caught on. Seems as though the good folks of Heavendale preferred to stroll by the lake than exercise indoors. Who could blame them?

I found Tina leaning forward on her mat right in front of the yoga instructor. She was right: He was positively cute. And a good decade younger than her too.

He tossed mysterious names at us that sounded like exotic flowers as the session went on. Sit in *Utkatasana*, a chair pose that burnt muscles in my thighs I didn't know I had. Go into *Trikonasana*, a triangle pose for which I required a foam block for support. I took several deep breaths as instructed and tried to bend sideways. In and out. In and out. The instructor rewarded me with a smile when my fingers finally brushed the floor.

'Now,' he said, turning to the small group of women, 'who needs any help?'

Tina waved her chubby fingers for attention. He moved behind her, holding both sides of her waist, and she effortlessly achieved the perfect pose, beamed at him flirtatiously through the mirror wall. Seeking bliss wasn't the goal for Tina. Not when her chest was heaving with excitement beneath a skimpy sports bra. For a wild second, I feared a wardrobe malfunction.

'So you found out, sweetie. I knew you would sooner or later.'

Tina was staring at the taped-up 'slut' note laid in front of her. We'd just grabbed a table at the empty juice bar when a bored-looking waitress called over to us. I ordered a black coffee and Tina a kiwi-cucumber smoothie with a sweet roll.

'Someone tacked it onto Suzanne's door, right?' I showed her the bits of Blu Tack at the back.

She nodded. 'Gave us all a nasty shock, that did. Done right on the evening those two died.'

'Hmm . . . convenient. So that note targeted Holly, then.'

'Could be. Or maybe Suzanne. Depends on how you look at it.'

'And how do *you* look at it?'

She propped her elbows on the table. 'Pretty girl meets handsome boy in town. No partners in sight. Of course they'll be open for a good time.' She smiled a saucy smile. I bet she loved it: Infamy coming to Heavendale.

'What about facts, Tina? I heard you saw them go upstairs to Suzanne's flat.'

'Well, damn. I'm sorry, sweetie, but I did.'

'Go on.'

'They both got out of his flashy sports car, and she rushed to his side, her hands stuck to him, as if he were made of glue. You should have seen the way she looked over her shoulder and slid her arm round his waist. Like the cat that got the cream.'

'Tina . . .'

'I'm not lying. She was staring straight at us.'

'Us?' A sudden flash of my mother in the loft, saying, 'There were witnesses.'

'Jade was driving by Market Square when she saw them and pulled over. Kimberley and I were sitting at the back.'

A doomed fling witnessed by three women, I thought. This sounded hopeless. 'Did Matt . . . enjoy what she did?' I cringed at the awkwardness of the question, but Tina cackled like a witch.

'Did he? Men usually do, sweetie. But it was too dark, and I thought he kind of looked embarrassed. He probably didn't expect her to be so open about it. Silly girl.'

'And you three just happened to be there?'

'Jade doesn't mind giving us a lift back home after our Monday meetings. See, I really don't want to ruin my lovely collection of Jimmy Choo boots.' Another saucy smile as she showed me her legs, wrapped in knee-high boots with stiletto heels. 'Did I tell you about the day I stopped traffic in them?'

'You did, Tina. Many times.'

The story varied mildly: She had broken down past Junction 36, propped the hood open, bent over the engine, wearing boots and a skintight red skirt. Once it was white. Last time, leather. But there was always plenty of honking and wolf-whistling from passing motorists.

The waitress came back with our order and Tina dug into her roll.

I tried to picture Holly, swooping in on Matt voraciously as she looked over her shoulder and lapped up the attention from these three women. Why had she done that? What was she trying to prove? I could feel the questions blowing back on themselves, going nowhere in never-ending loops.

'What's troubling you, sweetie?' Tina asked between chews.

I sighed. 'I just can't get my head around why Holly behaved so . . . indiscreetly.'

'Hmm, maybe she wanted to get caught. I wonder what Mrs Wilson would have made of that.'

'Mrs Wilson?'

Tina grimaced as she slurped green stuff through her straw. 'She always poured me a glass of her best gin when I visited her. A real nice house perched high on a hill, right on the outskirts of town, with old furniture and a comfy chair facing the bay window. That's where she liked to sit to do her knitting.' She leaned forward, voice down a notch. 'That's where she sat the night of the accident; "Can't beat the views of the lake," she always said. And the road too.'

I could feel my lungs contract, my throat close up while she took another bite of her roll.

She swallowed and finally said, 'There was another car that night.'

Relief washed over me. Someone to validate what Holly had shown me through the silk—a witness, at last. I took a sip of strong coffee before saying, 'Go on, Tina. Tell me more.'

'She saw them drive side by side moments before Matt's car swerved off the road and crashed into a tree. The other car apparently never stopped, and Mrs Wilson got very upset about it. I told her that maybe the driver got scared or confused, but she said no—something wasn't right. She couldn't understand why *she* drove away.'

'*She?*' I repeated. My hand tightened around my coffee cup.

'She,' Tina confirmed. 'But Mrs Wilson wouldn't give me the name. I doubt she could have seen the driver's face in complete darkness.'

'Maybe she recognised the car?'

Tina waved her hand before taking a sip of her smoothie. 'She was knocking at the door of ninety. And it was pissing down with rain that night.'

'But didn't she talk to the police?'

'Oh, she told them all right. Didn't seem like they took her seriously, though.'

No, they certainly didn't. No mention of Mrs Wilson's name in the accident report. Why had the police ignored her account of events? If forced to guess, I'd say they dismissed her as a dotty old granny. But I didn't need convincing that Mrs Wilson had all her wits about her that night.

'I need to talk to her, Tina. Urgently. Can you please arrange a meeting?'

'That's quite impossible, sweetie. She passed away in her sleep last December.'

I pushed my coffee away from my lips. It suddenly tasted bitter now that I knew Mrs Wilson had taken her secret to her grave.

'She was trying to make a point, Tina. I'm sure of that.'

'Of course she was. It's obvious she thought it was no accident.'

Tina's eyes twinkled with mischief as she went on. 'A sex scandal followed by murder! Damn, sweetie, it'd be the most exciting thing that's ever happened to this town.' She grinned. 'Now, if you want my two cents' worth, I'd say Daniel's got something to do with it.'

His name was familiar, thanks to my conversation with Suzanne. 'You mean Holly's boyfriend.'

She nodded, pulled a conspiratorial face as she lowered her voice. 'I always thought there was something not quite right with that chap. He's a dishy bloke, that Daniel, but too arrogant for his own good.'

'I thought he lived near Manchester.'

Tina rolled her eyes. 'So what? You think that'd stop him from driving a hundred miles if he got wind of his girlfriend flirting with Matt?'

I must have looked unconvinced, because she pushed the note

back to me, traced a gold glittery nail over the words. 'Now listen to me, sweetie. I don't fancy myself the next Miss Marple, but the message says, *Your daughter,* not *Holly.* You see, the difference is there because Daniel wanted to let Suzanne know why he bumped those two off the road. As for the word *slut,* well, it's proof enough he knew what was going on. Yes, death by jealousy. A crime of pure passion.'

I had a feeling Tina was reading a lot of Mills & Boons. But even as I played out the scenario of the jealous and murderous boyfriend in my head, there were two things that bothered me. One, how could it be Daniel if Mrs Wilson was adamant the driver was a woman? Two, that image of Holly throwing herself publicly at Matt didn't sit right with me. I didn't think Tina was lying. But I sensed something else eluded me, like a missing piece of a puzzle.

I finished my coffee, got to my feet and picked up my bag.

Tina reached across the table and grabbed my hand. 'Her name is Martika,' she said.

'I'm sorry?'

'Martika,' she repeated with a smug smile. 'Remember our conversation with your mother on Monday? She's the mysterious girl having an affair with Christian Drummond. You see, sweetie, whatever people try to conceal, Tina always finds out.' She let out a loud cackle as she released my hand.

I shuffled outside to my car, shut the door behind me, and picked up my phone. I tried to call Cordelia again. I needed more than ever to get through to her, someone who— unlike the other women in the group—I felt I could really trust. Who could help me see past my confusion. Who'd promised to come back to me with answers.

There was still no answer.

## 17

- Maple coffee table: apply thick layer of beeswax (*check*).
- Wooden bookcase: sand and antique (*check*).
- Victorian armchair: reupholster florals with ivory damask print (*in progress*).
- Parisian wardrobe: go for distressed shabby chic (*to do*).

'What about that old school locker?' I asked Suzanne, list and pen in hand. 'I was thinking of using warm primary colours. Paint it Bauhaus style.'

She nodded, wiped her brow with the back of her hand, then sat down.

The store smelled of glue and old wood. It was almost five, and we'd been working non-stop since midday. All afternoon I'd been thinking of ways to relay the news to her, but found none. Truth was, I didn't want to, I couldn't bear to break her heart or to sweeten the pill either: *Oh, you know Tina. She tends to read too much into things.* Or raise her hopes: *Who says Holly didn't trip over a broken slab and stumble by accident into Matt's arms?* And with a big, teasing smile, Holly had then swiftly turned her gaze towards those three women —*like the cat that got the cream.*

Sometimes, silence is best.

Sitting next to Suzanne, I realised I knew very little about her daughter. 'Do you mind if I ask you a few questions about Holly?' I asked, and she nodded, positioned herself sideways to face me.

'What was she like as a child?'

'She was smart, focused, such a joy to be around. I always thought she had a strong sense of direction in life from a very early age.'

'How's that?'

'I remember when I used to work at the garment factory. Only a handful of us were left at the end, and not much to do to be honest, so I was allowed to bring her on occasion. You should have seen her little face—only five and touching every dress we made. Always asking us plenty of questions. I knew early on it would be her passion.'

'Did she study fashion?'

Suzanne nodded. 'It's a hard field to get into, but I always believed in her. She eventually got to work for a prominent company in Manchester.'

I smiled. 'You must have been so proud of her.'

'I was, and grateful for Jade too. She helped Holly land that job. She still has connections in the industry, you see.'

'How did they know each other?'

'Holly did a summer work experience at Vintage Folly when she was a student. Jade always said my daughter had talent, that she was destined for great things. She couldn't pay her, but she made a few phone calls in return—Give and take, I suppose.'

I decided to change the subject. 'How would you describe her relationship with Daniel?'

Her mood darkened a bit. 'Hmm. Volatile, if I'm being honest. They were real intense from the start. They moved in together fast. Too fast.'

'What makes you say that?'

'Things had started to fizzle out towards the end. Not that Holly said much—she was too private for that—but I could tell something wasn't right between them when I last saw Daniel at your mother's New Year's party.'

The memory of the picture I'd found in the loft came back: Daniel with his arm stiffly wrapped around Holly, not smiling. 'Do you think she was having second thoughts?'

'Maybe. I think she realised she wasn't ready to settle down yet. She'd never had a proper boyfriend before Daniel—not that I knew of.'

'How did you get on with him?'

But Suzanne wasn't listening any more. She was distracted, her eyes flicking wildly behind me, out towards the front door. Someone had come in, settling the bell above the door jangling, and I whipped my head around to see a man standing there.

He was wearing an impeccably tailored pinstriped suit and a hat as black as his pencil moustache. Like a handsome, brooding protagonist stepping straight out of an American film noir. The incongruity of his attire alarmed me—something was wrong. A voice in my head told me to run, but I sat still, frozen in place and transfixed, like a pink-eyed rabbit caught in headlights. His were like pools of limpid blue, a shade of azure fixed on the space in the middle of the room.

Fixed on me.

'Miss Westfield?'

I stared, blinked at him as he moved closer.

'Miss Westfield,' he said again. 'I'm a private investigator. I'd like to ask you a few questions about the death of Matthew Thorne.'

I nodded dumbly, felt my stomach flutter. Fear. 'Your badge?' was all I managed to ask.

From his pocket he produced a leather wallet containing ID. My gaze blurred as I scanned the shiny metal and the name. It suddenly dawned on me why this man was here, why he wanted to question me about Matt. The texts, *those bloody drunken texts*—MysteryGeek had betrayed me.

MysteryGeek had hired a private detective.

He snapped his wallet shut. 'Mind if I sit down?' This time he looked at Suzanne, who promptly stood up and disappeared behind the counter. He scooted the chair around to face me, dragged the maple coffee table between us, now polished to a brilliant shine. A sure sign the beeswax was still sticky.

I assessed him quickly while he pulled a notebook out of his brief: tall, slim, dimples in both cheeks, mid-twenties at most. He looked awfully young for a private investigator. I assumed his hourly rate was reasonable, a likely reflection of his limited experience.

Not all was lost.

'Miss Westfield, someone—er—my client has raised some concerns about you. You sent each other a series of messages on Tuesday night, some of them referring to your now deceased fiancé. You wrote,' he glanced at his notes, '"I told him to go to hell." "I said I wanted him to die."' He looked up, slightly amused. 'That's pretty heavy stuff, isn't it?'

I shrugged, put on a casual tone. 'All couples have arguments. We were no exception.'

'Not everyone wishes their partner to die, though.'

'I think you're reading too much into that, Mr . . .?'

'Stanmore. Josh Stanmore.' He paused. 'Why don't you call me Josh and I call you Chloe?'

'Miss Westfield will do just fine.'

'Sure, Miss Westfield. So why did you tell Matthew to go to hell?'

'I can't remember.'

'What pushed you to say that? When did that happen? Where? You must have an idea, surely.' He grinned.

'As I said, I really can't remember.' I hated having to lie, having to pretend I'd forgotten, but he gave me no other choice. I couldn't bear to relive that moment again.

'You're not giving me a lot to work with here.'

'To be honest, this is really none of your business.'

'Private matters, right?'

'Yes, that's right. Private matters.'

His eyes smiled. 'What about your other message?'

'What other message?' I knew perfectly well about my *other* message. He glanced again at his notes. 'My client wrote, "He"— Matthew—"died in a car accident with Holly," to which you replied, "It was not an accident."'

A single, sharp exhalation from behind the counter. I glanced sideways and caught the shock on Suzanne's face. *I'm so sorry,* I mouthed to her. I truly was.

'What are you sorry for, Miss Westfield?'

The heat came rushing to my face. 'I-I think I might have had a little too much to drink that night,' I said, groping for a way out.

'Were you drunk?'

'No, no,' I lied. 'Just a glass or two.'

'Just enough booze to text my client what you really think, right?'

Blue eyes smiling again that had me biting my tongue. I disliked his shoddy tactic, his attempt to make me look guilty by pinning responsibility on me. I should have asked for a solicitor, although I couldn't think where I could find one. Time to play the trump card. If anything, I owed it to Suzanne.

'They weren't alone that night. There was another car.'

Josh Stanmore didn't say anything, just stared at me. He wasn't expecting that. I filled him in on what Tina had told me this morning.

'Where can I find this Mrs Wilson?' he asked.

'You can't. She died of old age.'

He rubbed his forehead. 'That's rather unfortunate. So can you clarify the relationship between Matthew and Holly?'

'They were . . . involved.'

'Involved in what way?'

'They had an affair, allegedly.'

'Allegedly?'

'Well, that's what the whole town seems to think.'

'And what did it feel like,' he said, leaning forward, his hands entwined, 'when you found out he'd been fucking her?' He slid the swear word in quietly, almost gently, like a stiletto between my ribs. I could taste sweat on my upper lip.

'How would I know? I only found out about their affair on Tuesday.'

'And you seriously expect me to believe that?'

'Ask my mother. It's the truth.'

'But you were angry, right?'

'Of *course* I was angry.' I tried hard not to sound angry.

'Because you hated him? Because you wanted him to die?'

'I've already told you, I only found out on Tuesday.'

'Kill two birds with one stone: You decided to bump off your fiancé and his mistress.'

'For Christ's sake,' I shrieked in desperation. 'I wasn't even in town when it happened.'

'You could have hired someone to do the dirty job for you. No awkward break-up, no emotional blackmail. Just an easy way out of a loveless relationship. Why don't you tell me the whole truth, Miss Westfield?'

'You're raving mad,' I snapped. 'I never killed them.'

I could feel the blood pulsing in my neck, sweat at the base of my spine, the sickening rush of adrenaline. I glanced back at Suzanne, who was swaying from side to side, her fingers pulling at the edges of a bright Indian throw. She caught my stare, but that made me so nervous that I glanced back towards the table.

Josh Stanmore rose from his chair and started pacing, hands behind his back.

'You were only twenty years old when you met Matthew Thorne. He was six years older, confident, self-assured. Or at least that was the impression he gave you. I suppose you must have felt quite vulnerable after your father's death.'

'Don't tell me you studied psychology too,' I muttered dryly. If he wanted to dredge up the past, he could do it alone.

'I didn't need to, Miss Westfield. I interrogated your mobile phone records.'

A black hole swallowed me whole. I could feel my limbs disconnecting, floating aloof and discordant in space, my mind stripped bare of its defences as I braced myself for his next words.

'It wasn't too hard to figure out your story once I tracked Matthew's last phone call. He was a deeply troubled, insecure, and abusive man.' He shook his head, as if he couldn't quite believe it himself. 'You must have thought of leaving him many times.'

I stayed silent, tried to thwart the memory but couldn't. Not this time. The images came through, one after another, each one like a blade dragged against my skin.

I'd finally left Matt on the evening he proposed to me. Stared at the bedroom ceiling until he was done and asleep, then yanked the ring off my finger and ran to my car. I didn't explain, didn't leave him a note, afraid that if he tracked me down I would surrender and never find the strength to leave him again. For days he tried to reach me endlessly, left me angry voice messages. On 3rd April, I didn't recognise the number.

'He called you,' said Josh Stanmore. 'Right from this house at 8:12 p.m. He used the phone upstairs to tell you he was staying at Stonebarn Lake.' He paused. 'You never told your mother, did you?'

I shook my head; I never found the courage to tell her I'd left him.

'Matthew shamelessly exploited the situation. He convinced your mother to move your wedding date closer, as soon as could be arranged. He warned you that if you didn't return, he'd come and find you. Drag you to the altar if he had to. Do you remember the last thing he said?'

I nodded. How could I forget?

*'You can never leave me, Chlo. You're mine. You will always be mine.'*

He knelt by my side. 'And tell me what you answered back.'

I stared down at the floor. His voice was so kind that tears gathered behind my eyes.

'Try,' he said gently.

Those ominous words—they gnawed inside me like a tumour. Like leeches to bare flesh. *Relief, peace, relief, peace,* was all my brain kept saying, almost begging me. All I wanted was a moment of peace and relief.

I cleared my throat and let the words fall off my lips quietly. 'Go to hell, Matt. I hope you fucking die.'

The admission hung in silence between us. Josh Stanmore rested his hand on mine and whispered in the shell of my ear, 'It wasn't your fault.'

I turned my face to him.

A tear dropped; the guilt stayed quiet.

Just then, a murmur through the air broke the moment. Something throbbed, like a rapid heartbeat. Edging nearer and shifting into a pounding drum—then the swoosh of rotor blades. I followed Suzanne, who'd rushed outside.

Two helicopters flew above our heads towards the mountains.

A woman's shriek shot above the pulsating sound—'Chloe!'

My hands began sweating as Kimberley stumbled towards us, curls bouncing wildly and face red, panic in her eyes as she pointed to the sky.

'My sister's gone,' she announced in a wail. 'She set off for the mountains this morning. Oh my God! It's almost six. She won't even answer her phone!'

'Kimberley, where exactly—'

She started to sob hysterically then, her head in her hands. 'Something dreadful happened to her,' she said through sharp breaths. 'Look at those helicopters.'

I turned to Suzanne, who was chewing her bottom lip. 'She's in no state to drive,' I said. 'We'd better go with her.'

Suzanne nodded and headed towards her car, parked on the side road adjacent to us, then she beeped open the locks. Kimberley sniffed back her tears, followed her, and slid into the back seat.

'Wait,' I called.

I hovered in the doorway, my eyes darting from left to right, scanning the store. 'Mr Stanmore?'

No reply.

'What is it?' Kimberley called miserably, peering out the side window. She was on the verge of tears again.

I took one last look around before I locked the door behind me.

'Nothing,' I said as I slid into the passenger seat next to Suzanne.

She started the engine.

## 18

The three of us travelled mostly in silence. Kimberley stared down at her hands clenched in her lap, her shoulders jerking with quiet sobs. She looked truly distraught, trembling like a quivering ghost, but I could think of nothing useful to say to soothe her nerves.

The road climbed and winded as Suzanne rounded yet another curve, hummed along to some 1980s rock ballad playing on the radio, her fingers drumming a restless beat on the steering wheel—a tic of anxiety. Outside, boats shaped like swans glistened gold in the dipping sun. Wisps of pink tinged the blue sky, like crushed rose petals on sheet glass. No clouds.

In the distance the cliffs beckoned, a mass of rock and dark greens towering in rugged magnificence, so sheer they looked as though they'd been sliced clean with a knife. Vertiginous, heart-stopping drops pointing into the void. A chilling foreboding seized me as I pictured a climber dizzy with fear and adrenaline: a foot slipped on hidden ice, a pulley snapped, the rope went slack.

A release, a scream.

A body plummeted five hundred feet.

I pushed the image away and stared ahead at the road.

We pulled up at the highest drivable point, where twenty-odd cars had already converged. I could just about make out the blades of a helicopter at the top of a rocky footpath trodden by scattered groups of people. A glossy-lipped teen stopped halfway up the path, held her phone up, and offered a variety of pouts and fish lips. Now all she needed was a tragic background for her next selfie. I bet she'd get a real kick from those extra likes on Instagram.

Mingling among curious onlookers was a familiar face, Tina, who'd dressed in cropped denim shorts. A senseless pair of black leather boots clashed with her red fishnet stockings glittering with rhinestones. I wondered what she'd been thinking. I also wondered what she was doing here (she seemed drawn to gossip like a moth to light).

Perhaps more surprising was my mother trailing her closely behind. Three days had passed since we'd spoken in the loft and mostly I'd avoided her since.

Kimberley spotted them outside the window and let out a little scream the way a sad puppy might suddenly whimper. She flung the door open, hopped down, and staggered towards them.

'Go,' Suzanne said to me when I looked at her. 'It's best I wait here.'

'You don't have to hide.'

'I'm not hiding. I just,' she jerked her hand in the direction of my mother and Tina, 'can't deal with those vultures.'

'Look, Suzanne, I owe you an apology. I should have told you about the other car.'

She nodded slowly, as if she was still absorbing the information. 'I heard what you said to that old-fashioned kid. Stanmore, right?'

'Yes. Josh Stanmore.'

'He's wasting his time. Nothing he can do will ever make a difference.'

'Not unless we manage to find who the driver was. Mrs Wilson did see something suspicious that night.'

'No, Chloe. That's what Tina wants you to believe. She should be ashamed of fabricating such stories. Putting lies in the mouth of a dead woman.'

'But what if it was true?'

'You don't know that.'

I *did*.

I waited a beat before asking, 'What about that slanderous note tacked to your door? Surely it can't be a coincidence.'

Suzanne snorted. 'Ah, that piece of crap. I almost forgot.'

'It certainly adds weight to the theory that someone resented Holly. I wonder more and more if she got tangled up with the wrong person. Someone who had reasons to hate her. Who deliberately murdered her.'

Suzanne whipped her head around, eyes blazing. 'How dare you say my daughter was murdered! Do you know what it's like to lose a child? Nothing can ever bring her back. Nothing ever will. Holly's gone.' She clamped her hand on her mouth, looking overwhelmed with a rush of emotion.

I wished I could tell her that Holly wasn't truly gone, show her what I'd seen, make her feel what I'd sensed, that in a realm beyond the visible her daughter too was in pain. But I could never convey the right words. They would sound trite and foolish without cold, hard proof, without tangible evidence from a CCTV or a living witness. Maybe Josh Stanmore would agree to help us. More likely, now that his job was done, we'd never hear from him again.

I took her other hand, squeezed it gently. 'I'm sorry I hurt you, Suzanne. But I can't leave Heavendale until I know what happened to Holly.'

Then I dropped her hand and stepped out of the car.


The path was steep. I puffed my way up, panting in the midst of a rowdy hum of speculation.

'Hmm, I'll put my money on some adrenaline junkie.'

'A bloody tourist, I bet.'

'Oh, those reckless youngsters.'

'Some crazy climber dude fell on his ass.'

Ten minutes later, I reached a flattish grassy area at the top and came face to face with Tina.

'Oh, sweetie, it's so nice to see you. How are you? Our poor blonde angel is such a bag of nerves.' I spotted Kimberley in the distance, clinging onto my mother, staring wildly at those two helicopters near the edge of the cliff as if they were living things. A sudden childhood memory: their green tails reminded me of giant grasshoppers in comic books; my dad's, I think.

I looked back at Tina. 'So how come you're here?'

'Oh, you know . . .' She cast a leering glance at a young paramedic passing by, her tongue flicking lewdly over her lips. 'Hmm, I've always had a thing for—'

'Tina . . .'

She dragged her gaze back to me. 'Yeah, well, can't blame a girl for wanting a slice of the action. Besides, I fancied a nice lungful of fresh air. I wanted to go out for a walk.'

I looked pointedly at her six-inch heeled leather boots: Jimmy Choo, no doubt. Tina caught my stare and let out a sharp laugh.

'Oh, back off, sweetie. Of course your mother gave me a lift.'

'Of course,' I said, twisting my mouth into a smug smile. Petty, I know, but she had it coming.

Somewhere a radio crackled out police calls. We both turned and saw a strapping policeman stationed twenty yards away, a portable transceiver close to his mouth, answering back.

Patting my arm, Tina said, 'Excuse me a minute, sweetie. I shall fetch information straight at the source.'

Off she went with a sharp wiggle of her hips. All those policemen in black uniforms, young flight paramedics, handsome doctors in white coats. All that testosterone in the air. This place had become a dream playground for Tina.

One of the helicopters lifted off the ground, blades slicing through the air. A crowd swarmed and clustered behind a length of yellow tape strung between plastic posts. Standing at the front, two officers clamped their ears and bent their heads, windswept.

Kimberley shivered.

My mother turned her head and waved me a stiff greeting. I slipped away from the crowd to avoid talking to her, catching a last glimpse of green tail as the helicopter plunged downward.

Retreating, I found a quiet spot where I sat cross-legged, sheltered from the wind, looking down at the valley. My eyes swept over isolated hamlets, some tucked into pockets like dots into folds. Heavendale stood eastwards, a flat stretch of ground easily spotted with its vast concentration of houses by the lake.

The garment factory perched on a hilltop, reachable through a rocky trail disused and shadowed by straggly fir trees. I could picture gnarled roots, slippery lichen, snapping boughs, the ground chock-full of dead branches and leaves. The source of pride and employment for a whole town had dried up and become an eyesore. Broken windowpanes boarded up with wood. Roofs caving in. A dozen desolate workers' homes crumbling into decay.

It was ruined and forgotten.

I found myself wondering about the generations of women who once worked and lived there: women in the industrial revolution, working-class Victorian women, women in both world wars. I imagined the factory filled with a small army of fabric cutters, sewing machine operators, ironers, trimmers, and packagers, all rushing amid the smells of steam and starch to supply soldiers' uniforms. I thought of past social movements that shook the country: strikes, women's rights, the fight for a fair wage. Were these women treated fairly? Had they faced the inexorable closure with courage? Had my grandma feared the whisper of cold dresses?

'You seem lost in contemplation.'

I turned my head around and saw Suzanne clutching a thin blanket, long and scarlet red, around her head. She looked like Little Red Riding Hood, albeit older.

'I'm afraid that's all I could find to pass incognito.'

'I'm glad you came,' I said.

She gave me a wan smile. 'I thought about what you said earlier. About Holly. I-I want to do the right thing, you know. Even if—'

A wail shot through the crowd. I sprang up, scanned the area, and saw people staring at Kimberley, who stood locked in a tight embrace with a slightly younger version of herself.

'Thank God! I was worried sick. Where were you?'

'With the police,' her sister said. 'I had to show them the location of the body.'

'The body?' Kimberley echoed hysterically. 'What body? Where?'

'Down the ravine. I was taking pictures when I realised someone lay crouched down there.'

The air rumbled with the whirr of returning blades. The crowd moved and pressed and squeezed closer. My chest tightened as that chilling foreboding struck me again. I craned my neck, stood on my toes to scan the crowd. Beyond dense rows of people, the helicopter hovered above the ground, ready to land.

'Come, Suzanne.'

Squashed but somehow grabbing hold of her hand, I jostled my way forward.

Someone shot me a stare.

Someone grumbled petulantly, 'Assholes!'

We ignored them and elbowed our way through half a yard. Then another, until we'd edged within touching distance of the yellow police tape. In the front row to my left was Tina. A woman beside me looked familiar, but I couldn't quite place her. As the rotors slowed to a stop, the door slid open and two men stepped out, holding a limp, lifeless body in their arms. Someone screamed behind us.

Suzanne's nails dug like claws into my palm. 'No. No, it can't be.' Her voice was almost inaudible.

My eyes picked up the scene in random flashes. A mass of dishevelled black hair. The left trouser leg torn at the knee. A long silk scarf dangling off her throat. Her neck bruised purple. I raised a hand to my mouth in horror.

It was Cordelia.

My legs went slack, and for a second I thought I might smack the ground. Suzanne laid a hand on my arm to steady me.

'Chloe, you look so pale.'

'I'm okay,' I mumbled, but I wasn't. I felt weak and sick and light-headed.

Cordelia's body was whisked onto a sheet-covered stretcher, then zipped up into a bag. Soon the crowd began to disperse, flocking to their cars and homes and evening routines. I caught sight of my mother hurriedly descending the path. The gloom of the evening was closing in, the sky casting an eerie lavender light, the colour of half mourning.

'Come on,' said Suzanne. 'Let me help you.'

I held on to her arm as she gently steered me away.

In the distance, a familiar silhouette came into view. He must have seen me, because he tipped the brim of his fedora. Then he turned his back and vanished once more, swallowed up by the dusk.

## SCISSOR SISTER

There's something fascinating about watching a crowd.

The tight horde of people. The fusion of faces. A thousand voices roaring as one.

No room for difference in a crowd.

No room for you.

Do you ever wonder who those people are? Why they're so hungry to belong?

Some have lost their way in life. Some have fallen by the wayside.

They hide their pain behind masks.

They assume social roles: busy housewives, caring mothers. Clerks, teachers, students, or nurses.

Some are men too.

They're angry and tired. They're lost and they hurt. They're disillusioned.

They need a voice.

They need certainty. Purpose. Clarity.

They're the people you see every day. They're your neighbour, your boss, your colleague. Your best friend. Your beloved mother. Your moody teenager.

You're shocked.

You think you know them better than that.

You're wrong.

These are the people who join Scissor Sister.

# 19

Saturday morning. In bed, I sat leaning against the pillows, still weak from the sight of Cordelia the day before. The sun pouring bright through my closed curtains seemed almost indecent.

I grabbed my iPad and browsed Scissor Sister's site, opened each of her social media accounts in separate tabs. For no good reason, I started calculating the number of new followers she had gained overnight.

Facebook: 289
Pinterest: 568
Instagram: 872
Blog: 1,320
Twitter: 2,501

New names on the Fake Brands list: Topshop, Zara, American Apparel.

Reason: Enemy of Scissor Sister.

Latest tweet: *The bigger they are, the harder they fall.*

I finally got up when it was almost noon, munched mindlessly through half a bag of Nacho Cheese Doritos, then guiltily ran to the bathroom and purged. Bright orange-yellow, like a hot sunset turned liquid.

At Suzanne's, I managed a few sips of coffee sweetened with brown sugar. Limply scraped the flaking paint off the Parisian wardrobe. Then we dragged it outside, beneath the awning, where I started brushing the doors and drawers with duck-egg blue.

A few yards away, a group of women congregated around the corner, murmuring to each other. Not an uncommon sight in Heavendale—women regularly discussed households, their own but mostly others. They craved gossip, extracted confidences and gleefully shared them with their friends. These were women with some degree of local influence, I supposed, judging by the presence of Mrs Adams (the grocer's wife) and her two fellow busybodies: Mrs Hughes, the salon owner (not Kendall—her trainee assistant—who'd botched Kimberley's curls last Valentine's Day), and Mrs Foster, the baker whose exquisite Arctic rolls were once firm favourites of mine. A bygone time when food wasn't a foe.

They listened hungrily to a fourth woman with short black hair and a booming voice. She stood before them, with her back to me, but I gathered something about her husband's pal, a car, her dog barking *that* night. Then, unexpectedly, the air stretched tight when I overheard a name drifting through the wind like a hushed whisper.

Cordelia's name.

She looked over her shoulder, gave me a quick, knowing smile, and startled, I dropped my paintbrush to the floor. I recognised this woman. Her name was Annie Dibben. Images of her came back: when she helped my mother settle in a decade ago, pinched my cheek when I was sixteen, came twice for Sunday afternoon tea. Then a long gap without seeing her after I left for London . . . Until yesterday, when she'd been standing in the front row.

A thought clanged in my head: she too must have seen the long black scarf pulled tight around Cordelia's throat, and peeking over the silk, a loop of bruised purplish skin.


Coffee break at 3 p.m., a call on Suzanne's phone. I glimpsed the name on her screen: Daniel Johnson. His voice through the speaker was clear enough for me to hear even though she moved away to answer the call. Seemed he had promised Suzanne to come to Heavendale this afternoon, to go with her to visit Holly's grave. Unfortunately, something had come up—a sudden evening engagement—and he had to cancel at the last moment.

'Shame,' he said. 'I bought a nice wreath of flowers for the first anniversary of her death.'

I guess he'd stupidly forgotten it was the week before.

Noticing Suzanne's look, I typed a quick note on my iPad, then waved it in front of her.

She read it over to him—'Chloe is happy to pick them up. Can I send her over now?'

A moment's hesitation on the other end of the line. Then, hurriedly, he said, 'Can she be here by five?'

Thankfully, given the time constraints, the journey on the M6 was smooth. Daniel lived in Prestwich, three miles north of Manchester city centre; the town I associated with a somewhat embarrassing memory—

I must have been nineteen when an old school friend called me one day, shrieking excitedly that her mom had given her two tickets to see U2 playing at the Longfield Suite.

'Ohmigodohmigod, this is too good. You're coming, right?'

'You bet I am!'

Turned out Longfield Suite wasn't really a concert venue but a ballroom with a wide sprung floor. We ended up seeing U2-2 (a tribute act). My friend had simply shrugged off the extra digit printed on the tickets. They'd cost her mother less money than I paid for fuel to drive there. Still, we had a good time.

My GPS showed I was only a mile away when I drove past Sedgley Park—which has no park. There used to be one a long time ago, but I guess they never bothered to change the name. A group of Jewish men with *shtreimels* (fur hats) walked along the tree-free road nearby.

Then Daniel's house appeared in full view: a residential interwar semi-detached, which boasted plantation shutters and two perfectly manicured box trees on either side of the front door.

I hit the bell, and he appeared immediately with a brisk, businesslike smile. Late twenties, clipped beard, blond hair neatly parted on one side, just like in the picture. A light blue polo tucked into chinos replaced the crisp tuxedo and bow tie he'd worn for New Year's Day.

'Chloe? Hi, thanks for coming by.'

He led me down the hallway, where a large wreath lay on a pristine console table. 'I had it delivered this morning from the best florist in Manchester,' he pointed out.

'It looks very nice,' I said. White carnation blooms as big as saucers, but the message on the ribbon was a let-down: *With deepest sympathy*. It felt cold and short, as if Holly wasn't even worthy of having her name in print. Daniel didn't look like a man caught in the throes of sorrow.

'I hope Suzanne appreciates the effort.'

'I'm sure she will,' I said unconvincingly.

He took the wreath in his hands and gave me another brisk smile. 'Right. I won't hold you up any longer. I'm sure you must be anxious to avoid evening traffic.'

He made a point of glancing at his watch: Breitling, steel, ten to five; dismissing me (nicely, of course) as if I'd already outstayed my welcome. Fuck it. I wasn't going to leave now without asking him a few questions.

'Could I trouble you for a glass of water?'

'Yes . . . Sure. Still or sparkling?'

'Actually, on second thought, I wouldn't mind a cup of coffee. Black, please.' I offered him my brightest smile.

His own smile dropped as soon as he ushered me into a severe living room, pointed me towards a sofa with a rigid back. Lots of stark lines and dark leather everywhere. I tried to picture Holly in this setting but struggled. Too stark, too uncreative.

A large arch connected the room to an open kitchen-dining area, where Daniel murmured quietly to a young woman standing behind a table. She grabbed the kettle then shot a nervous glance in my direction. Whoever she was, Daniel made no attempt to introduce her.

Soon he came and sat down opposite me, placing his hands palm down on his thighs. I could already imagine him counting the seconds in his head until coffee was served.

'So, Chloe, tell me what you do in life.'

'I'm helping Suzanne renovate her store at the moment.'

'Oh, I see. You're a decorator, some kind of *craftist*, right?' He seemed pleased with the neologism.

'Sort of,' I said. 'Actually, I haven't properly introduced myself. I'm Chloe Westfield. My fiancé died with your girlfriend last year.' There were gentler ways of putting this, but I couldn't think of a better one right now. No point sidestepping the issue.

Daniel froze, looked as if he was holding his breath underwater. 'What about it?' he blurted out after a deep exhalation.

'I was hoping you might help me find out what happened. Do you know why Holly decided to travel to Heavendale that week?'

'To visit her mother, I guess.'

'That's not what people in town are saying.'

'Ah, that note about Holly,' he said flatly. 'I take no notice of gossip.'

I hummed. 'But you heard about it, right?'

He let out a quick cough before he looked over his shoulder. The woman in the kitchen gave a tiny shake of her head, almost imperceptible, as if to send him some kind of signal. I could hear the kettle beginning to steam.

'Yes,' he finally said.

'Don't you think you owe it to Holly's memory to check if that rumour was true?'

He laughed at that—a bitter, sarcastic laugh—and for the first time he looked unpleasant. 'Please don't tell me you came all the way here to find out if my dead sweetheart was a slut. Mind you, I could say the same—whatever the male equivalent is—about your fiancé, Matthew Thorne. But I guess you haven't figured it out yet.'

My stomach clenched. 'Figured out what?'

He looked at me smugly. 'As an engineer, Chloe, I take a pragmatic approach. I rely on facts alone, not gossip.'

I said nothing, waiting for him to continue.

'I suspected long ago that Holly was having an affair. The signs were there from the moment she started that job in fashion: last-minute appointments here, impromptu business meetings there, overtime always. Never informed me once of her whereabouts. She behaved like she was running the whole show.' He laughed again. 'I decided to check her car mileage after a while; before and after each trip. She always clocked up two hundred and sixteen miles, which is precisely the return journey between Prestwich and Heavendale. Feel free to check that distance for yourself on your way back.'

I looked at him, unimpressed. 'You said yourself she visited Suzanne.'

'Yes, I did say that, but the truth is, Suzanne had no idea herself where Holly was. She started making excuses every time I called. Can't blame her for protecting her daughter.'

'Are you suggesting that Holly and Matt regularly met in Heavendale?'

He shrugged. 'What more proof do you want? A tape of their bedroom antics?' When he folded his hands across his chinos, I wished Josh Stanmore was here and had witnessed Daniel's degrading tone: *My dead sweetheart was a slut.*

A silver tray clanked down on the table—'Milk? Sugar?' The woman asked, suddenly standing over us.

'Just sugar, thanks,' I said.

She served Daniel first, brushed her free hand against his, and gave me a sidelong glance. It was a small gesture, but one I sensed was of importance to her. It was her way of asserting her presence in this house, her status or authority—whatever that was. Her black top slipped up as she stooped to spoon sugar into my cup, revealing the unmistakable swell of a baby bump. Four months, maybe five. She twisted her mouth into a small smile when she caught me staring, then put the lid back on the sugar pot and slipped out of the room. The sound of her footsteps faded up the stairs.

I felt a flare of anger. All that talk to convince me Holly was a cheat when he'd found solace in the arms of another woman, got her pregnant really fast. *Nice job, Daniel.* Time to crank up the pressure.

'Have you heard of a woman named Cordelia?' I asked.

He took a sip of coffee, bemused. 'Nope. Should I have?'

'She was found dead at the bottom of a cliff yesterday.'

'That's rather unfortunate. People should be more careful these days.'

'Cordelia didn't lose her footing by accident. She died because she knew who murdered Holly.'

Daniel coughed, almost spitting out his coffee. 'Holly? Murdered? That's just plain ridiculous.'

'Private Investigator Josh Stanmore doesn't think so.'

'Private who?' Daniel blinked. 'I have no idea what you're talking about.'

I decided to bluff, just to watch him flinch. 'There's a police investigation underway. It's fact, not rumour. A pragmatic man like you should appreciate that.'

'I . . .' He cleared his throat. 'I've got nothing to hide.'

'Haven't you, really? Mind you, Mr Stanmore is pretty good at digging into people's pasts. I'm speaking from personal experience here.'

His expression went blank, uncomprehending. 'What are you saying?'

'I see you had no trouble impregnating your new girlfriend.' I paused, letting the tension build. 'Tell me, Daniel, how long have you two known each other?'

'You're stepping over the line here. My private life is none of your business.'

'But it does drag you into the picture, doesn't it?' I perched on the edge of the sofa after I said this, brought the cup to my lips.

Of course he could have killed Holly. *They* both could have if they'd started their love affair before her death. I could picture the woman as an ambitious receptionist who greeted him every morning with a smile framed by scarlet lipstick. Who could talk *pragmatic* stuff and still blow-dry her hair to perfection. Who wore the kind of underwear you put on just to be taken off. Who demanded he choose between her and Holly.

*She*—the woman witnessed by Mrs Wilson—had travelled to Heavendale with Daniel at her side. I imagined his new girlfriend at the wheel, eyes trained on the car ahead, smiling huge and cruel when she drove Holly off the road . . .

But that scenario was so far-fetched, no one could possibly take it seriously. Even I struggled to turn the tables on them when so much evidence of Holly's infidelity had piled up against her.

I sighed and peeked over my cup at Daniel: his shoulders were slumped, his chin trembling, eyes wet with tears. He wiped them with the back of his hand. *What have I just done?*

I set down my cup with a clunk and stood up abruptly. 'I've got to go,' I said, breezing past him into the hallway.

He followed behind me, hovering over my shoulder. 'Please. I'm telling you, I've got nothing to do with Holly's death.'

I didn't reply, just grabbed the wreath off the table and pulled the door open.

'Chloe, wait. I was on an audio business trip to Munich that week. I have a dozen suppliers who can vouch for my presence.'

I turned back to gauge his sincerity. He certainly tried hard, although I was still not certain what to make of him.

'I swear to you I never would have hurt Holly. I just can't believe anybody would. I'm shocked, I really am.' He looked at me imploringly. 'Please don't tell the police or Suzanne, will you? I mean, about Tania's condition.'

So Tania was her name. Maybe I'd suspected right—maybe he and Tania had started their affair long before Holly's death. But somehow, I couldn't picture the pair of them as cold-blooded murderers.

'Daniel, do you remember anything out of the ordinary before Holly left? Any uncharacteristic behaviour that caught your attention?'

He nodded. 'She was working from home that day. At some point she got very upset and banged her fist on the table. Screamed something.' He scratched his head, thinking. 'I'm sorry. I can't remember what she said now.'

'Did you go through her belongings after her death?'

'Suzanne came to collect some of them. Tania—er—got rid of the rest.' He paused. 'Can you wait just a sec?'

He went back into the living room, where I could hear drawers being opened and closed. He resurfaced with two tatty green files in his hands: both bore the initials H.P.

'I found them by accident the other day. Not sure if you'll find them helpful.' He held them out to me then grabbed a card from his wallet. 'By the way, here's my number and email address in case you need to contact me.'

I scribbled my contact details down on a piece of paper and got into my car. Just as I started the engine, he put both hands on the edge of my open window.

'There's something else,' he said. 'I caught a glimpse of a strange logo on her laptop before she stormed off.'

I fished out my iPad and showed him the website page I still had opened. 'Like this one?'

'That's exactly it. I always thought those eyes and SS initials look a tad creepy.'

'Yes,' I said with a sinking feeling. 'They do.'

# 20

There was no rest on Sunday. With only six days to go before the fair, Suzanne and I redoubled our efforts to transform her store. By 2 p.m. we had cleared the floor of its sprawling paraphernalia. By four, I had taken pictures of all items worth listing on Etsy or eBay. The rest, Suzanne decided, would be stored elsewhere, so she crammed as much as she could into her car, strapped the old Regency mirror to the roof, then drove out of town.

I had plenty to do in her absence. It was such a lovely spring afternoon with a warm, light breeze that I started to apply a second coat of paint to the Parisian wardrobe. Locals strolled by and watched from a distance, craning their necks for a curious peek through the open windows. Judging by the puzzled looks and outright stares, the revamp was drawing mixed reactions.

I instantly remembered Suzanne's words: '*It was the committee's decision to launch a local boycott of my store.*' And Patsy's too: '*Suzanne didn't make the grade.*' Still, I made a conscious effort to smile back at the friendlier faces. Glad some of them tacitly supported our quiet rebellion against Denise Drummond and her biased crusade against immorality.

A German Shepherd sniffed his way down the square, made a beeline to nuzzle my hand, and rested his paws on my legs, tail wagging.

'Steady, fella,' a burly man in blue overalls called out from across the road. He was struggling to manoeuvre wooden planks into the back of his van. 'Don't worry, Miss, he won't bite or anything. He's just curious.'

I dropped my brush and crouched down to tickle the dog round his ears. He gave the side of my face a big lick in return.

'Come on,' I said, standing back up. He trotted obediently by my side as I coaxed him towards his master.

'Rudy likes you,' the man said, roughly patting the dog's head. 'He's usually not that friendly with strangers.'

I smiled, glad to have been singled out. Glad to have found a friend. 'Do you need help with those planks?'

'Not much we can do, really. They're too big. Even with the back seats lowered.'

'Why don't you chop them?' I suggested. 'Suzanne has three vintage hatchets at the back of her store. They're very sturdy.'

'Are you offering me the lot?'

'I'd be worried if you were a collector.'

He laughed at that. 'To be honest, I wouldn't mind getting rid of that wood. It's good oak if you're interested.'

I pondered his offer for a moment. 'Well, why not. I think I just might have an idea.'

'Ah, smashing! You're certainly saving me a great deal of trouble and time, Miss.'

'Please call me Chloe.'

He shook my hand. 'I'm Colin. Colin Dibben.'

I paused for a second. 'Are you Annie's husband?'

He winked. 'I hope the missus only told you good things about me.'

'Of course.' I helped him lift the planks back out of his van; Rudy trotting alongside us. 'Your wife was very kind to my mother when we moved into Heavendale.'

'She still remembers you—you're Kathryn Westfield's daughter, right?'

'I am.'

'She said she saw you yesterday.'

'I know. She was talking to her friends just opposite the store.'

'Well, I can't say I'm surprised here.' He shot me a comical grin. 'My missus always talks too much.'

153

Fragments of her conversation came back to me: her husband's pal, a car, her dog barking *that* night—Rudy, of course. Colin must know what it was all about.

When we unloaded the last batch of planks into the store, I poured him a large glass of water then said, 'I hope you don't mind me saying, but I was there when the police airlifted Cordelia's body. There was something wrong with . . . her neck.'

He frowned. Stared at me long enough to make sure there was no room for misunderstanding. 'Yes, that's what my wife said.'

'This was no accident, Colin.'

He drained his glass in one gulp, clanked it down. 'To hell with this. I might as well tell you the whole lot.'

'Something to do with a friend of yours, I heard?'

'Yes. Brad, a mate of mine. He left the pub on Thursday night and saw Cordelia drive up to the mountains. Very odd, because she ain't the type of woman to leave home after dark.' He looked at his dog. 'Maybe that explained why Rudy was behaving so strangely.'

'What do you mean?'

'He was restless. As if he needed a good walk or something before bedtime. So I took him to the mountains, which is no bother because I know all the shortcuts. Then Rudy started barking furiously when we reached the cliff. I had to steady him, put him on the leash and drag him back down. That's when I saw a shadow run to their car and drive off.'

'A shadow? You mean Cordelia?'

'Can't be. I heard the police found her car abandoned by the roadside yesterday. And Rudy would never bark at her. Not in a mean way, I mean. Cordelia fussed a great deal over my dog. She, uh, spoiled him twice with a free paw-reading session.' He gave me a look that said, *Don't ask.*

'Who did you see, then?'

He shrugged. 'Don't know. There was no moon that night. Some wicked type of fella. Ain't that right, Rudy?'

Rudy sat upright with his tongue lolling out of his mouth and his ears pricked, lapping up the mention of his name—if only dogs could talk.

'Have you told the police?'

'No, but I've told my missus.' He rolled his eyes in mock exasperation. 'It won't be long before it goes around town.'

I nodded. I imagined the news travelling like wildfire, from restless mouths to eager ears. Still, it didn't seem like such a bad thing this time. Maybe it was a chance to shine some much-needed attention on Holly. I had no doubt she and Cordelia had been murdered by the same person. Both knew who they were up against. And they must have come pretty damn close to the truth to pay with their lives.

'Got to get going. I can't keep the missus waiting too long,' Colin said, getting to his feet. 'I'll bring a ladder tomorrow morning to fix the roof, if that's all right.'

'The roof?'

He nodded. 'I noticed there were some missing slates and thick weeds poking through the cracks. You don't want a leak to spoil all your hard work.'

'Thank you,' I said, grateful. 'How can we repay you for your trouble?'

'Nah, ain't no trouble at all, Miss Chloe.' He looked around the room. 'You're doing a grand job, you know. That's what this community needs.'

I smiled at him and gave Rudy a big hug. With a happy woof, he trotted alongside Colin towards his van.


Thirty minutes later. I tipped my brush into the tin and froze when I saw his reflection in the old aircraft door. I didn't have to turn around. The shiny chrome gave me a clear image: twenty-odd, black-rimmed glasses, floppy brown hair. I'd seen this guy passing by three times in the last half hour. He stopped again by the bookstore opposite and stared through its window, hands stuffed into his pockets in a falsely casual pose, stealing furtive looks in my direction.

*Who is he? What does he want?*

I shivered at the thought of Colin's words: '. . . *a shadow . . . some wicked type of fella.*' Of course, maybe it wasn't the same man. But I wondered what would happen if I let him sneak inside the store. If I let him believe he was alone for a while.

I dropped my brush in the tin, stomped across the room, and slammed the back door shut, then crouched silently behind the counter. Two minutes later, I heard the first squeak. Then more as the floorboards creaked one by one.

*Squeak. Squeak. Squeak.*

Steady, measured footsteps getting closer, like the ticking of some huge clock beating in unison with my heart. When they stopped, I crawled quietly on all fours to take a peek: tennis shoes, skinny jeans, a grey shirt buttoned to the neck. Kept looking up until his gaze bored down straight into mine. I got such a fright that I jumped back and banged my head against a stool. Then, after lurching to my feet, I hurled it at him.

'Ouch!' The stool bounced off him and hit the floor.

'What do you want?' I shouted.

He removed his glasses and nudged the spot above his brow that was already a dark blue, like the outline of a plum. 'Shit. I think you dented my forehead.'

I studied him from behind the counter. That voice. That face. There was something oddly familiar. I scrutinised him from head to toe and back up again, scanning, searching for what eluded me, and gaped in shock when our eyes locked—his were limpid blue.

*A shade of azure.*

A shimmer of sweat quickly covered my skin. I could see through his deception now: the fedora, the old-fashioned suit, the clipped line of facial hair (a fake stick-on moustache, I figured). They were all gone, giving way to geek chic. He'd fooled me with his disguise, made me believe he was a private investigator.

He moved closer—'I can explain, Chloe. I mean, Miss Westfield.'

'Save your breath.' I yanked my phone out of my pocket and stabbed at the buttons only to realize the battery was gone. *Shit.*

'I just want to say it's not at all what you think. Dressing up isn't a hobby.'

I snorted. 'I don't care what you do in your spare time.'

He moved closer again, forcing me to shrink back against the wall. I glanced across the counter in panic, scanning its contents: sticky tape, rubber bands, paper clips. I snatched a plastic seam ripper and thrust it forward, almost jabbing him in the eye.

'Hey, take it easy with that . . . thing.'

'Then take a step back.'

He complied, flinging his hands skywards in an 'I can't win' gesture. There was something pitifully farcical about our act—me wielding a tiny crooked blade, him pretending I had a weapon.

I dropped it back to the counter and sighed. 'Who are you?'

'I'm Josh Stanmore. That's my real name. No lie.'

'I'm sure the police will be happy to know that.'

He put his hands down. 'Look, I understand why you're peeved about—'

'Peeved?' I shrilled. 'You think *peeved* comes close to describing how I feel? You are a fraud, Josh Stanmore. You're a liar, you fuck.'

'You're not being very objective here.'

I glared at him. 'Why did you trick me? To prove to yourself you can cut it as a detective? Make Daddy proud after you failed your entrance exams?'

'Okay, I get it, you're super peeved right now. But to be fair, you're the one who dragged me into this.'

'Dragged you into what?'

'You texted me that night you drank too much. Remember?'

'What? No! The only person I texted . . .' And then the penny dropped, and I pushed the tips of my fingers into my forehead. 'You mean you're . . . MysteryGeek?'

He grinned sheepishly. 'That's me, all right.'

I stood speechless, my brain starting to join the dots. I realised I had fed him all the information he needed to play his part. Or most of it.

'But how did you find out about Holly? I never typed her name once in my texts.'

'You didn't have to. I made the connection as soon as you mentioned Matthew Thorne.'

'So you were acquainted with her.'

'Actually, we were good friends. When you said you wanted Matthew to die, I really thought you'd killed them both. That's why I asked a contact at the Met to track the recording of your last phone call together.'

'But you already knew I was innocent before meeting me. Why bother with that,' I waved my hands around, 'masquerade?'

'I still had to find out what else you knew.'

'You used me,' I said defensively.

'I'm sorry, but you left me no choice. I had to take matters into my own hands.'

I nodded, trying to swallow my pride. I realised I couldn't shrug off responsibility for my actions and put all the blame on him. 'So you brought Detective Josh Spade to life. The character you played in our video game, right?'

He cracked a faint smile. 'Afraid so.'

'My God. You're sicker than I thought,' I said and started to laugh. It was as if all the tension bound up in me had been released in one steady stream of pure mirth.

He laughed too. 'Yes, well, go Google "private detective." They're all dead ringers for Humphrey Bogart, save for the stache.'

We both laughed again.

When we stopped, gasping, he said seriously, 'You were right, though. Someone did murder Holly.' He held my gaze longer than he needed to, his eyes shining with deep blue warmth. I made myself look away, picked at a nail and went quiet, the heat rising up my neck. A group of forty-odd Japanese tourists were leaving Market Square en masse from the window.

'The police should have been more thorough that night,' I said at last.

Josh nodded. 'They clearly didn't do their job.'

'No. They should have recorded Mrs Wilson's statement.'

'They should have interrogated Jade too. She pulled over to the side of the road to watch them. That can't be a coincidence.'

'You think Jade was the woman in the other car?'

Josh raked a hand through his hair. 'I'm not sure. Hard to imagine her Toyota Yaris would compete with a sports Maserati in terms of speed. Let alone force it to crash into a tree.'

'Unless she tampered with it beforehand.'

'Hmm, good point. There was a window of opportunity from the moment Matthew and Holly arrived until the time they left.'

'Twenty minutes, according to Suzanne.'

'Enough time to damage the brake cables.'

'Or slash a couple of tyres.'

'Yes,' he said, eyes brightening. 'A penknife would do.'

I cleared my throat. 'What about a pair of sharp scissors?'

Josh raised his eyebrows at me. 'You're thinking of Scissor Sister, right? What do you know about her?'

'Not much, except that she enjoys online anonymity and playing Mother Superior.' I shrugged. 'Seriously, though, it does broaden the number of suspects. Tina and Kimberley clearly had an opportunity too. Hell, anyone crossing the road at that moment could have done it.'

'Okay,' Josh said. 'So we know for sure our suspect is local. Now we need to find the motive.'

I turned my face towards the window again; Market Square looked deserted now. Some of the shops were starting to close.

'I went to see Daniel yesterday,' I revealed. 'At the end of my visit, he gave me two files full of handwritten instructions and sketched silhouettes. They all bore Holly's initials with dates in the bottom corner.'

Josh frowned at me, clearly not following.

'They were sewing patterns,' I went on. 'They all ended up being launched on the Scissor Sister website within weeks of Holly drafting them—including Amelia, their bestseller.'

'Okay, so what's the theory here?'

'Scissor Sister could have commissioned Holly. Either that or she approached Scissor Sister first.'

I had a flash of Holly, sitting on the sofa next to Daniel, screaming something at the SS initials on her laptop screen before she abruptly left for Heavendale. Everything pointed to a relationship gone awfully sour. Josh thought so too.

'Holly and Cordelia must have figured out something that cost them their lives. They obviously knew who *she* really is,' Josh said.

'But why Heavendale of all places?'

'Because this is the hub of all Scissor Sister activities, that's where Scissor Sister herself actually lives.' Josh looked me straight in the eye. 'Can't you see, Chloe? One of them is lying. One of them is our killer.'

It took a moment for the impact of his words to sink in. 'Are you saying . . .?'

But I knew very well what Josh was saying. My hand went to my throat as I wrapped my mind around the idea; the thought of it hitting me like a wall of solid stone. Too close to home.

He went on. 'Five women, five suspects. The question is, which of them is playing Scissor Sister?'

# SCISSOR SISTER

I hover close enough, pretending to stare at tomato boxes. Pretending to dither between plum and Tigerella.

How fucking mundane.

I am seething inside. I am livid.

Mrs Adams knows.

She's bending over the counter, whispering the news to Mrs Johnson, who will later tell Mrs Miller. Who in turn will blab to all her busybody friends.

By noon tomorrow, the rest of Heavendale will know.

I can't allow this. I must put an end to this.

I pay for my goods and stumble out of the grocery store.

Down my left arm, three dry lines of scabs are peeking out of my shirtsleeve. I can't bear the sight of them. Can't bear the memory of her nails digging into my forearm, drawing blood. She struggled terribly.

The strangling, though. That was careless. There were other ways, better ways. Ways to make it look like an accident or a suicide.

Never mind. I know what I have to do next.

I take a deep breath and remind myself what Scissor Sister represents to the world.

What *I* represent to the world.

The pleasure I feel whenever a new name joins me. The intoxicating thrill of watching my online numbers soar.

My grip growing stronger as each day goes by . . .

So can you see now? Do you finally understand?

Her treachery could not be left unpunished.
I never had a choice, I had to do it for them.
I had to do it for *you*.
Yes, you!
That's why I had to kill for you.

# 21

A tray of clinking silverware set outside my bedroom door, followed by a quiet knock. My mother—'Chloe?'

'Yes?'

'I brought you breakfast, sweetheart.'

'Thanks.'

I waited nervously in my bed until her footsteps padded away along the plush corridor and down the stairs. I had coffee first, then nibbled on a piece of toast, my bite spraying flecks onto a long strip of bacon oozing grease.

My stomach churning, I pushed the plate away and marched to the bathroom. I didn't make myself throw up. Just sat naked in the tub and ran warm water, with my chin on my knees, and inhaled deeply— the smell of cooked pork cloaked in lemongrass.

I started thinking then about what Josh had said the day before.

Five women.

Five suspects.

One of them devious enough to play a double game and fool the other four. A ruthless woman who wanted ultimate control. Who restricted her communication with others by means of Sister codes. Who wanted to protect her anonymity at all costs.

I closed my eyes and retraced my last seven days in Heavendale, tried to visualise who best fitted the grisly profile of Scissor Sister.

There was Jade Worthington, the fashion guru of the group. Also known as *Sister of Grace*. She had offered Holly a work experience at Vintage Folly three summers ago, made important calls to land her a job. An act of genuine altruism? Or did Jade exploit her drafting talents to secretly grow the Scissor Sister brand? She'd had a clear opportunity to murder Holly that night.

And so did Tina Williams, the self-proclaimed 'Queen of Gossip,' known in the group as *Sister of Love*. So far, I couldn't find any obvious connection between her and Holly. But that moment when she'd challenged Kimberley at the Monday meeting certainly raised question marks. How did she find out the exact percentage of the order backlog? Coincidence? Hunch? Luck? Hard to believe it was any of those when the information was supposedly confidential. Maybe she really had stolen Kimberley's passcode.

There was plenty to wonder about with Kimberley Gates, aka *Sister of Plenty*. Scatty, vulnerable Kimberley, whose store exclusively promoted the Scissor Sister brand. Who'd broken into tears during the meeting, and yet shown a very different side when she ripped up that note defaming Holly.

Patsy Carter—*Sister of Truth*—was an enigma too. I struggled to reconcile the image of her (successful fashion editor, glamorous magazine owner) with that of an employee blindly promoting a megalomaniacal dressmaking brand. As the brains behind the organisation, she would certainly fit, though.

And then there was Kathryn Westfield, aka *Sister of Trust*. Who'd claimed she hid the circumstances of Matt's death to protect me. Who'd called Holly a little slut. My mind stumbled from image to image—all ominous—of my mother. A flash of her arguing with Holly. A flash of her in the street sneaking under the car, fingers wrapped around a pair of long nose pliers. In the loft, a logo with gleaming scissors and watching eyes on her laptop screen, her fingers stabbing at the keys as she sacked Suzanne. A memory now of her in the kitchen, rubbing baby dribble off her floral cotton sleeve. Did she rub mud stains off her dress after killing Cordelia? Or was it blood?

I put my head in my wet hands—*You're crazy, Chloe. You're crazy to think what you're thinking*.

I grabbed a towel off the rack and stumbled out of the bath.

. . .

164

I met Josh at Mindful Wellness at ten. He was sitting alone at the back of the deserted juice bar, eyes fixed on his laptop screen. I plopped down in the chair opposite him and felt strangely happy to see him—comfortable and secure. A haven away from my own scary thoughts.

He looked up and grinned. 'Chloe. Good morning to you. Can I get you anything?' He took a sip of a red drink garnished with strawberry. 'I definitely recommend the ginger beet smoothie. Tastes amazing.'

'You should come here more often.' I glanced at the waitress who was slumped over the counter looking bored. 'Most Heavendalians favour lager and ale at the local pub.'

'Ah, the Old Swan, right? Good food. Comfy beds. Their Wi-Fi sucks, though.'

'Is that where you're staying?'

'Yup.' He rattled his glass between us. 'Tempted?'

I cracked a smile. 'Maybe later. So tell me what you're working on.'

'All business, huh?' He turned his laptop towards me. 'I'm trying to unmask our enigmatic Mother Superior.'

I stared at the screen. 'You're hacking into her website?'

'Trying to, but no luck so far. Whoever owns the Scissor Sister domain has paid to opt out of the WHOis directory—that's like a telephone book for websites.'

'Is there a way around it?'

'I've asked my contact at the Met to submit a data protection waiver to obtain her name and address, but he'd have to do it on the sly. My guess is she's probably using a proxy server to avoid detection.'

'But surely she must have left a digital footprint. There must be a way to ID her.'

'Not as easy as you think if the site is hosted abroad. She can still quietly operate in Heavendale and yet cover her tracks by having her details registered in Russia. In short, we stand no chance without full cooperation from the police or some cybercrime expert.'

'It's only a matter of time,' I said. 'They'll soon be investigating Cordelia's murder.'

'That's not what the police think.'

'What?'

He leaned across the table. 'Look, I've heard what people are saying in this town. That doesn't mean they're right. We can't know for sure—'

'I saw her, Josh. Her neck was bruised.'

'But that doesn't mean your version is right.'

I blinked. 'My *version*?'

'Everyone has their own version of a memory. Let me play devil's advocate for a moment. What if those bruises you saw occurred by falling?'

'They didn't.'

'What if they were scratches or deep cuts?'

'I can tell the difference between cuts and strangulation marks, Josh.'

He shrugged. 'Okay, fine. So for some reason, the police didn't see fit to request a post-mortem.'

'Something must have slipped through the net. It's negligence or incompetence—I don't know. I'll go talk to them,' I said, then stopped halfway out of my chair as I remembered my disheartening encounter with the chief inspector. Someone else would have to go.

Josh sighed. 'You'll be wasting your time.'

'Why?'

'They released her body last night.'

'I thought Cordelia didn't have any relatives . . .'

'She doesn't.' Josh cleared his throat, tipped his half-empty glass in my direction. 'It was your mother who signed the documents.'

I froze. My head was spinning, sickening thoughts racing inside me once more. I pictured her at the funeral home here in Heavendale, asking the director to beautify the corpse. *Put particular focus on the neck*, she'd say, slipping an extra wad of cash into his hand.

166

'Look,' Josh said, sensing my discomfort, 'maybe we shouldn't read too much into it. Maybe she offered to do it out of kindness.'

'Kindness?' I said, my voice hollow behind the blood in my ears. I tried to remember a genuine act of kindness from my mother. Wondered if the tray of breakfast from this morning counted. 'When is the funeral being held?'

'On Wednesday. It will be followed by a reception at Stonebarn Lake.'

I nodded absently then began rubbing my thumb hard across the table.

'She didn't tell you, did she?'

'My mother and I aren't exactly on speaking terms at the moment. To be blunt, I can't bear to see her. I'm having . . . trust issues.'

'I'm sorry, Chloe.' He reached over and covered my hand with his, stopping the movement of my thumb. 'I should have been a bit more tactful yesterday. I should have remembered I was also implicating your mother, after all.'

'No, it's fine. I'm fine. It's only one chance in five, right?' My laugh sounded more like a strangled sob as I dropped my gaze.

'You'll call me if anything's wrong?'

'Yes,' I said and freed my hand, then stood up.

'We're a team, Chloe.'

I tried for a smile. 'I'm glad.'

'Me too,' he said.


I drove back through town, still haunted by the memory of Cordelia—a limp cloak of black silk floating in the wind.

Across the square, Kimberley stood hunched inside her storefront display, busy plumping cushions on a bench and fussing over the giant pair of silver scissors and any SS envelopes that had turned floppy in the hands of her three mannequins.

This, I reminded myself, was the place where I had last seen

Cordelia alive. I desperately needed to believe someone else was guilty, not my mother. To turn my suspicions in other directions.

Once Kimberley skittered out of sight, I eased the door open and quietly slipped inside. She'd gone to join the Scissor Sister class at the back—running Mondays too, apparently, and again attended by the blonde and the brunette. I could pick out their voices among the intermittent clatter of sewing machines: syrupy when seeking approval, haughty when dispensing advice to the less proficient members of the group.

I brought my mind back to the day I'd found Cordelia in this store, right before Kimberley flew off in a rage. Before she tore the 'Your daughter is a slut' page into pieces.

There was that moment when Cordelia had slid a small card out of a label holder, gone back and forth between it and that page, a fountain pen in her hand, as if she was comparing something between them.

I knelt down by the tall shelving unit, right where she had, and examined the cards in front of me, trying to decide which one had piqued her attention. Most had the word *ribbons* written on them: Petersham ribbons, 10mm small ribbons, 45mm wide ribbons. Ribbons with blue flowers, green stars, Easter rabbits. Ribbons of all shapes, colours, and sizes. If the clue was in the name, I was at a loss to find it. As for the handwriting itself, it betrayed nothing in its pretty red curls and feminine loops. A far cry from that page of hard, overly precise lines tacked onto Suzanne's door.

The front door banged open, a tall man around the age of thirty stumbled in clumsily. The top two buttons of his white shirt were open, his tie undone. He looked smashed.

'Kiiiim!' he called, the syllable like a rising yell.

She came scuttling back with timid mouse steps, looking tense and alarmed. Underneath that, something else I recognised.

Fear.

'Rob, I thought you had a job interview.'

He snorted, swayed heavily towards the desk. He leaned back against a chair and picked up a pen from a mesh pot, then pointed it at me. 'Who the fuck is that?'

He stared me down as if I were some pesky gnat needing swatting. Kimberley squinted at me, registering my presence.

'It's only Chloe, Kathryn's daughter. Don't you remember Kathryn Westfield? She came over to help me last week.'

'Yeah, yeah, whatever. Get her out and shut the store.'

'But there's no meeting at Stonebarn Lake this afternoon.'

'None of my business.'

'But Rob, I can't. I'm running a class . . .'

He stayed silent for a moment. His jaw started working, and the air in the room suddenly turned stale and dark. In the background, the din of sewing machines sounded almost surreal.

'Who gave you permission?' he barked.

'I-I told you this morning. Oh, Rob, I swear I did. Please—'

'Who the fuck gave you permission?'

'Please, Rob, don't shout. I thought you agreed—'

'I agreed nothing,' he yelled, then staggered back to his feet. 'The lies you women always tell. Lies, lies, lies.' He took a step towards the back room.

'Rob, don't.'

'Don't you tell me what to do in my own house.'

'Please, Rob, I'm begging you. Let me handle this. They'll all be out soon, I promise.'

His hands balled into fists, then slackened when he noticed my stare. He turned around and, seized by rage, sent the mesh pot flying to the floor, pens bouncing and rolling off everywhere.

'Five minutes, that's all you have. Got it?'

Before Kimberely could reply he began staggering his way up the stairs and onto the first floor.

Kimberley stood like a quivering mess, muttering to herself, 'I'm sorry, Rob. I'm so sorry. It won't happen again.'

I rose to my feet, wrapped my arm awkwardly around her. 'He's gone now.'

She shook her head. 'He's never gone.'

I gathered the pens one by one, put them back in the pot. Then I marched to the back room and asked everyone to leave, mumbled some pitiful excuse about a last-minute meeting Kimberley had to prepare.

The blonde sighed heavily, sulked her way out the door with the brunette trailing closely behind. 'We'll come back tomorrow,' she said, her chin jutting. 'Ten o'clock sharp.'

I nodded, having nothing to add to that, and joined Kimberley, who had cowered in the back corner, head down, sobbing in silence.

'I'm sorry,' she said again when I sat beside her.

'Me too.'

A curl of her hair fell across her cheek, and in a flash a connection registered: her tears last Monday during the meeting, the tissue in her hand smudged with make-up. The faded line of a yellowish bruise on her left cheekbone.

Something inside me stirred. I needed to be gentle.

'Kimberley,' I said softly. 'Does Rob hit you?'

She flinched at the question and backed away from me, stunned, then shot a glance upward. I could hear Rob cursing upstairs, the clang of a beer can being cracked open.

'Please,' I whispered, 'let me help you. I know what you're going through. We must talk to the police now.'

'No, no, you don't understand.' She tugged at my arm, almost like a child. 'Look,' she said, and showed me her gold bracelet inlaid with green stones.

'I know, it's beautiful. But a present from him won't change—'

'Rob gave it to me yesterday.' She smiled through her tears as she held out her wrist.

'No, that's not true, Kimberley. You already showed me that bracelet last week.'

'It *is* true,' she said, her eyes fixed on it. 'It's true that Rob loves me very much. Aren't I the luckiest girl in the world?'

My mouth hung open—that same question uttered again. As if her mind couldn't cope with the ugliness around her and was stuck in a long-gone fairy-tale loop.

I tumbled out the door when Rob yelled her name from upstairs; my eyes were stinging and red. It was happening again. Like a mirror image of my old life. I could feel the heat of anger trapped in my throat, threatening to choke me like bile. Anger at Kimberley for protecting Rob. Anger at Rob for reminding me of Matt.

Anger at Matt, at myself, at my mother.

*Aren't I the luckiest girl in the world?*

I stumbled my way along Market Square, thick tears running down my cheeks before I'd even reached my car.

## 22

Back at Stonebarn Lake after a detour to an off-licence, my eyes were swollen and my emotions raw. I tucked a bottle of vodka to the side of my bed, rubbed away my tears, reasoned with my head, then pictured my mother telling me: *Wait until I cook you dinner, sweetheart. Bacon or fish pie?*

I wanted to drink to oblivion. There was nothing I wanted to do more than numb the pain away, wrapped in blankets, unconscious. I hated being in Heavendale, but my flat in Chertsey held no comfort either. I felt hollow and empty, with no sense of belonging, no roots, no home. Drifting through life in a constant state of weightlessness.

My iPad pinged, signalling a new email in my inbox. It was Daniel, who'd sent me a list of 'stealthy' car trips made by Holly in her last six months (assuming I could trust his odometer readings). I used to keep online diaries when I lived with Matt, recording compulsively my weight loss but also his trips away from London.

I looked for those dates, compared them with Holly's: one was a day or two before. The others didn't correlate at all. Nothing pointed to a long-distance love affair. In fact, I doubted they'd even known each other prior to April 2017. Though I couldn't completely debunk the quick fling theory, Holly must have made those trips to Heavendale with a sole purpose: To meet the woman who called herself Scissor Sister.

A second email pinged in my inbox; Daniel again. He'd suddenly remembered what Holly had said before leaving Prestwich: *'She stole it from me.'*

I read the words aloud, clung onto them. *Who stole what?* I immediately wrote back.

Within a minute his reply dropped: *I'm afraid your guess is as good as mine.*

I wasn't sure what drove me then to pad up the stairs to the loft. Curiosity? Suspicion? Fear? One chance in five?

*'She stole it from me.'*

With each step upward I had to fight a fresh wave of nausea. I stood in the middle of the room, forcing the bile down as I took a slow, careful look around. Everything looked tidy to the point of fastidiousness. The box of pictures was gone. The bulky A4 file with its Sister code and silhouette drawings had also disappeared off the shelf, as though my mother had wanted to wipe clean any evidence of our clash the week before. Only her laptop lay open on the cutting worktable. I pressed the space bar and the screen lit up with a white SS icon in the right-hand corner. I clicked on it, watched the Sister of Trust username appear atop a blank password box.

*What could it be?*

I tried her date of birth and a message flashed: *ACCESS DENIED: TWO ATTEMPTS REMAINING.*

I took another stab, this time entering my dad's name. *ACCESS DENIED: ONE ATTEMPT REMAINING.*

I didn't dare risk another try. I looked for the IP address, jotted it down, then made for the shelving units and trawled through every folder and file. When nothing caught my attention, I checked the filing cabinet and began pulling open the drawers. One was empty. Another contained a metallic box full of signed receipts. The last drawer pulled out only an inch and then jammed. My mother had padlocked it.

I pulled again and again. I could hear the faint rustle of paper followed by a rattling metallic sound. Not paper clips sliding onto each other. Something heavier. A pair of pliers? A garrotte? My face went hot. I couldn't bear to imagine the worst, so I searched for the key, ran my hand under the desk in case it was taped there, then looked at the underside of the top two drawers.

Nothing.

I clutched the side of the cabinet with one hand and the handle with the other—yanked hard. Harder. It didn't budge.

I was about to look for a prying tool when urgent footsteps clicked up the stairs—my mother. I grabbed the first book I saw from the shelf, pretending to be absorbed as she walked into the room.

'Chloe . . . What a lovely surprise.'

She looked disconcerted to see me. Her eyes anxiously scoured the room, drifted over to the table where her laptop was. When she frowned at it, my stomach roiled with nerves. Then she snapped it shut, swept past me, and dropped her coat on the trunk.

'How was your morning, sweetheart?'

'Fine, thank you.' I stared at the book in my hands: *Cook with Jamie*. I put it straight back on the shelf. 'How was yours, Mum?'

'Oh, busy-busy. Rushed off my feet as usual.' She gave a brittle laugh as she pulled out her phone and a key ring with a dozen keys from her handbag. One of them looked small enough to open the bottom drawer . . .

'I heard you'll be organising a reception after Cordelia's funeral on Wednesday.'

'Yes, poor thing. She was such a darling. It was the least I could do.'

'Her death must have been hard on you.'

'It was. I only wish I could have done more. I had no idea she was so . . . . unhappy.' Her voice cracked a little at the end followed by a wistful downward glance. I couldn't tell if it was genuine.

'She didn't commit suicide, Mum. She was strangled.'

'Good God, Chloe. Why would you pay heed to such viciousness? It's nothing but a nasty rumour going around. Started by some small-minded, petty people.'

'Some rumours carry a seed of truth.'

'Yes, well, certainly not this one. We'll give Cordelia a good funeral. I'm taking care of everything from now on.'

Goosebumps sprouted along my arms, the hairs on my flesh standing on end.

'Is everything okay with you, sweetheart? You look . . . dejected.'

'I'm fine,' I said, forcing a breath out.

My mother sighed and shook her head. 'I know you've been avoiding me lately. I know you've been seeing Suzanne too.'

'She's going through a hard time.'

'She should have handled the situation better.' I huffed out a laugh, but my mother was undaunted. 'Chloe, despite what you think, you don't know everything about Suzanne. She called in sick every day after Holly died. Then she didn't even bother to report for work.'

'She's been through so much, Mum. You should have reached out to her. Not once did you return her calls.'

'That is simpy not true. I wanted to clear the air between us, but she refused to see me. Twice she shut the door in my face. In the end, there was nothing more I could have done. Nothing Scissor Sister herself could have done. Suzanne had become unreliable. Unreasonable.'

'How convenient,' I muttered.

My mother leaned closer; I could feel her breath fill the hollow of my neck. 'Why do you care so much about her?'

'I made a promise to overhaul her store. I'm not reneging on it.'

'Your allegiance lies with your mother, Chloe. Not with a stranger.'

'She was your *friend*.'

My mother waved a hand. 'She belongs to the past now. Why waste your time when your future could be with us?'

I frowned at her, not following, but my mother simply smiled.

Her fingers brushed my cheek lightly. 'Cordelia's death is a terrible tragedy for us all, but we have to be practical. Soon Scissor

Sister will advertise a new vacancy. There'll be an opportunity for someone eager to fill that gap.'

I flinched. 'How can you be so heartless, Mum? Her body isn't even cold.'

'You need to learn to be tough, Chloe. Think about yourself. I could always put in a good word for you.'

'How? Via the SS intranet?'

'Of course, sweetheart. It's the only way.'

I didn't move for a moment, caught by the idea; considering the fantasy. A monthly salary, a regular job, my mother and I working side by side, exchanging pleasantries. Maybe even a little house by the lake, a husband, and a brood of children. A picket fence overflowing with roses and hydrangeas in summer. Sitting on the porch and eating a plate of food without feeling like retching.

'You can have it all,' my mother whispered at me. 'Scissor Sister is growing fast. With skills like yours, who knows how far you could go.'

A cold chill ran down my spine. My mother stared at me, her cheeks flushed, her green eyes fierce with belief—a frightening intensity I'd never seen from her before.

'I need to think about it,' I said, more than eager to leave.

She clamped a hand on my wrist, her fingers like claws. 'Think hard, sweetheart. You may never get an opportunity like this again.'

Only when I nodded did she release me from her grip. I could feel her gaze, white-hot on my back until I stumbled out the door.


I drove straight to Suzanne's. The roof had been cleared of its weeds and Colin was crouching on the floor inside the store, drilling holes and hammering nails into planks of wood. The smell of sawdust tickled my nose before I even reached the door.

'How can I possibly thank you?' I said in greeting.

'Nah,' he chuckled, embarrassed. 'I'm just doing my job.'

'But how did you know I needed the help?'

'I told him.' Suzanne appeared behind me, a sheet of sandpaper in hand. 'Colin offered straight away to help us.'

I smiled, grateful. 'I'm glad you guys didn't leave me wrestling with power tools.'

'Your four platforms should be ready by the end of today, Miss Chloe.'

I had envisaged each of them raised in a corner, furnished and bedecked with fabric and nostalgic memorabilia from a particular era. Everything had to be staged appealingly to stand a chance of selling, especially with the fair so soon in sight.

'I have a beautiful hand-painted Afghan shawl,' Suzanne said. 'I gave it to Holly when she turned eighteen but it would look good on one of your displays.'

I frowned at her. 'You don't have to.'

Suzanne shook her head, adamant. 'Maybe it's time to start letting go.' She sighed. 'Let me show you her bedroom, Chloe.'

She led me up a narrow staircase, then pushed open a door at the end of the hallway. Inside, blue-lavender walls paired with Andy Warhol art prints. Two plum sequined cushions adorned a single bed with a string of chilli-pepper fairy lights looped around barley twists. The wardrobe stood ajar, and I peeked inside at turtlenecks, two pairs of capri pants clipped onto hangers, a row of colourful dresses, mostly shades of green and blue. Ankle-high shoes slanted downward on a two-tier rack. An odd note: a pair of yellow rubber boots tilted against the back panel, their soles caked with dried mud.

I was frowning at the boots when Suzanne picked up the shawl from one of the drawers and handed it to me, looking down.

'I know this will sound crazy,' she started in a whisper, 'but sometimes I can feel her presence. Like a cold cocoon of greyness shrouding me.'

She shook her head as if she couldn't believe it herself, then squeezed her eyes shut and blinked hard. 'I keep hearing her voice. I lie in bed and I can hear her calling me at night. I keep thinking she's out there and alive.' She was trembling.

'Maybe death is a different form of life,' I offered weakly, my words too guarded and restrained to bring her any comfort.

We fell silent.

Suzanne pointed towards a desk then motioned for me to look down. Wedged beneath a square sheet of glass was a photo collage—about two dozen pictures of Holly, all of them as a child. One, in particular, tugged at my heart: a young Suzanne catching a three-year-old Holly at the bottom of a playground slide, her mouth wide open, her eyes beaming with joy. I felt a pang of envy as I tried to imagine the rest of their day together. Giggling daughter skipping alongside mother, small hand folded in big hand on their way back home.

Suzanne wiped a tear off her cheek. 'She was my baby.'

I nodded and let my eyes close.

For a desperate second, I wished I had been hers.


There was a bit of a commotion when I pulled back into the driveway at Stonebarn Lake. My mother stood inside the front door, arms crossed, face stern, head shaking. Opposite her were Tina and a tall slim man I recognised immediately—Josh.

*What's Josh doing here?*

I slid from the car, my gaze bouncing from one person to the next, trying to figure out what was going on.

Tina noticed me first. She was dressed in leopard-print leggings and a tight bodysuit, her rear and chest bulging out like four balloons.

'Sweetie, here you are. Your mother's being a bore. She's telling this handsome young chap you're fully booked.' Tina winked at me, and I knew straight away she didn't buy that story. I could either play dumb or expose my mother as a liar.

*'Your allegiance lies with your mother, Chloe.'*

Sod *that!*

'Actually,' I said, 'the green room is free. I checked it this morning and it's all clean and in perfect order.'

My mother looked aghast. 'Which green room?'

'Right opposite mine.' I turned to Josh, feeling daring. 'I hope you don't mind floral motifs on your bedspread and curtains. It's very English country.'

He grinned at me. 'I love it.'

My mother glared at me, then slapped her forehead dramatically. 'Good God! How could I possibly forget?'

There would be consequences, but for now I decided not to care.

Tina lowered her voice. 'See, Kathryn? It wasn't that hard.' She linked her arm through Josh's and pulled him towards the house. 'What's your name, sweetie?'

'Josh,' he answered, allowing himself to be dragged along.

'You and I will get along just fine,' she purred.

Twenty minutes later, footfalls and the sound of suitcase wheels gliding down the corridor—Josh knocked at my door.

'Hey,' he greeted. 'Thanks for bailing me out. I don't think I could have done it without you.'

'You should thank Tina. She takes a shine to any man under the age of thirty.'

'Ah, and here I thought she fell for my charms.' He winked.

I shrugged then asked, 'What are you doing here?'

'Figured I'd visit. I read somewhere online your Wi-Fi's awesome.'

'Says who?' I crossed my arms. 'Seriously, Josh, my mother hasn't had a guest in donkey's years. Why did you leave the Old Swan?'

'I was worried about you. I saw you crying this morning in Market Square and just thought you could use some moral support. Like me staying closer.'

'I'm not sure that's a good idea.'

'Hey, don't knock it. I could cheer you up a little, make myself useful. Set up a firewall on your laptop? Bring you coffee in bed?'

'Hmm,' I said, letting myself enjoy the moment more than I dared admit. 'Try again.'

'Okay, what about we play side by side and solve a murder mystery? In fact, we could do something suitably film noir.'

I raised my eyebrows, intrigued.

He grinned. 'You got any plans for tonight?'

# 23

It was 10 p.m. when Josh and I sneaked outside. Our breath smoked through white fog so thick, it was like peering through a veil of diaphanous gauze. Even the street lights let off a feeble, bleached glow, like dandelions gone to seed.

We crossed Market Square, turned a corner that led into a lane, then another onto Coleridge Street. Two long rows of stone cottages huddled like ghosts in dull slate-grey. No street lights here. The only glow came from random windows lit blue from a television.

'First time?' Josh whispered.

'First time for what?' I whispered back.

'Trespassing on private property.'

'Does it look like it's a hobby of mine?'

'No. It's just you're . . . quiet. Calm. *Something.*'

'Concentrating,' I supplied, squinting at house numbers before turning my eyes to him. 'I don't mean to spoil the mood here, but what if we get caught?'

'We won't,' he said, without a twitch. Then he raised his eyebrows a notch. 'You're not having second thoughts, are you?'

'No, I'd just rather avoid another trip to the police station.'

'Just relax, everything will be fine. We're only breaking the law because no one else's going to get the job done. Anyway, look at it this way: we're working for the greater good now. Or something like that. Right?'

'Sure,' I said. 'Someone should give us a medal.'

He smirked and dug me in the side with his elbow. 'Smartarse.'

I turned back to hide my smile, spotted number 84—stopped and stared, the smile fading from my face. I couldn't help but shiver.

Cordelia's house lurked with its two front sash windows, baleful panes of glass rendered impenetrably black. It felt as if the house were watching us from inside. I took a deep breath before I followed Josh who had already pushed open the gate—it quietly closed behind us.

The door key I had plucked surreptitiously from my mother's key ring. It had been easy to spot with a tiny piece of paper labelled *Cdl* taped over its metal head. I supposed it was part of an arrangement between them—my mother going in when Cordelia was away, checking things for her, twitching curtains, watering plants, picking up the mail off the floor, and making it look as though the house was occupied.

Inside, we flicked on our torches. Their beams cast distorted halos across the walls, our silhouettes like German Expressionist shadows creeping along a black-and-white film set. Josh pointed to the living room on his right: baroque furniture, oriental carpets, scrollwork ornaments, odd curiosities, and way too many candles. Cordelia clearly hadn't been a fan of minimalism.

'So what exactly are we looking for?' I asked in a hush tone.

'Clues.' He slid his torch beam along a dining table, winced at the sight of a dried-up animal's paw. 'Anything suspicious like . . .' He coughed. 'Really?' He dangled a pair of fluffy pink handcuffs between his thumb and forefinger.

'A joke present from Tina. I know because she offered my mother purple ones.'

He put them back down. 'I bet that didn't go down too well.'

I shrugged. 'My mother's always suffered from a sense of humour deficiency.' I beamed my torch on a stack of envelopes, trawled through them: mostly junk mail and begging letters. 'By the way, did you manage to hack into her laptop?'

'Yeah, like ten seconds tops before something shut me down. Not a virus or Trojan, but some kind of tracking device implanted there to stop access.'

'Who the hell knows this stuff?'

'Someone who's very smart about technology and knows exactly what they're doing.'

I struggled to reconcile the idea of my mother with a computer guru. As for the other women, I was at a loss to pick one who was a wizard on their keyboard.

Josh echoed my thoughts. 'My guess is they all have that device stored somewhere in their system file, some kind of spyware. I wouldn't be surprised if it worked hand in hand with the SS intranet. The type of network complex enough to protect Scissor Sister against cyberattacks and still track every movement of her staff online.'

*Scissor Sister is watching you.*

'The Orwellian nightmare come true,' I said.

He nodded. 'Big Brother is everywhere these days. She may well have recruited a techie to do the job for her. Some kind of expert.'

'What about you? I thought you were some kind of expert.'

'Me?' He shook his head. 'Just because I dabble in computer programming doesn't mean I'm an authority on the subject.'

I felt foolish for a moment. I'd made assumptions about Josh, pinned some pretty ridiculous high hopes on him: press some buttons, crack the codes and *bam*, the whole truth revealed. That hushed sense of expectancy placed upon the brightest geeks. I was regretting not being more curious about him.

'So Josh, what do you do in life?'

He bent to look inside a sideboard. 'I'm a video game designer.'

'Really? Just like the nineteen forties detective game we're playing?'

'Ah, yeah, that one.' He gave a short cough, trained his torch on the ceiling, and made a loose, random loop. 'Actually, I designed it. I even commissioned Holly to work on the characters' clothes.'

'Oh, right. I see.'

And it was true. I could really *see* it in my mind in a way that made perfect sense. Josh thinking through the concept and the plot. Holly, index finger clicking the mouse button, designing vintage dresses for Vixen in 3D software—not a stretch for someone used to sketching silhouettes by hand and creating her own patterns.

'Have you two ever been lovers?' I ventured timidly.

He gave me a puzzled look. 'Why do you ask?'

'I-I don't know,' I said, hoping the semi-darkness hid my blush. 'I'm just trying to get a sense of who she was, I guess.'

'Well, I can tell you she was very smart. Talented and—'

'You're not answering my question.'

He gave a long sigh. 'Okay, fine. We had a brief fling when we first met at uni if that's what you want to know. It lasted a few weeks before we realised we were better off as friends.'

'Why didn't it last?'

'Jesus, Chloe! I don't know. Who wants to rush into a relationship when they're eighteen? Anyway, Holly wasn't the type who liked to be labelled.'

He went silent after that and started scouring some more drawers. I felt I'd been too intrusive, as if I was a parent asking prying questions about his first experience of sexual intercourse.

I decided to lighten the mood, slinking quietly towards him. 'So you know how the game ends, right?'

He turned back and caught the smirk on my face. 'Hey, that's not fair. You can't expect me to remember every single storyline.' He began ticking excuses on his fingers. 'And the gameplay flow charts, and the role-play mechanics, and the challenges and puzzles.'

'Oh, I'm sure you know them all,' I said. 'No wonder you played so well, *Inspector Stanmore.*'

I winked at him then left him to rummage through the rest of the room.

Back in the hallway, I padded into the kitchen on my left. The decor was dated, with a battered-looking brown stove and 1960s units. The top cupboards were filled with all sorts of canned and dried foods. A copy of the *Westmorland Gazette* lay folded on the table, exposing a partially completed crossword. In the sink stood a chipped enamel mug stained dark brown on the inside—probably Cordelia's last coffee.

I walked up the stairs, past the bathroom, and peeked inside a tiny room filled mostly with clothes and the scent of a white musk candle.

I returned to the landing, checking rooms: something clinked when I pushed open the last door. Strung on a hook behind it were talismans on chains, swinging crystals and charms—the clatter of metal on glass. I put a hand out to still them, swept my torch over the room: a double bed stained a rich mahogany, a vanity with a mirror, a chest of drawers. Facing a sash window stood an old Singer sewing machine on a cast-iron table. Two open shelves lined the walls; one had black tins full of strange esoteric objects, while the other was crammed with books on astrology and numerology.

'I'm wasting my time,' I said to myself with a groan.

Just then I heard a rattling noise.

Someone was raising a window, or so I thought.

Here.

Now.

Downstairs in the house.

A shuffle of a chair. Quick, furtive footsteps. The faint creak of hinges. A door shut with barely a click, and the snick of a lock.

*Josh?*

My spine sent me an alarm. There was something unnerving about scouring a psychic's home, a disquieting sense that there could be ghosts roaming out in the dark. I shook off the chill, beamed light onto a spiral notebook, and shivered at the sight of the SS initials on its cover.

Some of Cordelia's scratches I couldn't understand, most of them involving minutes of their Monday meetings. A page discussed marketing ploys and expansionist strategies. Then, written inside the back cover in capital letters was *Sister of Peace*. Beneath it, a dozen lines with one-word names. All crossed through except for the last one.

A hand tapped my shoulder—'Find anything?'

I startled, but it was only Josh. I quickly showed him the page and whispered, 'I think I've just found Cordelia's password.'

'Good job.' He smiled. 'Now have you seen her laptop? Don't want to risk being kicked out of mine again.'

'It's not in her bedroom.'

'What about the back room downstairs? I heard you open the window.'

The breath froze in my chest. My mouth opened, closed, and opened again, the words a cold scream in my throat.

He looked at me, alarmed. 'What is it, Chloe? What's wrong?'

'There's someone else in the house.'

Instantly we flicked off our torches and moved out of the bedroom. On the landing, we leaned over the balustrade and peered down into the dark. I could hear the ruffling of paper, the low clink and shift as things inside drawers were being moved. Then, a beam of light slid down the bottom of a door, there and gone in an instant.

Josh turned to look at me, pressed a finger to his lips, and grabbed hold of my hand.

We crept our way down the stairs. On the bottom step he pulled away from me, held me at arm's length, and ordered quietly, 'Stay here.'

I clung onto the newel post, watching him edge along the hallway, wrap his hand around the doorknob, and slowly twist it, my heart thudding hard in my chest. A push, a clang.

Someone had locked the door from the inside.

*She* had locked the door from the inside.

One of the five Sisters—it had to be.

Fear clogged the back of my throat, cold and salty like sweat. I tried to picture her face, her features, the name floating there before my eyes, not quite within reach. And yet I had a terrible sense of familiarity, could almost . . .

*No . . . Wait . . .*

*WAIT . . .*

*DON'T GO!*

A window clattered open; Josh dropped his torch and began to throw his weight against the door, ramming it hard with his shoulder. Plywood cracked, then split at the third attempt. I rushed forward, pushed my arm between the cracks, groped for the key then clicked the lock. The door swung wide and slammed. A rush of cold, misty air. I could see a movement through the open sash window, fuzzy and darting, a flash in the darkness. Josh jumped over the sill and ran after her until the fog swallowed them both.

In the dimness of the room, I could make out an object on the floor: a fountain pen. I reached down, pulled off the cap, and glided the tip along the palm of my hand. A smooth red line, with a tiny splash of blotted ink at the end. I dropped it mechanically in my pocket and explored the room—Cordelia's consultancy cabinet, by the looks of it.

Drawers had been pulled open, most of them filled with manila files labelled with client names. Sheets of papers were strewn across a Gothic desk, some likely dropped in a panic on the floor. A tatty pack of tarot cards, a flat-screen monitor sitting on one side. I pressed the power button and noticed a large envelope addressed to me in Cordelia's handwriting. Torn at the top, with two pages spilling halfway—two photocopies of old newspaper articles.

The first one was dated February 1964 and was about British fashion designer Graham Holmes. The name was unfamiliar to me, but the article hailed him as a promising talent who had taken the fashion world by storm with his previous collection. His spring-summer line was, at the time of publication, reported stolen three days before the start of his London fashion show. Holmes had launched a heartfelt appeal to whoever would come forward with information about the theft and released pictures of the missing dresses. My torch slid across each of them until I gasped in shock.

'What is it?' Josh's voice, his breathing ragged and fast.

I whipped my head around: beads of sweat covered his brow and his jeans were torn and soiled with damp earth. He managed a pained smile.

'Bloody fog,' he said with a groan. 'I think I tripped over a rock.'

'It's okay,' I reassured him. 'She had the advantage of home ground.'

I showed him the page, pointed to the last picture. 'Look, that's the teal-blue dress! Graham Holmes designed it before his whole collection mysteriously vanished back in 1964. He named it Cleora.'

Josh leaned over. 'Do you think Holly knew about it?'

'Yes, I'm sure she did.'

Undoubtedly, Holly had wanted me to own it for good reason. A dress she'd replicated into a pattern. A dress that had ultimately brought about her death.

Cordelia had promised to come back to me with answers, and that's exactly what she did, or tried to, with a clue that lay right before my eyes, somewhere on this page—the crucial link to Scissor Sister.

My thoughts were running in circles, yielding nothing but questions. What could possibly lie behind the craftsmanship of the dress? And if it had really been lost, how had Holly ended up owning it?

Josh sat in the chair and started tapping on the keyboard. He asked, 'Did they ever recover the collection?'

I stared down at the second page in my hand; March 1966. The headline read: FASHION DESIGNER COMMITS SUICIDE.

Underneath it, a black-and-white portrait of Graham Holmes, a young man with a slicked-back hairstyle, smiling at the camera. The article explained that he'd built his collection on hope and money, but its loss drove him to drink and despair, impairing his creativity, and the debts he amassed forced him to shut his own fashion house. A stellar rise for an equally steep and devastating fall, the article concluded.

He was only twenty-five when he took his own life. The same age as Holly.

When I looked up, I could see Josh's eyes probing mine in the half-light.

On the computer screen, a message flashed red: *ACCESS DENIED—LOGIN DEACTIVATED.*

# SCISSOR SISTER

CHART-TOPPING RAPPER SLAIN BY BULLET

LOVE ISLAND STAR FOUND DEAD IN FLAT

FASHION DESIGNER COMMITS SUICIDE

Your eyes flit from one headline to the next. Greedily. Hungrily. You're dying to know more, aren't you?

A chance to fill the void in your life.

A chance to make their loss your own.

A chance to be a part of something bigger.

Dead celebrities, it seems, hold a special place in your heart.

Who doesn't love a story that restores their perfection? A story that makes them the hero once more, flawless and adored, keeping the feeling of nostalgia alive.

Yes . . . Nostalgia . . .

An inevitable by-product. A thriving and lucrative market too.

All those Marilyn art prints in hot pink. All those Purple Rain T-shirts for sale. All those ceramic mugs with *The King* printed in light bulb lettering.

Your appetite for memorabilia is decidedly high. Inexhaustible. There's always a gap for someone else.

A gap for a new name like Graham Holmes.

A young talent gone to waste.

A bright star gone too soon.

Soon he'll be worth more dead than alive.

## 24

Four hours of tossing and turning; my brain was buzzing like a hornet's nest, but somehow, between an umpteenth nip of vodka and daylight, I finally managed to doze off. I dreamt that Cordelia had sneaked out of the morgue. Her face and neck pampered to perfection, skin glowing like wax. She flew over a churchyard where a decayed Graham Holmes had clawed his way out of the grave. They mumbled quickly and unintelligibly to each other until my mother loomed out of thick fog and swatted them both away, them vanishing in puffs of magic smoke.

Then she turned to me with a cruel smile, her eyes rolled up to shiny whites, crooning, *'Come to me, sweetheart. Come work for Mother.'*

I sat bolt upright in my bed, panting and covered in sweat. Outside, the sun was just rising, white fog giving way to colours and dew and morning birdsong. In the distance, the same group of women scuttled downhill.

The sound of cackling laughter downstairs: I peered into the kitchen and saw the back of Tina. She was sitting on a stool with a tray of coffees between her and my mother, who caught me staring. No white eyeballs, I noticed.

'Morning, sweetheart, what would you like for breakfast?'

'Just coffee. Black and strong, please.'

'What about a fruit? A piece of toast, maybe?' she asked in the overdone tone of a concerned hostess.

'I can't. I'm not staying long.'

'Of course you're not.' She flicked on the kettle, smirking as she rose to grab a clean mug. 'I hope you'll have a nice a day at Suzanne's.'

I ignored her, sliding onto a stool next to Tina.

She winked at me. 'Slept well, sweetie?'

'Like a baby.'

'You look terrible.'

'Thanks, Tina. How are you?'

'Oh, terrific. Isn't your friend joining us?'

'What friend?'

'You know, what's his name . . . Joshie something. The cute sweetie who came in yesterday.'

'He isn't my friend,' I said, my voice defensive. 'Why are you asking?'

'Relax, sweetie. Just making a little light conversation.'

I saw a flicker of something in Tina's eyes and wished then I hadn't sucked down so much vodka. My thoughts were vaporising; I couldn't read the look on her face, couldn't decide if she was disappointed not to see him or insinuating something else. Shifting in my chair, I glanced at her tight skirt and podgy thighs and six-inch heels, tried to picture her outrunning Josh in the fog last night . . . It beggared belief.

'Did I tell you about Martika?' she asked, nudging my elbow.

'Yes, Tina. You mentioned her name last time.'

'Well, you ain't heard nothing yet.' She leaned into me and whispered, 'Someone caught her having sex with Christian Drummond again. Seems like they enjoyed a good bonk in the woods.'

I rolled my eyes in mock consternation, but Tina would not be distracted from her story.

'That Martika is such a naughty lass. I heard she rode him like a mare in heat. All thrusting hips and naked flesh.'

I stared at her. 'You seriously believe that?'

'Damn right I do,' she snapped. 'I have proof this time, I have compromising pictures that could ruin her reputation.'

'I thought no one knew who she was.'

'Sweetie, I don't give a flying hoot about that Martika girl. I'm talking about Denise here—I'm after big fish.'

'Why? You think Denise Drummond is a shark? What has she done to you?'

Tina just cackled again like a witch then raised her mug to her lips, not adding another word on the subject.

My mother brought my coffee over; I gulped down a couple of burning swallows and quickly stood up.

'Right. I have to go,' I said, annoyed with a vendetta I didn't understand.

I was out the door and on the front step when I heard Tina call to me—'Have a nice day at Suzanne's, sweetie.'

In truth, I wasn't planning on going to Suzanne's. Not yet, anyway.

More questions had come rolling in since I'd learnt about Graham Holmes. I needed to go back to the source—back to where I'd first found the dress. So I drove to Market Square and parked in the side alley next to Vintage Folly, right behind Jade's black Toyota. A rusty scratch had chipped off the paint on her boot. Scuff marks dented the driver's door, and inside, the front leather seats looked cracked and worn. She must have owned it for quite some time, I presumed. I put my hands up to the rear windows, but the glass was tinted so dark, I saw nothing except my own reflection.

I suddenly remembered Tina's words: '*Kimberley and I were sitting at the back . . . You should have seen the way she looked over her shoulder and slid her arm round his waist. Like the cat that got the cream.*'

But Holly couldn't have looked over at Kimberley or Tina. She couldn't have seen them—not behind those dark tinted windows, not in the falling darkness. If she'd looked over her shoulder and recognised the car, there could have been only one reason why she slid her arm so overtly around Matt.

Because she knew Jade would be watching her . . .

. . .

I didn't spot her right away when I entered the shop. She was standing inside the dressing room at the back, behind the half-open door, where it appeared she was trying to squeeze the life out of a fat woman in a sugar-pink prom dress, its fabric dangerously stretched over her bosom and belly. It looked as though there would be no *symbiosis* or magical spark between woman and dress this time.

Jade then tactfully suggested a bigger size.

'Chloe,' Jade called once she'd clinched the sale, weaving her way between the clothing racks to lightly touch me on the arm. 'It's so good to see you. Is there anything I can do for you today?'

She was wearing a cute gingham dress that matched her hoop earrings and headband tied into a bow. She looked like a retro cool Betty Boop.

'I was hoping you could give me some information about the teal-blue dress.'

'Oh,' she muttered, frowning. 'I'm sorry. I hope you understand, it wasn't my place to tell you about it. Your mother wouldn't have approved.'

'She kept you all on a tight leash, didn't she?'

'Kathryn's had a hard year,' Jade said diplomatically, then gestured towards the till.

'Now, if you'd like a refund, I can—'

'No, that's not what I'm here for,' I interrupted. 'I found out who designed it. Someone called Graham Holmes.' I watched her face for a reaction: shock, alarm, surprise. But Jade only tapped her lips thoughtfully.

'I've heard of the name. Died tragically young, in his twenties. His entire collection is considered lost.' She flashed me a sympathetic smile. 'I think you might be mistaken.'

'Apparently not.' I reached into my bag and showed her the article. 'The Cleora dress was designed in 1964 and stolen that same year.

Still lost when Holmes took his own life in 1966. But somehow, in 2017, Holly Paige wore it on New Year's Day at Stonebarn Lake.' I paused, adding, 'You were there too.'

Her smile became a little more fixed. 'Your mother invited so many people. I really can't remember.'

*Lie.*

'But you knew Holly pretty well,' I said.

'Who told you that?'

'Suzanne said Holly worked for you when she was still a student. You thought she was destined for great things. You thought she had talent.' *You even found her a job, for Christ's sake.*

'Did I really say that?' she scoffed. 'I hire interns every summer. I'd like to think they have some kind of talent and a bright future ahead of them.' It was a sentence so generic, it was worthy of a beauty pageant.

'Did you know that Holly had a strong interest in dressmaking?'

'I thought she was rather into fashion.'

'She created many dress patterns. Some of them ended up being launched by Scissor Sister herself.'

Jade stared at me, her eyes gaping wide. She looked genuinely shocked. 'That's impossible. Holly was never part of the team.'

'Not that you knew of, maybe. Either that or we're looking at plagiarism.'

'Are you questioning Scissor Sister's integrity?' She sounded appalled.

'I would if I'd never met my boss in person.'

'That's the twenty-first-century way to do business, Chloe. You should know that Scissor Sister has done more for this community than anyone else. She gave women in this town a new lifeline after the garment factory shut. Now, are we done?' She glanced over at her desk. 'I really ought to go back to work.'

'Just one more question.' I paused for a moment, looked her straight in the eye. 'How did it feel when Holly finally chose Daniel over you?'

Jade took a sharp breath as though I'd stabbed her in the heart. Her face drained of colour and a charged silence pulsed between us: a tightening of the air, the ticking of a clock. I counted the beats, one, two, three—like counting the seconds between lightning and thunder.

'What did you just say?' The fight was gone from her voice.

'I know, Jade.'

She exhaled slowly—walked to the door and flipped the sign to CLOSED. I thought she might ask me to leave then, but instead she pulled a soft pack of Gauloises from her dress pocket and beckoned me to follow her outside.

We stood in silence against the wall in the side alley. Jade glanced warily up and down the square as she lit her cigarette. She took a drag, fingers trembling, and held the smoke so long, I wondered if she'd inhaled it. When she blew it upward, she gave me a sidelong glance.

'How did you find out?'

'Part hunch, part deduction,' I answered. 'I found nothing to prove that Matt and Holly kept up a long-distance love affair. But I just couldn't explain why she slid her arm around his waist that day. It just didn't feel right, like the gesture was deliberate. Like she was trying to convey some kind of message to *you*. A way to break the bad news, I suppose.'

'A way to hammer her point home,' Jade said softly.

'Is that what Holly was trying to do?'

Jade nodded. 'She dropped in a few hours earlier to say things were over between us. She was kind of hoping I'd be more understanding, that I could turn the page just like that.' Jade snapped her fingers.

'When did you two start your affair?'

'About three years ago. Things weren't too rosy between her and Dan.'

'That's the impression I got too.'

Jade sucked down more smoke anxiously. 'Holly told me she'd never loved him. I stupidly believed things would be all right if I gave

196

her more time, that she'd make up her mind to leave him in the end.'
She laughed, a low rasp. 'I met Dan at Kathryn's New Year's party last
year. To be honest, I thought he was a bit of a dick.'

'Didn't you try to change her mind?'

'Try? You have no idea. I practically begged her to rethink, but she
wouldn't—oh no. Holly was too proud, Holly wasn't *that* kind of girl.
Said she didn't like to be labelled.'

Echoes of what Josh had said last night at Cordelia's. I could only
speculate as to why Holly had feared to be *labelled*. Clearly she'd
struggled with her feelings and her sexuality, but for one reason or
another, she had seen fit to choose Daniel. I suddenly felt very sorry
for Jade—she seemed truly distraught—and I could certainly
sympathise with a life that didn't turn out as planned.

'But why didn't you come clean after Holly died?' I said. 'It seems
like Tina *misunderstood* the gesture.' I hated the choice of verb. Too
PC. 'You could easily have stopped the rumour. You could have saved
Suzanne from being fired.'

'And say what, Chloe? Shift the talk to me? Let the whole town
know I'm a dyke?' Jade blew out angry smoke. 'No—I won't let that lot
throw me to the wolves.'

She had a point. Tina had shown she was ready to go to great
lengths to defame Denise, who'd done the same to destroy Suzanne
the year before. It didn't take much for some women to make life hell
for others. In a town as small and conservative as Heavendale, I could
see why Jade would hold tight to her secret.

'I told Holly we should move in together, somewhere like
Manchester to be close to her workplace. The two of us were making
enough money to rent a nice one-bedroom flat. I wish we'd given it a
try.' Jade's last words came out as a gasp. Her eyes filled with tears and
she dropped her chin into her chest. 'I would have uprooted my entire
life for her.'

'I'm so sorry,' I said. 'If only things had turned out differently.' The words sounded beyond trite, but Jade looked up and cast her eyes to the sky.

'If only she'd told me what truly bothered her.'

My heart started to race. 'What do you mean?'

Jade stubbed out her cigarette against the wall. 'Just a hunch, nothing more. Holly said something like she had no choice, that it was the only way she could stop *her*.' Jade narrowed her eyes in concentration. 'It took me a while to realise Holly was really scared. Then she said she had to go back to finish it.'

'Finish the pattern?' I asked hopefully.

'What pattern?'

'I . . . Never mind. Carry on.'

'That was it, she left. I saw her jump into Matt's car and he drove off.'

'Do you know why Matt was with her?'

Jade frowned as she popped a breath mint into her mouth. 'To be perfectly honest, I thought you'd be the one to answer that question.'

# 25

For the funeral I wore the teal-blue dress with a navy shawl. Black was hopeless and nothing else in my wardrobe suited the occasion.

By the time I reached the ground floor, I realised that Stonebarn Lake had been turned overnight into a shrine. Sympathy cards and candles dotted old lace tablecloths at meticulous intervals. Floral arrangements in crystal vases: creamy roses, lilies, hyacinths—mostly white and still bound in luxurious cellophane ruffs.

In the kitchen, the collection of china wall plates had given way to a very large framed photo of Cordelia, pale faced and dark clothed, like the subject of an old daguerreotype. I immediately had a memory of staring at a black-and-white picture of Matt looking stern, right on that spot. My mother was repeating her creepy little shrine, twelve months apart.

A chill ran down my spine when her voice spilled out of the living room—'No, I don't want to hear your excuses. You find me a third catering staff by midday, or I'll make sure no one ever books you again.'

Heels thumping the floor, she stormed through the door, a pillbox hat pinned to the crown of her head. She slammed the phone down; her anger was like a stench under a billowing cloud of blooms. Her eyes snapped critically over my dress through her wide-mesh veil, then shifted back with a frown to my face. She said nothing, just snatched her clutch bag from the table, me trailing behind her.

We drove in complete silence, past Lake Avenue, past Market Square. We exited Heavendale and bumped along a sinuous road for a couple of miles. I glanced at my mother behind the wheel and started shivering in my seat. Something was clogging up my throat.

For a stupid moment, I wanted to jump out of the car.

*Deep breath, Chloe. You're being paranoid.*

Last night, I'd made my way quietly down to the living room where I perused the tall glass bookshelf and dug out a copy of *1984*. Back up in my room, sleepless and restless, I reread some of the chapters, and it shocked me how Scissor Sister had derived her terminology from Big Brother.

Telescreen (SS *Intranet?*), Hate Week (*Fake Brands list?*), Doublethink (*Blog?*), Ministries of Love and Peace and Truth and Plenty (*just like the Sister names*). Sickening resemblances. Like an updated version of a classic, but this wasn't fiction. This wasn't an imaginary dystopia—this was real. Someone had mirrored the rules of a totalitarian regime, erased and eliminated all opposition. Someone had exploited collective fears to whip up division and hate.

I glanced back in my mother's direction; the thin black veil floating over her face like a malevolent mist. I dug my fingernails into my palms.

*Who are you, Mother?*

*What have you done?*


St Peter's Church was a mishmash of styles due to partial destruction during the Blitz. It had a restored belfry sitting atop a Gothic tower and a gold-leaf-painted dome above the chancel.

Fifty to sixty people had already arrived and more were queuing outside to gain entry: friends, neighbours, and numerous unknown faces too. I supposed no one could resist being part of the excitement now. A clump of women formed a huddle by a pillar, all wreathed in black and fake pearls, trading whispers behind cupped hands, their painted lips parted like birds' beaks. No doubt the news of Cordelia's murder was making its last rounds.

Someone shrieked excitedly behind me: 'Look who's sitting at the front.'

I turned to a familiar face: the brainwashed blonde I'd met at Kimberley's store. Twice. She slipped onto the pew next to her brunette friend, who chortled, 'Oh my God, I can't believe she showed up. They all totally showed up.'

Then looking straight at me, the brunette said, 'Oh, hi.'

The blonde glared at me. 'Oh, right. You're the one who stopped our class.' She crossed her arms and I shrugged—guess she was still peeved about that.

'Who were you just talking about?' I asked.

The brunette pointed to a peroxide bob flanked on either side by a pair of equally dyed blonde bobs.

'Denise and her clique,' she said.

The infamous residents' committee, at last. All bundled on a pew right in front of the pulpit as a sure sign of their rightful importance. Denise Drummond briefly turned sideways, her fifty-plus face half hidden behind outsize smoky glasses, as if to shade herself from the speculation surrounding her marital troubles. No husband in sight. Probably wisely. He'd likely been left tucked away at home.

The organ pipes exhaled the muffled tones of *Adagio for Strings*, and everyone scurried to their seats before four men carried in a shiny white coffin—closed coffin.

As the procession moved past, I suddenly wished Cordelia had worn a silk dress the day she died, not trousers. Maybe through touch I could have sensed a memory.

An interruption. Heels clicking on the stone floor.

'What the heck is that woman wearing?' the blonde whispered behind me.

I turned my head and caught sight of Tina, who made a late but eye-popping entrance. It wasn't so much a case of what she was wearing, but what she wasn't. Her black skirt passed her crotch by an inch and her neckline dipped so low, it showed off two protruding mounds of bronze-painted flesh. She tottered down the aisle on dangerously high heels then broke into a coquettish giggle when she squeezed herself between two blushing young men. Another one near the end, not so young, must have ogled Tina with far too much interest, because his wife jabbed him in the ribs.

The pew groaned in protest.

After the priest murmured the opening prayers, we stood and sat several times. Then my mother made her way to the podium, clutching a piece of paper. Her voice was solid when she delivered the eulogy:

'This is a letter to Cordelia, my dear friend.' She took a deep breath. 'My heart weeps, but my mind knows you are in a better place now. A place where there is no pain. A place where you are at peace. Your memory will forever live in our hearts. We will miss you at our Sunday roasts and our Monday meetings. We will miss your joy and your laughter. Mostly, we will miss our friend and beloved sister.'

A few sobs echoed around the church. As she walked back to her seat, Patsy rushed up to her, but my mother needed no steadying.

'Losing a close friend is always a tragedy,' the priest intoned solemnly. 'Naked came she out of her mother's womb, and naked shall she return there. The Lord gave, and the Lord has taken away—it was His will. Blessed be the name of the Lord.'

'What's all that naked business about?' grumbled a man beside me.

I wondered if the Lord's will to take Cordelia away disturbed anyone else.

The crowd got to their feet for the final hymn and gradually ebbed away into the day's glare. Small groups gathered outside, kissing each other in greeting. My mother was gone, the other four Scissor Sister women forming a Gothic little tableau by the churchyard. I walked over to them and saw Kimberley dab her wet eyes, one suspiciously redder than the other, with a lace handkerchief.


Cordelia was buried south of the church next to a gentle stream. There was no more burial space in Heavendale, hadn't been for almost two years. Her headstone was made of upright marble, white and simple. The epitaph read: *In loving memory of Cordelia Phillips.*

I said my last goodbye. Picked my way alone among the graves, still and silent in the grass and spared my old ghosts a thought—those I'd seen when I was a child but was too afraid to listen to. Those whose bodies slept underground but souls roamed the sky.

I pictured Cordelia entering their world.

On the north side of the churchyard, where a budding elm tree stood, I could make out the shape of Suzanne. She was on one knee, adding fresh flowers into a clay pot. White roses, I noticed. I drew closer and put a hand on her shoulder, stilling as I stared at Holly's name carved onto the stone.

Suzanne turned her head, giving me a thin smile. 'I thought it was supposed to get easier with time.'

'Some days it's not so rough,' I replied, crouching down next to her. 'Other days it feels like you've been swallowed into a black hole.'

Suzanne nodded. 'Kathryn never spoke much about your father.'

'No, she wouldn't. Sometimes I just think my mother's like a block of ice. Frozen from the inside. Maybe she can't help it.'

'Maybe she's starting to thaw a little,' Suzanne replied pensively. Then she pulled out an invitation card from her handbag and handed it to me.

Looping black letters beneath a spray of purple flowers—

*The honour of your presence is requested on Wednesday, 14 April from 2 p.m. to 5 p.m. at Stonebarn Lake.*

My mother had scrawled Suzanne's name on top in her own handwriting. Was it a catch of guilt after our conversation two days ago? Her way to extend an olive branch to Suzanne? Such magnanimity on her part surprised me.

For a moment I had a swell of hope that maybe my mother was taking a baby step towards reconciliation.

Suzanne shrugged. 'I don't intend to go.'

'Maybe you should,' I said.

'No, Chloe, I'm not ready to face your mother. Not yet. And it won't be the time or place for a little heart-to-heart.'

'But it's not all about her, is it? There'll be plenty of people who want to enquire about your store, the makeover. Can't hurt to let them know it'll be relaunched in time for the fair.'

'But Denise—'

'Denise has got more pressing issues right now. She won't object—I'm sure she won't even be there. The tide is turning, Suzanne. Go show them all how strong you are.'

# 26

The mourners arrived at Stonebarn Lake at two o'clock sharp, lining up like workers waiting to punch their clock cards. The robust four-dozen flock—again, mostly women—soon swarmed into the living room and out into the kitchen. They formed polite little circles and exchanged condolences around clusters of lit candles. On the wall, Cordelia was gazing down on us with mellow amber eyes.

'How are you holding up, my dear?' The question came from a random woman who suddenly approached me to give me a limp hug.

'Fine, thank you,' I said, bemused.

She nodded at me, then stammered Matt's name and burst into tears. A white-haired woman came in between us and decided to hold both of our hands in a peculiar gesture of comfort. I'd barely been here twenty minutes, and already the reception felt too much like a repeat of last year.

Josh I couldn't find. Twice I'd gone up to his room, before and after mass, knocked on his door, but there was no reply. My sense of disappointment was acute. Silly, I know. But strangely, I found myself missing his presence.

Someone waved at me from across the room, catching my eye. It was Colin, so I gave him a little wave back.

A couple of waiters (yes, just two—no third one in sight) manoeuvred their way through the crowd with canapés and drinks. I grabbed a flute of champagne and meandered through the rooms, startled when my mother bustled through the door with a silver tray. Her smile was so stiff it resembled a pained grin—like a cross between the Joker and a Stepford wife on autopilot hostess mode.

'Do you need help, Mum?' I said, trailing after her.

'Don't be daft, sweetheart.' The smile twitched. 'Now, be a darling and have a slice of Mrs Pickering's homemade chocolate bavarois.'

She just passed me off to the white-haired woman who'd held my hand minutes earlier.

'I made three batches.' The woman beamed proudly, handing me a paper plate of cake. 'What a gorgeous blue dress you have. Nice to see someone in this room isn't wearing all black.'

Some distance behind her, I spotted Kimberley. She was standing against the wall by the bifold doors, her head bent low, her golden curls drooping on her cheeks as if she were a shamed nymph. Next to her, Rob, guzzling down the rest of his beer. He blinked angrily at the crowd, put a proprietary arm around Kimberley's waist, and swiftly hustled her away. My skin began to crawl.

'Bastard,' Jade muttered. I turned to face the remaining trio of Scissor Sister women. 'I can't believe he's showing his face.'

'Stair fall, my ass!' said Tina haughtily. 'Same old excuse. We should report him.'

'You'd be wasting your time,' replied Patsy before she drained the rest of her champagne glass. 'She'd never admit to it.'

'Patsy is right,' said Jade. 'She denied everything the last time Cordelia talked to the police.'

'A really sensible woman Cordelia was,' reflected Tina. 'I'm glad we buried her beautiful. Flowers and everything. All set to meet her invisible little friends.'

Patsy glared at her. 'Don't be ridiculous, Tina. What are we going to believe in next, magic?'

'I'll say what I please, sweetie. You can't bad-mouth the dead's beliefs.'

'She had a good sense of humour, though,' Jade chipped in to lighten the mood. 'Remember the day she joked that one of my nineteen forties cocktail dresses was possessed by the spirit of Joan Crawford?'

Tina chuckled as she crammed a smoked salmon blini into her mouth. 'And what advice did she give you, sweetie?'

'Get rid of the wire hanger.'

A well-worn joke, but Patsy didn't find it one bit funny. She stared glumly at her empty champagne glass, mumbling, 'Why do they make these so damn small?', then flounced off, making a beeline for one of the waiters, only to bump into Suzanne.

I was glad to see she'd come despite her reservations. The two of them quickly engaged in conversation and melted away into the crowd; I hoped it would go well.

I moved away from the others, making my way through the room without any sense of destination or purpose. I told myself to spy on more conversations, but really, I didn't have the heart to do that. What did I expect? The truth to tumble out of someone's mouth?

I sat on a chair in the back corner and felt irretrievably glum. I didn't touch the cake. I wanted to drink.

A waiter appeared, smiling over me. 'Would you like some more champagne?'

Wordlessly I held out my flute, took another long swallow, and let my gaze flit idly across the crowd. A movement just behind the doorway caught my eye—it was a shoe. A man's shoe. Someone was leaning against the wall, a shadow watching us all in silence.

I could feel the burp of a shocked bubble pop back up my throat when he finally emerged into the kitchen: I saw the back of his tailored pinstriped suit, his black fedora. He turned around, and now I caught a glimpse of his pencil-thin moustache. He rapped a spoon against a crystal glass.

The crowd murmured and wondered and huddled until Josh's voice soared.

A disguised Josh.

Again . . .


'Ladies and gentlemen, my sincere apologies for interrupting your afternoon. I'd really appreciate if you would just indulge me for a moment.'

I rose from my chair, stood at the back of the crowd, my head spinning faster than it should have. A few feet away my mother poured recklessly into Patsy's flute, champagne foam spilling over her white tablecloth. She stopped only to frown at Josh as though she should have remembered his name from somewhere. He certainly wasn't on her guest list.

'Who are you?' she demanded.

'Please forgive the intrusion, Mrs Westfield. I'm a private investigator. My name is Inspector Stanmore.'

'Inspector?' Her nose wrinkled as if she smelled something nasty. 'Is something the matter?'

'As a matter of fact, yes. I have a serious announcement to make.'

'Your timing is not appropriate. We're all mourning the loss of our very dear friend Cordelia.'

He smiled, unfazed. 'Which is precisely why I'm here, Mrs Westfield. There has been a lot of talk lately about the dire circumstances surrounding her death. Regrettably, most of it is true. I'm afraid Cordelia Phillips was well and truly murdered.'

The crowd erupted in a collective gasp.

'What do you mean, murdered?' The question came from a slightly built woman who had to crane her neck to be seen. 'My husband works as a police support officer, and all he heard of was a cranial fracture.'

'At the very least, she likely suffered a concussion from the fall.'

'So it was an accident, then.'

'No, Madam, she didn't slip off the edge of the cliff. Although we have no coroner's report to corroborate it, the injuries on her neck are consistent with strangulation.'

Another wave of gasps.

Mrs Pickering's hand flew to her chest. 'How can he sound so reasonable and say such things?' she whispered to me, coming to stand at my side.

I caught Patsy twirling the stem of her flute between her fingers, her face stoic. At the front, Kimberley's shoulders were shaking with sobs.

Josh cleared his throat. He wasn't quite done yet. 'Last year, you may remember that two more people died tragically. Their names, I know, are familiar to you all: Matthew Thorne and Holly Paige. Both found dead in what was widely regarded as a fatal car crash.' A pause, a shaking of the head. He certainly had a flair for the curtain line.

'I'm afraid they too were murdered.'

'That's impossible,' someone sputtered.

'For Chrissakes,' someone else said. 'I mean, that's crazy stuff. I'm just a lass working at the local launderette.'

I squeezed my way into the crowd and watched Mrs Dibben nudge her neighbour, muttering, 'I told you so, didn't I?'

'You only mentioned one murder, not three.'

Mrs Dibben shrugged. 'Just keeping you on your toes.'

When I reached towards the front I caught his gaze, just for a second. His eyes looked a different shade, still blue but much darker, probably covered by coloured contact lenses. I supposed he'd learnt from his mistake last time. He put his hands up to hush everyone and looked back at the crowd.

'Everyone, please. I have good grounds to believe we're dealing with the same person. I'll need everyone's full cooperation from here on out. I'm sure that together we will finally bring our killer to justice.'

At the room's silence, Josh raised his glass and everyone else raised theirs obediently. 'Justice for Cordelia, Matthew, and Holly,' he said.

'Justice for Cordelia, Matthew, and Holly,' the crowd repeated. Some of them burst into spontaneous applause.

Shortly after that there was a sort of Q&A session, and Josh showed he wasn't fazed, easily adjusting into the fantasy character he'd brought back to life. To me it sounded like he missed his true calling—acting.

'Well, Inspector, do you have any suspects?' someone asked.

'Suspects?' He nudged the brim of his hat up. 'A few, but I'm not at liberty to reveal their names.'

'Have you decided why Cordelia was murdered?'

'Hmm, I have a theory on this.'

Now he was being as cryptic as a spy in a thriller. A woman next to him almost summed up the mood to perfection: 'It's like being an extra on *Midsomer Murders!*' she declared excitedly.

Someone behind me jostled for space.

'Inspector,' Tina said in breathy tones, as if she were Jessica Rabbit, 'I was Cordelia's closest friend. Do feel free to drop by my place any time.'

She pressed a thick, creamy card into his hand and shouldered her way back into the crowd. I could see she'd actually handwritten her home address across the back with a little heart at the end.

I moved away, caught a glimpse of Jade standing on her own in a corner, looking dazed and shocked, and another of Mrs Dibben, frantically texting on her phone. Suzanne waved at me from the back, giving me a sad smile.

Someone by my side held up one hand and cocked her head. 'Was that the doorbell?'

I strode to the door and welcomed the oh-too-familiar sight of the blonde and the brunette. The latter wielded her phone in front of my face and shrieked, 'Oh my God, I totally can't believe this. There's a killer in our midst!' I glimpsed the name of the message sender: Mrs Dibben, unsurprisingly.

Ten minutes later, the agitation was reaching a fever pitch. Two more rings of the doorbell. More people. More champagne popping open. The two waiters glided through the rooms like ballerinas balancing silver trays on their fanned-out fingers.

I kept on scanning the crowd.

Of my mother there was no sign.

# SCISSOR SISTER

Nothing resists me. No one.

No rumours, no police.

Not even a private detective.

Not even you.

It's fight or flight. There can be no half measures, no time for drama. I will dispatch anyone who threatens my own existence.

You'd rather have a strong *Sister*, wouldn't you?


I sneak out of the house and see more cars than usual parked along the road. That black Toyota, I know, belongs to Jade Worthington. The dirty white Transit van is Mr and Mrs Dibben's.

I've lived long enough in this town to spot the odd one out. Deep Brunswick green, with a wooden dashboard and a retractable canvas roof. Too retro, too different—just like its owner. I don't even have to second-guess myself.

I get my hacksaw out of my bag and swiftly slide under his car. Four or five minutes are enough. After all, it's not like I've never done this before.

You have to cut the brake line, you see. Just enough to produce a hole. Just enough to force the fluid out.

There are so many slopes and hills around Heavendale.

So many opportunities to press hard on the brake pedal.

So many opportunities to die.

Then I puncture the two front tyres for good measure.

On my way back I almost bump into him in the doorway. Make a quick excuse, but he only half listens. He tells me he's in a hurry.

Good . . . Good.

When I re-enter the kitchen, I flash the crowd my brightest smile.

## 27

I rushed up the stairs to my room, taking a moment with my back up against the door, the breath trapped in my lungs. I could still hear the noise, the chaos downstairs.

Josh's voice echoed in my head: *'We're a team, Chloe.'*

Lies, damn lies—I'd been such a fool to believe him. He didn't warn me, didn't trust me enough. He'd kept me in the dark, and now I couldn't help but feel he'd betrayed me.

I glanced at my alarm clock. It was only gone four, but daylight had faded so fast, it almost looked like nighttime. Outside my window, clouds had grown thick and close. Above the mountains loomed a daunting mass of black.

I didn't care.

I was feeling wild and in need of open air.

I ripped at the zip, flung the dress onto my bed, and changed into jeans. Then I rushed down the stairs and out the front door.

'Chloe, wait.'

Rapid footsteps clattered behind and followed me down the road; I didn't reply, quickening my pace.

Josh broke into a run to catch up to me—'We need to talk. Where are you going?'

'None of your business,' I muttered.

'You can't walk to town. We're minutes away from a storm.' He put a hand on my arm, but I shoved him away.

'Just look at yourself,' I spat. 'What the fuck are you playing at?'

'Ah, so now you're peeved about that.'

I glared at him. 'Was it too much to ask, to inform me of your plans?'

He sighed, ripping off his moustache. 'Why don't you and I clear the air, all right? Go back—'

'Noooo.' A long wail like a child's, my finger pointing to the house. 'I'm not going back there, Josh. Do you understand? My mother is . . . My mother is . . .' I put my hand over my mouth to muffle a cry.

'Chloe, what's wrong?'

I breathed in hard, the word *guilty* itching to come out like a bad tooth. 'My mother is gone,' I made myself say at last. 'Gone.'

A lone rumble of thunder in the distance. A laugh echoing in my head—Matt's. *'Wrong G, Chlo!'*

'Hey, hey, easy.' Josh's voice coming to my rescue. 'Your mother's gone nowhere. She just popped across to a neighbour to ask if she could borrow some more glasses.'

'Did she?' I shook my head in disbelief. 'How do you know?'

'Because she just told me so.' He looked at my face, gave me a gentle smile. 'Look, I'll tell you what we should do. Let me take you out of here and we'll go eat somewhere, see if we can chase the clouds away. Keswick? Windermere? You choose.'

I nodded, still shaking, and he put an arm around my shoulder and walked me to the passenger side of a car that wasn't his: a vintage Comet convertible, the colour deep Brunswick green.

'Rental.' He winked. 'I picked it up this morning. Can't blow my cover, right?'

We drove the first couple of minutes in silence. Heavendale loomed behind us, but with distance its shadow sank beneath clouds so low, they cloaked the horizon. Ahead of us chevrons and catseyes flashed along the road. A streak of forked lightning cracked across the sky.

'I had to shake things up,' Josh said then, breaking the tension. 'I was going nowhere with the Scissor Sister intranet, couldn't hack into it so I thought, why not? It all was spur of the moment, really. Just like when you texted me the first time.' He glanced in my direction. 'It's our only chance, Chloe. We need to ramp up the pressure, push her to make a mistake.'

'What about you?' I said. 'What if you get yourself in real trouble?'

'It's a risk I'm willing to take. Anyway, there's no turning back now.'

A lump rose to my throat at the thought of him getting caught. Then, slowly, I swallowed my fear and began to see his point of view. Part of me resented his underhand methods, but the other part admired his courage and resourcefulness. Besides, what other choice did he have, knowing the police hadn't seen fit to investigate?

'We're only looking at four suspects,' I said after a pause.

'Four?'

'We can discount Jade.'

'I'm guessing the two of you had a talk?'

The truth about the affair I couldn't disclose, not even to Josh. When I left Jade yesterday, she'd made me promise not to betray her secret. But I could tell him a simpler truth. One that, once I'd had a chance to reflect on it overnight, was pragmatic and made sense: 'Jade didn't recognise the Cleora dress. She never would have sold it to me if she had.'

'And you reckon that's proof enough?'

'I know she's innocent,' I said with finality, and Josh simply nodded, keeping his gaze on the road.

The sound of thunder rolled closer, an ear-splitting crack. Then a shriek of tyres, followed by a screech of brakes, high and urgent.

'Josh?' I said, my heart thumping.

The car swerved and skated across the other side of the white line; Josh's jaw clenching as he jerked the steering wheel hard to the left.

Instinctively, I looked out the side window. Something odd was following us: a nebulous shape, a cloud, but it hovered far too low to be one. It veered around curves the same way we did and passed through rock slopes as if they were no obstacle.

*Holly* . . .

Another lurch to the left. A shift of gearstick, the pedal slammed to the floor. Squealing brakes. Josh kept his eyes trained on the road, his face a tense mask. 'Change of plan,' he said, trying too hard for a casual tone. I stared out the side window again.

Holly was gone.

Josh floored the accelerator—the engine groaning like a dying ox, coughing and roaring as we limped up a steep curve, struggling for speed. Behind us smoke was spewing out, as black as soot. Inside the car, the air turned acrid and hot. Dread sank into the pit of my stomach.

Something was horribly wrong.

My lungs felt like ash, sweat bubbling to the surface of my skin. Another bolt of lightning streaked across the clouds, a glimpse of something flashing in the distance. Something familiar. And then, caught in the glare of headlights near the edge of the cliff, I saw it. Down the slope. As clear as a flashback.

*The oak tree.*

A terrible panic leached all logic from my brain. It was happening again, just as it had for Holly and Matt—a gruesome replica. We too were going to die. Unless—

'Josh,' I urged. 'Stop the . . .'

Rain came pelting down on the roof, drowning my words in a deafening drum—the downpour like sharp needles clicking through metal.

'Josh!'

I clutched his sleeve and pulled, a desperate tug, my eyes transfixed on the wipers slapping furiously across the windscreen, my vision blurred through the thick sheets of hurling water.

Suddenly we hit a pothole.

The wheel jerked out of Josh's hands. The tyres lost their grip against the wet, slid inexorably out of control. I braced myself for impact when the speedometer needle rose to the right of sixty miles an hour.

And yet everything turned into a slow motion dream.

The tree started to grow right out of the ground, twisting from crown to root. Branches swelled and curved and coiled into knots, from which leaves grew like webs of tiny flexible fingers. There was no crush of metal, no shattering of glass. Instead, just a smooth and supple cushioning.

And then, silence.

A billowing movement through stillness.

She appeared to me then, teal-blue silk rippling like water in suspended air, her face haloed in white light, smiling. And it was such a luminous smile, a blast of warmth and ice, like a shower of sparks doused in soft flakes of snow. Crystals soared in a dance of iridescent colours lighting up the grey skies—not a single drop of rain.

Through my head rushed a million emotions: awe, wonderment, gratitude . . .

And a thousand questions too—*Is it a dream? Am I dead or alive? Could I still discern between the two? Holly, tell me what happened . . .*

Soon my eyelids grew heavy, the teal blue blurring my vision into a mist of grey.

Then everything went black.

## 28

I woke to the harsh glare of fluorescent lights. Rolled my head from side to side and blinked at the sight of shiny chrome rails—two of them, propped high on each side of my bed. The air had a tangy, antiseptic smell that caught in the back of my throat.

I raised myself up on my elbow and spotted a glass of water in a plastic cup, brought it to my lips. Cool, but not ice cold. Sipping, I assessed my new surroundings: the sterile floor tiles, the bedside table, the moulded plastic chair, a pale blue tunic glimpsed through a gap in the cubicle curtains.

Someone peeked her head in; a nurse.

'Good afternoon.' Her voice as bright as singsong. 'How are we feeling today, Miss Westfield?'

'Fine.' My voice croaked. 'Where am I?'

'You're at the Westmorland General Hospital. We're taking good care of you now.' She breezed in and plumped the cushions behind my back. 'You had a big scare, didn't you?'

I nodded, and for a moment I found myself back in the car: spurts of black smoke, raindrops like bullets, the oak tree twisting and stretching like a living airbag. Flashes of memories too sharp and surreal to put into words. Then I remembered Holly and rubbed a hand over my eyes.

'How did I end up here?'

'The young man in the hat called an ambulance.'

'Josh!' My heart throbbed in my throat. 'Where is he? Is he okay?'

'Oh, don't you worry about your friend. He's perfectly all right. We discharged him from our unit last night.'

'Last night?' I repeated, certain she was mistaken. 'You mean this afternoon. It all happened this afternoon, right?' And then doubt set in as I squinted at a window through the curtains. No storm, no dark clouds. Just a frame of bright blue sky.

The nurse broke into a sympathetic smile. 'You slept for a solid twenty hours. This isn't unusual after a traumatic accident.'

I wanted to tell her this was no accident, then thought better of it. Gingerly, I started testing my body. Palpated my arms and legs, flexed my fingers and toes. Nothing broken or bandaged—I was unscathed.

I kicked the white sheets off me.

'Wait,' the nurse said, startled. 'Where are you going?'

'I'm leaving.'

'You can't leave without the doctor's permission.'

I didn't reply, just grabbed my clothes and shoes off the chair. I turned to go but she was blocking my way.

'Please, Miss Westfield. I must insist you get back to your bed.'

'I'm fine, I really am.'

'The doctor wants to see you first.'

'I don't need a routine inspection.'

'This isn't a routine inspection.'

'Then what is it?'

We stood locked in a stare for a moment, silently challenging each other. As if we were playing a game of who blinks first. How old was she? Maybe late forties. She was tiny with kind brown eyes, but her face was pink and resolute as she handled the situation like a seasoned professional. I found myself wondering if she had seen much death in her life. In this type of environment, more than a little, I should think.

'Fine,' I said, glancing at the wall clock showing ten past two. 'How long will I have to wait?'

'Not too long,' she said, her voice bright again. 'I'll get someone to bring you lunch first.'

I tried not to grimace as she exited the cubicle. Seconds later she bustled back in with a book in her hands and my iPad.

'Oh, I almost forgot. You'll be glad to know that your mother came to visit this morning. She said you might need some light entertainment when you wake up.'

The book I grabbed first. It was just a fuchsia-coloured paperback, with cute bows and high heels and a drawn outline of the New York City skyline on a glossy cover.

So why did I feel a chill run through my fingers?


Twenty minutes later. Still no sign of food or a doctor. I kept fidgeting in my bed, my thoughts dark and tense and dwelling once again on my mother. I could feel them slipping into unhealthy obsession and pounded the mattress with both fists.

*No, Chloe. Just. Keep. It. Together.*

On the bedside table was a pad of graph paper, half used, with pale grey lines forming small squares. I thought of calling the nurse for a pen, then patted my jacket pocket and found one. I decided to work methodically and chronologically. I wanted to sum up what I knew, force it into structure, starting with the day Holly had left Prestwich with those enigmatic words: '*She stole it from me.*' The issue, really, was that *it* could mean a number of things. The Cleora dress? A pattern? A project in common?

Something else eluded me, just one small detail: Daniel said he'd caught a glimpse of the Scissor Sister logo on her laptop. I tried to picture Holly sitting on the sofa, glaring at the Scissor Sister website, but I couldn't see how it led her to think she'd been *robbed*. A sudden realisation? Or was she actually staring at something else?

Next, the day Holly and Matt died. From my conversation with Jade, I'd gathered Holly was under tremendous pressure by then. '*She said she had no choice . . . She had to go back to finish it.*' The pattern for the Cleora dress, of course.

I found my attention briefly wandering from the page. Poor Jade. Would Holly still have chosen Daniel over her if things hadn't turned out so wrong?

Then I tried to piece the events of that evening together: a twenty-minute stop at Suzanne's, where Holly wrapped up the pattern and scratched my name on it (I could only assume Matt played a part, although his overall involvement remained largely a mystery). Two women—Kimberley and Tina—had a clear opportunity to tamper with the car. But what about the note tacked onto Suzanne's door? Why would Scissor Sister pour out her hatred in writing once her deed was done? Somehow, it seemed excessive.

And then there was the not-so-small matter of narrowing her identity down to one woman. I'd Googled Scissor Sister again yesterday morning, browsed the News section, and found more evidence of her expanding online influence.

Press articles bloated with glorious, florid words praising her upcoming appearance: ' . . . *our trendsetting leader whose utmost relevance is to grace the fair in Heavendale . . .* ' Nice job, Patsy. As for Kimberley, her store was literally an advertising façade for the brand. These two women fitted the profile of Scissor Sister to a T. At least more than Tina or my own mother.

Lunch arrived at three: chicken with mash and chunks of broccoli. A carton of juice and what looked like strawberry jelly. I left my food on the bedside table and grabbed my iPad. I brought up the Scissor Sister blog and resumed my reading where I'd left off last time, patiently working my way back through each post. I needed to understand who she really was, see if I could catch some clue between the words to help me unmask this egomaniacal woman.

At first, nothing unusual struck me—the same relentless propaganda, the aggressive self-promotion. But as I wound back through much older entries, a very different picture came into view: her enthusiasms, her achievements, her hopes. Someone selfless. Someone who wrote from the heart. Hard to imagine it could be my mother. In fact, the difference in style was so startling, it completely caught me off guard. What had provoked that sudden change in her? Was the rise of success to blame?

I tried to picture a woman whose empathy had dried up over time. Who'd reinvented herself as a female Big Brother on the net. Whose ruthless ambition had driven her to kill.

'Miss Westfield?'

I looked up at the man who had just entered my cubicle: mid-thirties, about six feet, broad-shouldered, and thick-chested, the type people would label as 'beefy.' I had a clichéd image of him in a pair of rugby shorts instead of his white coat.

'I'm Doctor Andrews,' he said. 'My apologies for the wait. How are you feeling today?'

'Much better, thank you.' I wanted to get out of here as quickly as possible. I straightened myself up in my bed and made a confident face. I smiled.

He smiled back. 'I'm glad you rested well. I believe you had a narrow escape yesterday.'

'I did, but thankfully I'm unharmed.' I cleared my throat. 'Do I need to sign a form before you discharge me?'

Doctor Andrews nodded, almost absently. He pulled the chair close to him and sat down, tilted his head towards me. No smile this time.

'There's something I need to talk to you about, Miss Westfield.'

'Sure.'

'We did a blood test this morning while you were asleep.'

'Is it standard procedure?'

He cleared his throat. 'No, not really. We just thought it would be the right thing to do in your case.' He let the last words hang in the air between us—*in your case*. I imagined them holding hands like three little girls, whispering in each other's ears and sneering at me.

'Miss Westfield,' he went on, 'the results show that your red blood cell count is lower than normal.'

'How low?'

'Low enough to keep you under observation for a while.' He

clasped his hands on his lap, as though the gesture was adequate for the situation.

I had to shut my eyes for a moment. I didn't want to hear what he had to say, what I knew he was going to say anyway.

'You suffer from an eating disorder, Miss Westfield. Anaemia is a common complication related to your condition.'

The *A* word was out—admittedly, the least taboo of the two *A* words, one unspoken, his turn of phrase careful as if I was the victim of some flu. I pictured a woman lying on a bed with smooth white sheets, a feeding tube taped to her nose.

I had to make myself breathe.

'Listen,' I said. 'I've had a bit of a hard time lately, okay? I know I've skipped a meal or two in the past, but I'm fine, it's over now. I'm back in control of my life.'

Doctor Andrews briefly glanced at my plate of food, untouched, then back at me with an understanding smile. When he spoke again, his voice was smooth and soft, a voice wearing silk gloves. 'We have a fantastic team of specialists at our disposal: psychiatrists, psychologists, dietitians. Nutritional counselling is an essential part of our programme. What we can do here is try to work on your feelings, help you identify and label your emotions so that you can reprocess experiences related to past trauma.'

Matt's voice coiled in my head, burrowing inside like a poisonous worm. *'You want to make me happy, don't you, Chlo?'*

I shook my head to blot him out. 'No, please. I don't know if I could handle it.'

Doctor Andrews leaned over, put his hand over mine, and squeezed it. 'I understand.' His eyes were so kind, it made my own swim. 'Have faith in us and yourself, Miss Westfield. The first step is always the hardest.'

Silence for a few long seconds. 'If I agree,' I managed to say, 'how long will I have to stay?'

He rose from his chair, rubbing his chin thoughtfully. 'I suggest you have a rest while I make the necessary arrangements. There will be more tests to follow, but if everything goes to schedule, we should be able to discharge you on Saturday.'

*The day of the fair.*

'I can't.'

'Please, Miss Westfield. You must understand that your condition is very serious. Give us the chance to offer you excellent treatment.'

I nodded dumbly. Then felt a bolt of panic. 'You won't tell my mother, will you?'

Doctor Andrews shook his head. 'No, but I strongly recommend you do that yourself. The success rate for our patients is noticeably higher with the care and support of loved ones.'

When he left, the curtains swaying behind him, I exhaled long and hard, wishing I had something other than water to drink. The thought of spending two more days and nights in hospital was unbearable.

I returned my attention to my notes and somehow found myself squinting at the page. Something was nagging at me, twitching inside me all of a sudden. What was it? The answer was almost there. Something not in the meaning of the words but rather in their shape: the turn of a *T*, the tip of an *S*, the cusp of a *V*, or the crook of a *Y*. It was that tiny blot of red ink on the final letter of each word. Always. Like a pause, a small but resolute squiggle. It looked oddly familiar.

I stared for a moment at my fountain pen. Not mine, really. I remembered picking it up off the floor in Cordelia's office, by the window, when Josh was chasing after . . .

And then I jerked upright, my heart in my throat. I understood now—it was right in front of my eyes.

I knew who'd sneaked into Cordelia's house that night.

I knew who *she* was.

I bolted out of bed, scrambled into my clothes, and stuck my head through the curtains: I glanced right. Then left. An elderly woman lay inclined in her bed. Next to her was a nurse, holding a glass syringe with the needle pointing up. I scuttled away down the corridor and stabbed at the lift button, breathing hard.

The doors opened downstairs to a scene of commotion: paramedics rushed in with a stretcher upon which a man lay strapped, an oxygen mask on his face. A woman ran after them in a fit of frantic screams. Two nurses scurried behind to grab hold of her.

I kept my head down and quietly dashed towards the EXIT sign.

## 29

Rush hour. The three-lane motorway was clogged. I sat in the back of an Uber, my mind besieged by traffic frustration and the blasting radio. My driver, a man in his early thirties, had turned the music up and bobbed his shaved head comically to the autotuned plastic voice of a teenage girl. She was screeching something about 'doin' it good and keepin' it real.' Keeping it dumb, rather.

Looking out the windscreen, I saw we were still slogging behind the same sickly yellow Jag at little more than trotting speed. I wished now I hadn't dropped by the Tesco opposite the hospital, fussed endlessly over low-carb chocolate cookies, only to devour a whole pack in a flash. I was tapping restless feet on the floor, the sugar rush still coursing through my bloodstream—Doctor Andrews would surely not approve.

The black digits on the dashboard clock flipped to 18:00. There was no flash news on this radio station. Instead, a candid interview of Kim Kardashian revealed that motherhood had made her reassess her life priorities. The driver laughed at that and flung his head back.

He informed me then that Ms Kardashian's latest selfie on Instagram showed nipples flashing through her neon-pink latex dress. 'Still,' he reflected thoughtfully, 'it was kinda lame. Not jack-off material like the shot of her butt on *Paper* mag cover.'

I made myself nod politely, grateful when the Jag in front began to roar at a faster speed.

The roads cleared as we left the M6. We whipped through Windermere, past the National Park, past a group of cyclists sprawled on a grassy verge, past Helvellyn pointing sharp-topped ridges three thousand feet to the skies. I couldn't stop the sharp intake of breath, the tiny cry of relief, when we drove past the oak tree. My driver pulled up just outside Market Square, and I ran as fast as I could, my heart pounding, the cobblestones spinning before my eyes as though they were a kaleidoscopic carousel and the clang of church bells striking half six in my ears.

I feared I might be too late.

But I wasn't.

Through the display window between the giant blades of suspended scissors I glimpsed her face. She was standing still behind her desk, gazing vacantly at the opposite wall. Cutting a lone figure lost in her own thoughts.

*Kimberley.*

I stormed through the door, darted for the haberdashery shelves, and peered at the cards in their plastic holders.

Her voice behind me sounded stunned. 'Chloe?'

I didn't move, didn't reply. My gaze was solely focused on the words, scrutinising the shape of their letters and the tiny squiggle of red ink at the end of each of them. It was like seeing every card with a fresh pair of eyes. I slid one out and delved into my bag, producing the taped-up note.

I slammed them both on Kimberley's desk.

'Your writing, right?'

She looked down, then up, twiddled with a lock of blonde hair and said defiantly, 'I don't know what you're talking about.'

I pulled the pen out of my jacket pocket, wedged it between my thumb and index finger, and saw her blanch. *The look of recognition,* I thought. Now it was time to drive my point home.

On a blank page, I patiently duplicated the note, '*Your daughter is a slut,*' drawing harsh and even letters similar to the original ones. I showed Kimberley the end result, my finger hovering over each squiggle of fresh ink, then pointed to the haberdashery card that read, *Petersham ribbons,* with its pretty curls and feminine loops and red squiggles.

I looked up at her. 'Your pen betrayed you,' I said, and whacked it down on the desk between us. 'You tried to disguise your handwriting, but Cordelia knew it was you who wrote that vicious note. She knew you tacked it onto Suzanne's door.'

'No,' she cried. 'That's not true.'

'Drop the act, Kimberley. I saw you rip it to pieces when Cordelia confronted you. I was watching you from the back of the store.'

She gasped, then pressed her fingertips to her mouth. Her eyes flicked anxiously from the pen to me.

'After Cordelia died,' I went on, 'you got wind of the rumour that her death was no accident. That's when you started to panic. What if the police decided to search her house? What if they found your pen with a copy of the note, then put two and two together just like Cordelia did? You couldn't take the risk, could you? You couldn't risk them asking you some pretty unpleasant questions—How about, "Did you murder Holly and Matt?"'

She shrieked, made a quick move to snatch the pen, but I was faster, cupping it with my hand on the desk. 'Game over, Kimberley. You just missed your last chance.'

'I didn't kill them,' she shrilled. 'Give me back my pen.'

I shook my head. 'You're in no position to bargain.'

'Please.' Her anger turning into begging. 'What do you want from me?'

'Tell me everything you know. No lies, no half-truths. Then maybe I'll consider not turning you in to Inspector Stanmore.'

It wasn't the straightest of deals, but the impact the name had on Kimberley was undeniable. She nodded frantically, took a shaky breath, and asked, 'Where do you want me to start?'

'How about your beginnings with Scissor Sister?'

So she did.

## 30

Kimberley had always been a fan. She got hooked on the very first line, the very first blog, the very first tweet—the one showing the Amelia dress made of Union Jacks ('So inspiring! Just like watching Ginger Spice on TV when I was a child'). I'd seen it myself, and the sentiment couldn't have differed more from Girl Power. More like Cool Britannia cloaked in garish patriotism.

Still, Kimberley thought it would be *totally fab* to redesign her store. Emulate the image of the brand and commission a giant pair of display scissors ('Turns out plenty of kids just come to yank the damn thing'). Then she stocked up on every single SS pattern and taught classes on how to use them ('I mean, I was bound to get noticed sooner or later, right?').

*Smart move, Kimberley.*

I asked her if she suspected who might hide behind Scissor Sister and she just laughed. A laugh full of possibilities. A laugh that suggested she knew how to play dumb but was far from stupid ('I've always wondered why all six of us happened to live in the same town').

Whoever Scissor Sister was, Kimberley had once entertained high hopes of meeting her. ('I thought she'd pay me a visit some day. See what I did, applaud my efforts. Maybe make me her right-hand woman. Silly of me, I know'). She looked so dejected that I asked if ambition had prompted her to write the note. Kimberley went silent for a minute, then said she'd simply snapped. It was just a silly flash of violence. She saw Holly put her arm around Matt, but really, she never meant them or Suzanne any harm.

Was her answer a cop-out? Perhaps. But somehow, I didn't think she was lying. She looked down at the floor, and I could sense her reluctance to say more. Fear, I was sure, played a major part.

And violence.

Constant put-downs, seething frustration, the seeming unfairness of life—I identified with Kimberley in more ways than she could imagine.

One day, it all catches up with you.

You just *snap*.

You act violently because you too are a victim of violence. Physical and verbal violence perpetrated by men like Rob or Matt. Sometimes violence is so insidious and pervasive, it almost slips by unnoticed—the aggressive language, the fiery rhetoric used by the likes of Scissor Sister. Who do you hold accountable when there are no bruises to show?

'Kimberley,' I said, after the room had been silent too long. 'Does Rob—'

'Don't,' she said, raising her palm to stop me.

'Why don't you want to talk about it?' I pushed on.

She clamped her lips shut, head bowed into her chest. I thought she was going to clam up, but then she said, 'If I don't talk about it, I can pretend it never happened. I know it's all my fault. Part of me feels strongly that I'm to blame.'

'You think the abuse is your fault?'

'I know it sounds ridiculous, but it's how I feel. Sometimes I think I must deserve it. Otherwise I don't know why it would happen. But if he's in a bad mood he'll just . . . he'll just . . .'

Something upstairs smashed on the floor: a glass bottle. A groan followed by a shuffling of feet, then silence.

'Kimberley?' I said, dropping my voice to a whisper.

Her lips had begun to twitch. 'Yes?'

'Come and stay with me at Stonebarn Lake. You'll feel safer if we discuss things there.'

She looked back up at me, her gaze now resolute. 'No, Chloe. He's going through a hard time, can't you see? You don't know the real Rob like I do.' She paused. 'I can change him, I can make him love me again.'

I shook my head, knowing all too well she'd only be wasting her time. She had to understand that he'd never loved her, that love for Rob was indistinguishable from the basest and most abusive forms of violence. She had to pack her things now, leave him while it was still not too late.

Run away before things worsened.

And then the words choked in my throat when I caught a movement on the stairs. Standing halfway up was Rob, staring straight down at us. His hand was gripping the railing so tight, his veins bulged dark blue.

'Who the fuck do you think you are?'

The words hit me like a bomb. Rob thumped down the stairs, slowly, purposely, not stopping until he was an inch from me. I could smell his anger mixed with stale beer.

'You think you can come to my house and make me look like a fool. Fill Kim's head with your feminist crap. Just because you lot can't handle a real man.'

'You're no real man,' I said quietly.

'Rob,' Kimberley pleaded.

He snapped his head towards her. 'Shut up and go upstairs.'

'But we were only—'

'Liar!' he yelled, slamming his fist on her desk. 'I heard everything. You two were plotting behind my back.'

'No, no, Rob, I swear to you. It's not at all what you think.'

Rob lunged then, grabbed one of her wrists and squeezed it until she cried out in pain. His face twisted into a sick smile. 'Don't you ever tell me what I should think, sweetheart. Now get the fuck upstairs.'

He released her, and she moved silently past him, head down, then looked back up at him. 'Please, Rob, don't get mad at me,' she said. 'I love you.'

He stared at her, his face carved in contempt. 'You're so pathetic.'

When she bit down hard on her lip, he stepped closer. 'You're just like one of those sad puppy dogs, aren't you? The ones you push and kick, but they still come back to you, whining and yelping and pleading. Hoping their owners will take pity and make them feel loved. Isn't that right, Kim? You're a dog.'

Kimberley clung to the railing and began sobbing, sucking in loud gulps of air.

Rage filled my mouth like spit. 'No,' I said. '*You're* the fucking dog.'

They both stared down at me, stunned—Rob recovered first. 'What did you just say?'

'You heard. She's not your bloody punchbag.'

He released his hand from Kimberley and smiled at me then—that sick smile again, twisting my insides. My eyes flew to the door: left open, I noticed, although I could have sworn it was shut only moments ago.

Rob followed my stare and spread his arms out wide. 'You and I aren't finished just yet.'

I tried to move past him to the door. 'Get out of my way.'

'I'm afraid I can't do that, sweetheart.'

'I'm not your sweetheart.'

He laughed, his face a twisted mess. He started walking towards me, forcing me to retreat towards the back of the store.

'You women are all the same,' he said. 'You think you're so special. Think you can play hard to get when things go your way. And when they don't, you come back begging.' He rolled up his shirtsleeves. 'Do you like begging too, sweetheart?'

'Fuck you,' I said, my heart slamming hard against my ribcage.

'*Fuck you.*' He mimicked me in a coy, girlish voice then poked me in the chest with two fingers and laughed again.

Another step back, then another. Closer and closer to the back wall at the end of the room every time he took a step towards me. I was trapped. I snagged a fabric roll off a shelf in sheer desperation and waved it at him like a sword.

'Good,' he said, his fists clenched into tight balls. 'I like a challenge.'

Then the fists slackened when I bumped into something solid. Not a wall. I looked over my shoulder and my heart surged with relief when I saw Josh—or rather Inspector Stanmore, who was staring straight at Rob, a pair of handcuffs dangling from his hand.

'I'm happy to provide that,' he said coolly.

'You cops,' Rob raged under his breath. 'Nothing better to do than throw your weight around. Why don't you go arrest that foreign vermin? Those bloody women are all over town.'

*You misogynist, racist scum,* I thought. Plus, his comment made no sense at all in a town that was predominantly white British.

Josh kept his cool and asked, 'What do you mean?'

Rob snarled. 'I already told the police. Don't they pass on information?'

Josh moved to his side and put a hand on his shoulder. 'I'll come and check on Kimberley tomorrow. If I find out you've touched even one hair on her head, you're done.'

Rob muttered something unintelligible, then turned and flew out of the store, the door slamming behind him.

I rushed to Kimberley. 'Are you okay?'

She was trembling, one hand clutched to her mouth, the other hanging limp at her side. I found myself reaching for it and squeezed her fingers.

'Men like him don't change, Kimberley. They never change.'

At first she began to nod, the words seemingly reaching a place inside her. But when she slid her gaze to the window the nodding stopped, Rob stumbling away in the distance, her hand slipping away from mine, and in a rush I could sense his power all over her again.

I dug her pen out of my pocket. 'Keep it,' I said, a catch in my voice, and dashed towards the door, Josh's footsteps following close behind me.

Outside, the sunset burned the sky a bright liquid gold. It made my eyes water to even look at it.

'So you really think she's innocent?' Josh asked after we'd returned to Stonebarn Lake.

He'd been cooking in the kitchen for the last fifteen minutes, chopping basil and tomatoes on a cutting board, stirring inside a boiling pot with a wooden spoon. The air filled with the smell of garlic and olive oil. My mother was still an unseen presence in the house.

'Kimberley was only interested in the pen,' I said. 'Not in the articles about Graham Holmes. She left them on Cordelia's desk because they meant nothing to her.'

Josh nodded as he bent over the stove and dipped a finger in the sauce, put it to his mouth.

I grinned at him sideways. 'I thought geeks only guzzled Coke and binged on crisps.'

He winked. 'True enough. But I still owe you dinner.'

'Dinner?'

He nodded. 'I said I'd take you somewhere to eat yesterday, remember? I thought it'd be best to forgo the road journey this time.'

'Oh, of course,' I said when I noticed the two plates. 'But really, I'm not hungry.'

He said nothing for a moment, busy serving the food on the table: a linguine dish. 'I called the hospital earlier and spoke to Doctor Andrews. He said you left without warning.'

I tried a jokey smile. 'I thought I might as well spare you a visit.'

But Josh wasn't smiling. He held my gaze long enough for me to think, *That's it, he already knows*. It was there in his eyes, the deep blue strangely overcast. Maybe not the ugly specifics, but the general outline—which was bleak enough.

'Do you want to talk about it?' he asked.

'I really don't—'

'Sit down,' he said gently, pulling out a chair for me.

I sat down next to him. Watched him twirl the linguine on his fork and blow over it to cool it off. Without a word, he brought the fork to my mouth. I didn't know why I let him feed it to me. He had a tender, sweet look on his face.

Some of the food fell out, so he scraped the sides of my lips the way an adult would wipe the mouth of a small child. He chuckled, and eventually I began to chuckle too. Blushing.

When I finished swallowing, he placed the fork in my hand. 'Try,' he said, the blue of his eyes cloudless again.

My heartbeat throbbed as I gathered a forkful, our knees touching under the table, hoping the tremor in my fingers looked like clumsiness.


Upstairs, in my bedroom, the dress was gone—vanished. Not lying on my bed any more, where I'd left it the day before. In a panic, I mentally ran through the faces of people who'd attended the funeral reception. It could have been anyone. Anyone could have sneaked up here.

Then I suddenly thought of the nurse's words: *'You'll be glad to know that your mother came to visit this morning. She said you might need some light entertainment when you wake up.'*

My iPad! I was sure I'd left it too on my bed. So if my mother came to pick it up, she must have seen . . .

My hand flew up to my mouth.

I rushed to her bedroom, tore open every drawer of the dresser and combed through the wardrobe. Nothing. Then I searched the entire ground floor before I raced back up the stairs to the top of the house.

The door of the loft had been locked.

# 31

Friday morning, I handed Josh his second cup of black coffee. No sugar, no milk. He said he needed the extra boost to keep his wits sharp. He also bemoaned his lack of progress while I was in hospital.

Tina, it seemed, had played her usual flirty routine. Shrugged off all knowledge of the order backlog as a sheer stroke of luck ('Did I really say thirty-two percent? Our Kimberley can be so melodramatic at times'). And no, there was no chance in hell she would give him her SS password—even if he had to drag her to jail ('Mind you, Inspector, I do love a man in uniform'). He sighed as I pictured her chubby finger toying teasingly with his tie.

As for my mother, she'd reluctantly agreed to meet him at Mindful Wellness. Stomped her way in angrily and spilled her outrage: 'Three murders in Heavendale and you suspect *me*? Have you lost your mind, Inspector?'

She refused then point-blank to answer a single question about Scissor Sister. Said she had urgent matters to attend to and simply walked off.

Her defiance baffled me. I couldn't reconcile the idea of my mother with a woman who showed so little regard for 'the law.' Like Bonnie Parker—a posh version for the gentrified.

Thank goodness Patsy had shown a less rebellious spirit. Arranging the meeting point, though, took some fussing over the phone. She wouldn't let Josh into her lakeside villa ('Surely, Inspector, a woman in my position should be spared gossip and bad publicity'), while he drew the line at driving out of town (Who could blame him after our last stint on the road?).

So they settled on Stonebarn Lake. Today, at a quarter past ten. Enough time for Josh to put on his detective uniform and immerse himself in his character. Enough time for me to drag the chintz sofa an inch closer to the glass table, to make sure I'd enjoy the best vantage point to the living room through the gap in the kitchen door. The doorbell rang its cheerful three-note chime.

*Showtime.*

The first thing I noticed was that Patsy wasn't wearing her customary dark power suit. Instead, vintage sandals and soft linen folds, a dazzling shade of white, swung back to fall around her calves. The sort of dress you'd wear to radiate purity and righteous innocence. I wouldn't be surprised if Patsy was reading books on fashion psychology.

'Is Kathryn here?' she asked. No hello, no hi. That Frisky Lady smell wafted off her again like a discordant note.

'No. I haven't seen her for a while,' I replied.

'Oh, good. That ghastly murder business is such a nuisance. I mean, do I look like a fucking serial killer, darling?' She waved her hand extravagantly and sashayed past me towards the kitchen. I doubted she'd lost much sleep over Cordelia's death.

'Inspector Stanmore is waiting for you in the living room,' I said. 'Tea or coffee?'

'Skinny Teatox, please.' She sighed dramatically. 'Oolong and black liquorice. Your mother always keeps a box for me in the upper cupboard.'

'Sure.'

I plugged in the kettle and readied a teabag: smelled foul— punishment for the calorie-conscious. Patsy's kind, I must say, are different from mine. They're food fascists who thrive on public approval. They love small gestures of sympathy that praise their strength of character, which is often tested by secret binges behind closed doors. In short, you're supposed to feel a little sorry for them.

When I brought Patsy her mug, I gave her a half-comforting, half-pitying smile. She was sitting very properly on the edge of the sofa, her hands folded in her lap.

She took a demure sip and smacked her lips at me in pained contentment. 'That's lovely, Chloe. Thank you.'

'You're welcome.'

I couldn't bring myself to look at Josh. I quickly retreated to the kitchen again, where I pulled the door ajar behind me and spied through the crack.

'Mrs Carter,' he began, 'thank you for your time. I'm sure you must know the reason I brought you here.'

'The same reason you met with Tina and Kathryn, I suppose.'

He smiled. 'News travels fast.'

'I'm afraid this town is just as prolific as Trump on Twitter.' She let out a croak of laughter, as if amused at her own joke. 'Anyway, how can I help you, Inspector?'

'I'm curious to know more about you, really. You graduated from a prestigious fashion school and worked your way up to the top of *British Vogue*. When you left you founded your own magazine, *Retro Mode*. And now Scissor Sister.' He smiled again. 'I find your career path quite fascinating.'

'Fascinating?' Patsy made the word sound distasteful. 'Some would rather call it successful.'

'Why Scissor Sister?'

'She sent me an email last year. She needed an expert in fashion advertising, which is exactly what I do on a daily basis.'

Josh raised an eyebrow. 'That must involve an awful lot of extra travelling. That must eat away at your very precious time.'

'Women tend to multitask better than men, Inspector.'

'Ah, true enough, Mrs Carter. You make it sound so plausible.' He leaned forward, his sharp gaze assessing her. 'Seriously, though, do you expect me to believe you?'

Patsy snapped her mouth open and shut. For a second, she seemed lost for words. 'Scissor Sister pays good money,' she sputtered defensively.

'How much?'

'How am I supposed to answer that?'

'As truthfully as you can.'

'I can't complain.'

'That's not an answer,' he replied. 'I found out that *Retro Mode* has recently expanded worldwide. And with your husband as the CEO of Deutsche Bank, you don't *just* do it for a bit of extra cash, right?'

Patsy shot him a hard stare. 'I thought this was a murder investigation, Inspector. Not a discussion of how many zeros sit in my bank account.'

Josh leaned back in his armchair. He tugged at the brim of his hat then nodded. 'Very well, Mrs Carter. So who do you think killed Cordelia?'

Patsy let out a mocking snort. 'Isn't it your job to figure it out? I'm only one of your suspects, after all.'

'Oh, you aren't a suspect at all, Mrs Carter.'

Behind the door, I clamped a hand over my mouth to muffle my gasp. Patsy stared at Josh for a long second. His face was unreadable.

*He's onto something,* I thought.

'You couldn't have killed her,' Josh continued. 'I checked your itinerary last Thursday: You left Heavendale late afternoon and drove straight back to London.' He waved his mobile at her. 'I checked your phone records as an extra precaution. You have a perfect alibi.'

'Well, that's me off the hook, then.' Patsy stood up to leave. 'Now, if you'll excuse me—'

'I'm not done yet,' Josh said, the words flying out of his mouth like bullets. He beckoned her to sit back down.

I glimpsed the first signs of nerves on Patsy's face: the twitching under her left eye, the slightly open mouth, the shiny brow (a touch of Botox, perhaps?). I still remembered what it felt like to sit opposite Inspector Stanmore. My feet began fidgeting in sympathy.

'I want to meet your employer, Mrs Carter.'

'I ... sorry?'

'I want to meet the woman who passes as Scissor Sister. I think you know very well who she is.'

He scooted his armchair forward, his eyes unflinchingly on hers. I noticed the slight tremor in Patsy's hand as she raised her cup to her lips.

'You're scared, Mrs Carter. You put on a good show, but it's obvious she's controlling you.'

'You know nothing about her,' she whispered.

'I know when a woman is afraid and pretending not to be. I can help you.'

'I don't think so.'

'Let me try.'

'How?'

'Tell me her name.'

'Can you arrest her?'

'Someone has to.' He smiled.

Patsy broke into a quick laugh, glum and hollow, like a deflated balloon. 'What's the penalty for blackmail, Inspector?'

'What has she got on you, Mrs Carter?'

I couldn't help but picture my mother. My hands began shaking nervously against the door, which slowly swung open on its hinges —Creeeaaak.

Both heads snapped towards me and I smiled, embarrassed. 'Tea, anyone?'

Shaking his head, Josh shot me a quick wink. Patsy asked in her most pleasant tone, 'You wouldn't have something a little stronger, would you, darling?' She clearly didn't mind my intrusion.

'Sure. We have some leftover champagne in the fridge.'

'That'll do just fine, thank you.'

I left to grab the bottle, twisted the cork, and necked down a good swig. I too needed a bit of reinforcement to deal with this particular situation. I reentered the living room and handed Patsy a glass—she drained it in one shot.

'I wish I could go back to that day and do things differently. I should never have trusted that woman.'

'When was that?' Josh asked.

'March last year, that's when I met her for the first time, in Market Square, shortly after my husband and I purchased our holiday villa. She seemed nice enough, helpful and welcoming. So much so that I invited her for a drink the following weekend.' Patsy nudged her empty glass towards me. 'I barely drink at all, Inspector. But I can be partial to a treat once in a while. You know that, don't you, Chloe?'

I nodded in sympathy and refilled her glass. I imagined she was referring to that wine-flavoured chocolate mousse I'd ordered last week. If I remembered correctly, she'd wolfed down the whole thing on her own.

'Anyway,' she went on quickly, 'I don't know what came over me. I started discussing my private life.'

'And?' Josh prompted.

'And the whole thing just bubbled out of me,' she said, her voice rising. 'I told her about my sex tape.'

Silence stretched for a few long seconds: Patsy drained her glass. Josh's mouth hung open. I recovered first and asked, 'Do you actually mean a private tape with your . . . banker husband?'

'Don't be dim, darling,' she said breezily. 'He's a London MP from the Tory party.'

'Oh,' I cleared my throat, 'right.'

Josh recovered his wits. 'So Scissor Sister stole that tape from you, then.'

Patsy nodded. 'Sort of. She hacked into my private cloud account.'

'I see. But why didn't you tell the police?'

'And say what exactly, Inspector?' Patsy huffed in outrage. 'Discuss the ins and outs of my extramarital affair? Imagine the scandal if the press gets hold of it.'

Indeed I could already picture a few choice headlines:

FRISKY LADY GETS KINKY

TORY MP: MY THREE-HOUR ROMP WITH DIRTY PATSY

I bet that tape would notch plenty of views on YouTube before its shock-worthiness faded.

Patsy thumped her hand on to the table. 'I had no choice. I tried to confront her, but she simply denied everything. She would only address me via the SS intranet. She said I had to promote her brand or else she'd leak the tape.'

'Patsy,' I said, 'does the Cleora dress mean anything to you?'

'Of course,' she said. 'It's about to be splashed everywhere—fashion magazines, social media, national press and news channels.'

'When?'

'Tomorrow.'

'Isn't that a bit excessive for just one dress?'

'Just one dress?' Patsy scoffed. 'Are you kidding me? There's not just *one* Cleora dress. There are thousands of them.'

Josh and I exchanged shocked looks.

Patsy went on—'Anyway, I don't have the details. She promised to release me as soon as the launch is over.'

Josh shook his head. 'You can't trust her, Mrs Carter.'

'There will always be something else,' I said.

'She's already killed three people,' he added.

'Goodness.' Patsy gasped. 'I surely don't want to end up at the bottom of a cliff.' She grabbed the champagne out of my hands, refilled her glass, and as she did so, I couldn't help but feel a hard lump in my throat. There were only two suspects left: Kathryn or Tina. My mother or her best friend.

*My mother.*

'Mrs Carter,' started Josh, 'I need her name now. Who is Scissor Sister?'

Patsy buried her face into her drink. She looked back up with glazed eyes and sighed. 'It's Tina, Inspector. Tina Williams.'

. . .

A brief moment of elation followed Patsy's departure. Half glee, half relief, and a certain sense of accomplishment too. And maybe a little something else when Josh lifted me off the floor, his hands clasped around my waist. He swung me around once, quickly, then set me back on my feet. His eyes lit up when he kissed my forehead.

'We did it,' he said.

I could feel my skin tingling hot red where it met his lips. I stared down at my shoes to hide my blush. 'We need to be sure, Josh.'

'Why? You think Patsy could have lied?'

'No, it's not that.'

'Then what is it?' He gently hooked his forefinger under my chin and lifted it until I was looking at him. He was frowning at my sudden silence.

I had no idea how to say it. Part of me, I had to admit, was angry at my own laxity. I'd never thought Tina capable of pretending to be anyone other than herself. I knew she was a gossip, I knew she nurtured some obsessive grudge against Denise Drummond. But Scissor Sister? Blackmail and murder? I had seriously underestimated Tina, I supposed.

'Nothing,' I finally told Josh.

In the distance, the faint wail of a siren. It grew louder, drawing closer by the second. Flashing lights pulsed through the panel of frosted glass in the front door.

Flashing blue lights.

The sound of tyres crunched gravel in the drive.

The siren abruptly stopped.

*Something was wrong.*

*Bang! Bang! Bang!* 'Police! Open the door,' a male voice demanded.

Josh made a move but I reached out. 'Don't.'

'Maybe they figured out something we don't know.'

I clamped a hand on his wrist, my body pulsing with every beat of my heart. 'I have a bad feeling about this.'

243

'We need their help, Chloe. Now's our chance—let's grab it.'

*Bang bang bang.* 'Police. Open up right now!'

'No, Josh. Listen to me—'

'It's okay.' He freed his hand and smiled. 'Let me handle this.'

'Josh, please.'

He turned and opened the door. A cop in body armour stared at him head-on. Grimly.

Three yards away, another stood in a falsely casual pose against the hood of a patrol car, his eyes flitting from me to Josh. 'Are you Josh Stanmore?' he called.

Josh had barely nodded when a pair of handcuffs were slapped on his wrists.

'You're under arrest for usurpation of official authority,' the cop closest to him said. 'You are to be questioned immediately at the police station.'

'Hey, no. Just let me explain—'

He didn't have a chance. The cop dragged him out of the house, hauled him into the back of his car, and slammed the door shut.

I rushed after them. 'No—please get him out. You're making a terrible mistake.'

But the two cops ignored me and slid into their seats.

Josh looked out the window; he was pale but he attempted a brave smile, mouthed, *'Don't worry,'* as the car began to peel out of the drive.

Our eyes locked.

When he vanished into the distance, I sank to the ground and cried.

# SCISSOR SISTER

I don't lose.

I *never* lose.

I slay the enemy.

I crush the resistance.

I dispatch the treacherous.

Of course, I had to be a little more cautious this time. You don't want a new death to spoil your fair tomorrow, right?

I watch the police thwart his pathetic deception and enjoy a smug moment.

Good riddance, *Inspector* Stanmore.


Nothing will stand in my way now. What I have set in motion cannot be stopped.

I might just as well relax and enjoy my own show.

But I don't. I can't.

There's a nasty lump lodged in the back of my throat. Like a bad seed taking root when I see her.

Crouched on the ground . . .

Crying . . .

And then I know . . .

I *know* . . .

She too has conspired against me.

She has *betrayed* me.

No loyalty. No allegiance. None at all. Haven't I always been kind to her?

Haven't I?

I grip the steering wheel until my knucles turn white, my seething breaths misting the side window, my mind wrangling over her fate.

I mull over the same question again and again:

*What am I going to do with you, Chloe?*

## 32

Indoors, I dried my tears and began pacing the hallway like a rodent in a cage. Sat down, stood up, picked up things, and put them down. The frequency with which I checked my watch didn't make the time go any faster. I couldn't stop thinking about Josh.

*Where is he now?*

I pictured him sitting inside a tiny interview room at the end of a grey slate hall. Or confined to a cold, dark cell between three narrow walls. Solid metal bars, a small square window covered with barbed wire. The image made me shiver.

I needed Patsy to save Josh. Someone who could help me prove Tina was behind Scissor Sister. Who could point out the connection between all three murders. I looked up her address online, grabbed my car keys, and marched out of the house.


Patsy's villa was only a few minutes away, a luxuriously converted cottage overlooking the east side of the lake. A small section of them stood there, all boasting cherry trees in full bloom and vast expanses of greenery behind high electronic gates. Her gate had been left open, courtesy of a gardener's van. A man whose uniform matched the grass was bumping along on his lawn tractor. I pulled over to the side of the road and slowly walked up the drive.

The house itself was not exactly private: tall glass windows facing front and back, through which I could glimpse the outline of an outdoor hot tub (bubble frolics with her Tory lover?). I took in next slabs of Italian marble in a glossy kitchen, sticks in tall vases next to an ivory modular sofa, a wet bar—everything inside looked obscenely white.

Then there was Patsy.

With her arms flailing wildly in the air, she looked like a manic ghost as she shouted into her iPhone, cradled on her shoulder.

'Is that a joke? Are you fucking kidding me?'

Sounded as if Patsy had sobered up quickly. She didn't say anything else, just flung her iPhone on the sofa when she spotted me and slid the glass door open.

'What do you want?' The question sharp like a dog's bark.

'I need your help, Patsy.'

'Help? Do I look like a friggin' Samaritan? I need some help too. I've just found out the police arrested Inspector Stanmore.'

'I know,' I said. 'It's all a terrible misunderstanding. You must come with me at once. Tell them everything you know about Tina. We have to get him out.'

'Get him out? Are you out of your bloody mind? Haven't you heard?'

'I can explain—'

'He's a fake, Chloe. He's an impostor. I should never have trusted him.'

'Josh was only trying—'

'Josh!' She gasped and narrowed her eyes. 'You knew all along, didn't you? You were in cahoots with him.'

'Patsy, no. Just listen to me one second—'

'Oh, I see now. The two of you were plotting to sell my story to the press. How much did they offer? Tell me how much. Was Tina behind it?' She was getting completely paranoid now. I couldn't get through to her.

'Please, Patsy. We must go—'

'Oh no, young lady, we're not going anywhere. You've got some serious explaining to do.' She grabbed a remote control on the table and pressed a button. The buzz of an electric motor . . .

I whipped around and saw the double gates sliding shut.

I broke into a sprint.

Twenty metres.

Ten.

Five.

Slipping through a narrow gap just in time, I scrambled my way back to my car. My heart throbbing fast, my foot pressed on the accelerator, I drove away to the squeal of tyres and the sound of Patsy's hysterical shrieks, 'I'll pay you double. Triple. Name your price —anything!'

I whipped down the road past Stonebarn Lake, the sight of it making my stomach lurch. The image of Patsy screaming on her phone just wouldn't leave my mind.

*Who'd tipped Patsy off about Josh?*

Even by Heavendale's standards, the news of his arrest already having made the rounds was highly unlikely. No—someone had engineered the whole situation. Someone who'd been spying on us, hovering at the edges. Someone who'd been watching us all along.

My thoughts inevitably turned to Tina.

From memory I knew she lived only a couple of streets away from Cordelia, in a cottage I'd visited once in my teens, in which the rather bland decor belied a saucy picture of semi-naked firemen holding their hoses in interesting places. '*All proceeds go to the Cumbrian burns unit,*' she'd reassured my mother, then winked at me mischievously. I remembered suppressing a laugh at the time. Now the memory threatened to spill more tears.

I rang the doorbell. An ugly tabby cat sat on the window ledge of next door's house, where the din of a lunchtime talk show rumbled behind closed curtains. Someone was watching *Loose Women*. I rang the doorbell again, waited. Rang it again and waited some more, the TV babbling on in the background. Then, seized by sudden anger, I flung my fists against the door, knocking and knocking and knocking with throbbing knuckles.

I yelled Tina's name at the sky.

When the last sound died out, I noticed the cat was gone. The TV next door had the volume turned down low. A thin blue-veined hand twitched the curtains ajar, a hushed voice scolding, 'Crazy, crazy girl. How dare she scare my sweet little baby.'

The cat leapt back on the window ledge, cool green eyes fixed on me, a strangled territorial growl rising from its wide-stretching jaws. The TV blared again before I'd even reached my car.

Downtown it was almost impossible to park. People clustered around vans to unload crates, boxes, awnings, tables, and poles—all to be erected into stalls in preparation for tomorrow's fair.

When I finally wound my way across Market Square, the sight of SUZANNE'S SHABBY CHIC had me awestruck; a gorgeous, arresting sight. The façade, repainted sage green, had put oomph into the name. A warm grey colour gave the shutters a stylish contrast. The old faded door sign was gone, now replaced by smart cursive letters nailed onto an oblong piece of carved wood.

Suzanne jumped to her feet when she saw me enter. 'Just the person I wanted to see! I was wondering whether to go for country or Georgian. I'm a bit short on both, really.' She pointed to a platform partly dressed in eighteenth-century furniture. The other three, I noticed, had been beautifully furnished in styles recognisable as modern, shabby chic, and art deco. Suzanne and Colin must have put in a lot of extra hours to finish the store on time for the fair.

'What do you have in mind?' I asked.

Suzanne showed me a pile of floral fabric squares pinned together on an antique Singer table. I guessed she wanted to make cushions.

'You could combine both. The Georgians were quite fond of their chintz.'

'Oh, that's an excellent idea, Chloe. I'll get cracking as soon as I finish clearing up.'

'Let me help you.' I sat behind the Singer and began to operate it. *Tik tik tik tik tik.*

It was the first time I'd touched a sewing machine in the last three years. My hands soon remembered their old, bittersweet routine.

*Tik tik tik tik tik.*

'Have you heard anything back from Inspector Stanmore?' Suzanne suddenly asked.

I lifted my foot from the cast-iron treadle; felt my throat close up when I pictured the disappointment on her face. *Not today*, I thought. *Not yet.* I made myself breathe through the lie.

'I heard he's making progress. Good progress.'

Suzanne dragged a tilt-top table onto the platform and smiled. The sewing machine resumed its *tik tik* sound.

Two hours later, I sat on a terrace fifty yards away, wanting a stiff drink. I ended up ordering a cold Frappuccino like the person at my neighbouring table: a snobbish woman with gold Chanel sunglasses. Maybe because I had a change of heart. Maybe because I didn't want to draw a snobbish glance.

No matter. I was still desperate to help Josh. But acting out of a desperate impulse had yielded zero results so far. No, I had to think more methodically. Devise some kind of strategy. So I grabbed my notes from my bag and began browsing through them while I waited.

Matt's section was by far the sparsest, and the most dispiriting too. All I had were two questions slotted sideways in the margin: *How did he meet Holly? Did he play an active role, or wrong place, wrong time?*

I chewed at the end of my pen and stared at the other paragraphs. There was very little I could answer. At least I took comfort in crossing out a few lines: the note Kimberley admitted writing, the extensive press coverage pointing to Patsy being blackmailed. Those two mysteries had now been solved.

Then I remembered something new. Something crucial Patsy had said: *'There's not just one Cleora dress. There are thousands of them.'*

Thousands of Cleora dresses. I tried to get my head around the idea, but I knew it could only mean one thing: Scissor Sister had cloned the dress. Had launched it into mass production.

It wasn't hard to imagine how the dress could be the start of something big. Scissor Sister had grown powerful and gathered an impressive following over the last year. And with Patsy's PR machine sent into overdrive, all she needed was to put her own spin on it: the tragic story of Graham Holmes, the lost and found dress. Play into high drama. The fair being a perfect backdrop for the big reveal. Everyone would want to snatch a piece of history.

*But what about logistics?*

Producing such a vast number of dresses was no small task. Did Scissor Sister make use of overseas facilities? Factories in Bangladesh? India? Vietnam? Almost every high street retailer was going down that route these days.

But something bothered me when I looked back at my notes: the Fake Brands list. Popular streetwear brands she'd repeatedly vilified on her blog and cast as her enemies. No way would she have formed a partnership with any of them. No, Scissor Sister had decided to do it all on her own: cut the costs, cut out the middleman. Everything was kept under her strict control. Which meant it could only be a local enterprise.

When I raised my head, I saw it through a gap between the shop roofs, perched in the distance on a hilltop. Heavendale's glorious past. The answer was staring me right in the face.

The garment factory had been brought back to life.


I let Google Maps determine the most accessible route, bumped along a stony track for less than a mile, jolting and shaking past a deserted barn, then stopped at the bottom of a rocky trail, long disused, and left my car there. I hiked up and ducked my way below fir trees. A low branch scratched the side of my face. A bird abruptly took flight. I ploughed through, head down and panting towards the hilltop.

By the time I reached the factory, I was out of breath, panting and wheezing, my brow wet with sweat.

It stood there like an old, windswept ghost. But a ghost well and truly back in business by the looks of it. Patches of bright light seeped through the boarded windowpanes, some of which had been smashed into pointy shards, jagged and sharp. I could hear the rapid staccato of sewing machines escape through them.

I took my phone out and turned on the camera. *Click. Recording.* I couldn't help but wonder how many people were working inside.

The front metal door creaked open and I jumped, then ducked behind a tree before I could get caught. I peered over one side, where two young blonde women had slipped out for a cigarette break.

*Click.*

They spoke in a language I didn't understand, although their intonations suggested an Eastern European tongue.

*Recording.*

They exhaled the last of their smoke. When they slammed the door shut behind them, the blood came rushing to my head. Like going too fast on a roller coaster, light-headed with adrenaline. I sank against the tree and gently slapped my cheeks.

*Easy, Chloe. You'll be okay.*

I realised I hadn't eaten a thing all day. I wanted to catch Tina red-handed, but I wasn't sure I was strong enough to do it on my own. Then again, if she wasn't inside, no doubt these women would immediately warn her that a stranger had been looking for her. They'd clear the space overnight, remove all evidence and proof.

No, I couldn't afford to take that risk. Not yet. Not when Josh's freedom was at stake. I slowly retraced my way down to my car in the waning sunshine.

There was one more thing I needed to do.

. . .

Back in Heavendale, I hurried down the street with a gooey candy bar in my mouth, fighting hard the urge to gag. I dropped by the police station; I knew they wouldn't be keeping Josh there, but I hoped the young sergeant on duty would be accommodating enough to tell me where he was being held.

He wasn't.

It took fifteen minutes of begging and a desperate flirtation with sugar-sticky gums before he relented.

'Carlisle,' he said, looking up from his computer.

That was almost thirty miles away: I jotted down the address, and ended up whizzing through the A66 and the M6, which were luckily clear.

When I arrived, Chief Inspector Gordon Smith was leaving through the main door, a smart leather briefcase hanging by a strap at his side. He seemed none too pleased to see me.

'Miss Westfield, please don't tell me police stations are a regular part of your travel itinerary. What could possibly bring you to Carlisle?'

'Josh Stanmore,' I said.

His eyes barely flickered. 'Ah, our deluded detective impersonator. He stirred up quite a fuss in town.'

'Are you keeping him overnight?'

'Miss Westfield, it could well be the first of many nights. His offence is punishable by up to six months in jail.'

My stomach dropped. 'You've got to release him. We need his help. Three people have lost their lives so far.' I stomped my foot on the ground. 'For God's sake, Chief Inspector, all of Heavendale knows that Cordelia was strangled. I can't believe none of you are acknowledging this.'

'That's not what our coroner's report says.'

'Sod the report,' I snapped. 'You have a killer on the loose. We suspect it might be Tina Williams. She trades under the name of

Scissor Sister and will stop at nothing to eliminate whoever threatens her expansion plans.'

'So I heard. This story doesn't stand up, Miss Westfield.'

'Well, see for yourself. It does.'

I held out my phone, showed him my videos and pictures, let him listen to my audio files, all from the garment factory. Something changed in him; his eyes glistened with an intent fever. He watched me closely. Seeking. Probing.

'Tell me the truth,' he ordered.

I told him about the Cleora dress, the other women, and the way they worked. I told him everything I knew about Scissor Sister. That her stage presentation was scheduled for tomorrow afternoon at three during the fair.

There was no more time to waste.

Gordon Smith nodded avidly. He said he would carefully look into it. He agreed to dispatch police forces to the factory right after Scissor Sister's presentation. As for Josh, no visiting was allowed until he made a final decision on the matter.

When we parted ways, I blinked the sudden wetness brimming behind my eyes. I tried not to picture again the small square window, the three narrow walls and the cold dark cell with solid metal bars.

And Josh locked inside.

# 33

I woke up the next day feeling off. Groggy. *Something's wrong*—that's what I woke up thinking. A burst of words, followed by a quick realisation: someone was knocking on my bedroom door.

'Chloe?' My mother, whispering.

I remained silent, my hands tightening over the blanket, pulling it up to my nose. I hadn't seen her for almost three days. Then again, I mostly hadn't been home since my stint in hospital. I wasn't sure she'd been home much either.

Another knock, the handle jiggling followed by a key rattling in the lock. I never knew my mother had a spare key.

She breezed into my room, smiling brightly. She wore a vintage bluebird dress with crimson blossoms and carried a tray with coffee and a blueberry tart. 'Your favourite,' she said, her voice almost girlish. 'I made it especially for you.'

I eased myself up against the headboard, still not letting go of my blanket. The plate, I noticed, was one of her finest blue china ones—one she saved only for special occasions. My mother had never fussed over me, never got her danged china out for me once, not even on my birthdays. Now, though, I was given special treatment.

She poured me coffee into a dainty cup and sat on the bed beside me, patting my arm. 'I was worried sick about you, Chloe.'

'Were you?'

'Where have you been?'

'Just . . . out.'

She laughed, leaned her head towards me. 'Oh, sweetheart, you're such a bad liar. You know you can talk to Mother. To your mother.'

I took a bite of the tart then, chewed it slowly, staring down at my plate. Silence except for the sound of my swallowing and something compressing tight inside my chest.

My mother sighed. Her voice turned sombre when she said, 'I've been thinking a lot about you lately.'

I raised my head. 'Yes?'

'I tried to understand you. I wanted to know what drove you to make that choice.'

'What choice?'

'You know . . . *your* choice.'

'I don't understand, Mum. Are you talking about me helping Suzanne?'

A quick shadow passed over her face: a frown, a veil of disappointment. She scooted closer on the bed and stroked my hair behind my ear, fixed her smile back in place. 'It doesn't matter any more, sweetheart. Eat your tart now.'

I nodded, feeling oddly feverish. My mother watched me eat for a moment, then rose from the bed and took one last glance at me over her shoulder—'Today is the day Scissor Sister has been waiting for. It shall be a day we will all remember.'

She padded away down the corridor, humming to herself *Oh, what a beautiful morning* in a tuneless, high-pitched voice.

When the front door shut behind her, I stumbled to the bathroom and threw up a long stream of purple slime.


Four hours went by in which I stayed locked up in my room. Lunchtime with no lunch. I was watching the minutes blinking by on my alarm clock when finally I dragged myself out of bed, feverish, and turned on the cold tap in the bath. I stepped into it with my nightgown on, chin on my knees, teeth chattering in my head.

Part of me just wanted to lie there and die. Face still, lips blue, and eyes frozen underwater. All my troubles gone.

I dressed sensibly, put on jeans and a pair of jaunty wellingtons.

Somehow they reminded me of Holly's with their cheerful canary yellow colouring and clumps of dried mud caked on the soles. I could picture her climbing the long disused trail, her head ducking under a fir branch, her boots treading on damp soil as she neared the hilltop.

Closer and closer.

One last time.

All streets and roads converging towards Market Square had been closed off to traffic for the fair. Lake Avenue was no exception. By the time I reached the bottom of it, I could see a trestle table with a collection of plaid tote bags. On my left were shell and turquoise pendants strung on plaited cords. Someone had embroidered aprons with the slogan *From Heavendale with Love*. Two orderly rows of stalls stretched into the distance and, between them, an endless parade of people.

I moved along, checked the time on my phone (only two twenty), and caught sight of a tiny bamboo hut on wheels. Inside, a collection of kimonos hung on wooden poles. All luxuriously hand-painted: tangerine blossoms, turquoise wave motifs, water lilies. I peered at one that looked like a bewitched forest, all dark greens and shades of black.

'Very very old,' the tiny Japanese saleswoman assured me. 'Pure silk. You like it?'

I dashed out of the hut before she could say more. I didn't want to find out what old spirit could lurk inside. Some peeved witch or a vengeful geisha?

As I drew closer to the town centre, images of food sprouted before my eyes. A pop-up bakery selling artisan bread on chunky timber crates. A marmalade-making competition being judged by a food writer from *The Times*. A table laid with snow-white napkins displaying cupcakes dressed in piped buttercream; creations flavoured with vanilla and honey, chocolate and cinnamon. Pockets of food smells everywhere. I was desperate to escape, so I rushed to the heart of the square, gripped by an energy I'd never felt before.

The buzz of excited voices.

Someone behind me shouted, 'Come on, girls. Let's find a good spot.'

One of them barrelled into me as she forced her way past. The woman in front of me barely flinched, brushed off my apology with a flick of her hand, her gaze firmly locked on a stage where a giant video screen was propped. Between wide-open scissor blades was a projected human face hologram, and beneath it, the glow of SS initials pulsing white.

And the crowd kept swarming in towards them from all sides.

Like moths to light.

Like bees flying to their queen.

At 2:55, a five-minute countdown appeared on the screen. By the end of it, the lights on stage went up a notch, a more dramatic set-up. The crowd went silent. Then, the opening scenes of a short film: black-and-white shots accompanied by the beautiful singing of a Wagnerian soprano. We watched people working in fields and factories, sowing and sewing, ploughing and trimming. All smiling. All white.

The singing faded to give way to a female speaking voice, powerful and mesmeric:

**'This is the land of our fathers and mothers. They lived at a time when work was abundant. A time now long gone.'**

The soprano voice soared, high notes building to a rousing climax; a British flag rose up a mast.

**'This is our great nation. The factories, the fields—**

259

**they were once the marks of our great nation. The home of our products. The pride of our hard-working people.'**

Red flames burst through the flag, turning it to ash. The crowd gasped at the sight and grew tighter, as though afraid to be consumed by fire, the air around us choked with body heat.

The film cut to colour pictures of factories, their machinery operated only by Black and Asian labourers. Country names popped onto the screen: India, Vietnam, China, Ethiopia, Bangladesh.

**'These are the people who steal our jobs. They are a threat to our great nation. A threat unleashed by the destructive force of globalisation.**
**But what is globalisation?**
**WHO. ARE. THEY?'**

The voice had grown harder, more commanding with each word. A young couple by my side was staring fiercely at the screen, their attention rapt as company names started rolling up.

One by one, I read the names of all the major fashion retailers that featured on Scissor Sister's Fake Brands list.

**'They are our enemies. They are traitors to the working people. Their only goal is to grind our great nation into ruin. Do NOT trust them.'**

The crowd began to cheer and clap, the applause building steadily.

*Flash, flash.* I suddenly realised there was a private section near the stage, where journalists took notes and clicked away with their cameras.

**'Globalisation is the root of all evil. Globalisation is destroying our families and contaminating our minds. They are taking everything away from us.**
**I repeat: DO. NOT. TRUST. THEM!'**

Someone raised his fist in the air. 'Get them all out.'

A few people laughed; others whistled approvingly. Then the music got darker; the film showing now heart-wrenching images of workers trapped under rubble. Howling screams, colums of smoke ascending to the sky, the background of a garment factory set ablaze.

Dhaka.

My stomach lurched.

**'Their fates are only a matter of consequence. He who steals from us shall not go unpunished. He who plunders our great nation shall pay the ultimate price.'**

A fresh cheer broke through the crowd who basked in the unshakeable belief that the voice addressing them could never be wrong. They wholly embraced the nationalistic rhetoric, gave up all pretence of moderation to unleash their latent xenophobia, safe in the knowledge that their behaviour was not only acceptable but justified in the eyes of Scissor Sister.

**'My dear countrymen and women, the time has come for us to take back control. We will show the world the power of our brand. Only together can we put an end to this rotting culture of greed and profit. This is a battle between tyranny and freedom!'**

The applause swept forward like thunder. Feet stomped the

ground as the voice grew more urgent—a deliberate drowning of consciousness.

**'We are standing on the threshold of a new beginning. I, Scissor Sister, pledge to represent your voice. I shall be your one and only true choice. For only by putting your trust in me will we triumph over our enemies.'**

'Scissor Sister,' the crowd chanted in a thousand-voiced roar. 'Scissor Sister.'

On the screen, two giant SS initials throbbed white, like strobe shots matching the collective pulse.

I shuddered and stumbled out of the delusion of the masses.

## 34

At Stonebarn Lake I picked up my car, followed a short diversion route, and parked under a copse of fir trees near the garment factory. It was just me at the bottom of the trail—no patrol cars, no police in sight. No Gordon Smith.

I rested my head against the seat rest and listened to a sad Billie Holiday song on the radio. I was still reeling and shaking from the language used by Scissor Sister. Not that it came as a surprise, really—I was less shocked by the content than by the fact it fell on so many receptive ears. A crowd prepped and groomed, their minds polluted. Ready to eat straight out of her hand.

The minutes passed. Jazz gave way to blues, and still no sign of a police car. I thought about my options: Go home, wait there . . . I pictured myself pacing the hallway again and shook my head. I could then stay in the car, listen to more blues (which was making me dangerously sad). Or I could go up the trail, check out the situation— which was the only way I would know what was going on.

But there was nothing going on when I went up the trail. No women smoking. No light seeped through the boarded windowpanes. Not a single sound of a sewing machine.

I cautiously made my way around the factory when I noticed with surprise that the front metal door had been left unlocked—not only unlocked but ajar. Cold sweat trickled down my spine.

'Gordon?' I called, peeking through the door. Slowly, I pushed it open. 'Hello. Chief Inspector? Anyone there?'

But there was only silence.

I peered through the semi-darkness, ran my hand along the wall until I hit a light switch. The humming of fluorescent tubes overhead, the ceiling as high as twenty feet, and the shop floor as big as a basketball court. It was filled with machinery: ten rows of industrial sewing machines side by side, fifty in total. I ventured in slowly, taking in every detail, wondering if the police had already searched the place and simply forgotten to shut the door.

A large calendar, faded and damp, hung on the wall. An autumnal landscape of the National Park showed moody skies and rolling hills streaked with red and gold; October 1997, the last official month of activity before the factory's closure.

Next to it, a set of steel pigeonholes where names in faint black ink appeared on stickers yellowed with age: *Sally, Beck, Nat, Louise* . . . These women, I imagined, had long moved on. But then a new row caught my attention, eight names precisely, which stood out for different reasons. They were written in blue marker, and the paper hadn't yet yellowed or the ink gone faint.

I slowly peeled at the edges of *Agnieszka*, uncurling the sticker to reveal a faded *Angie*. In fact, the whole row of blue names was distinctly foreign: *Aniah, Elena, Magda, Tsvetana.*

My heart leapt in my chest when I read the last name: *Martika.*

The elusive, mysterious girl in town.

A memory rushed to mind: me, in my bedroom, glimpsing a group of distant silhouettes scuttling downhill at sunrise. Thrice.

These women, I realised now, must have been working at night. I pictured them living outside town lines, sneaking up and down the rocky trail like vigilant little ferrets. Sworn to secrecy, they had to be discreet and mostly succeeded—except, of course, Martika. Her fling with Christian Drummond had certainly got some attention.

I searched through the filing cabinet and a few drawers—at least those I found unlocked. Apart from spare needles and thread spools, nothing caught my eye. The floor looked meticulously tidy and clean too. No fabric scraps, as if yesterday's hubbub had never happened.

It was only when I passed the rows of sewing machines that I noticed a glass-enclosed office at the back. Inside was a desk, and on it a laptop, the screensaver flashing a picture of two white SS initials. I pressed the space bar, and something immediately appeared: a transcript of text messages; all dated 3 April 2017.

11:50 – **Matt:** Need to talk to you now.

11:53 – **Holly:** I've already told you. It's impossible.

11:54 – **Matt:** I don't want a damn copy. We're talking about my wedding, for Chrissakes.

11:56 – **Holly:** ███████ will never forgive me if she finds out.

11:56 – **Matt:** She doesn't have to know.

12:10 – **Holly:** Meet me at Vintage Folly. 2 p.m. I'll bring the original.

One of the words had been deliberately blackened—a name. Only once I'd reread the messages did I finally understand their meaning.

*So that's what you were after, Matt: the Cleora dress.*

*How did it happen? A chance encounter with Holly, perhaps? Did you really think I'd come running back into your arms for a designer piece?*

*I can picture it in your sick mind: me, walking down the aisle in teal blue and crowned with a Swarovski tiara. Or was it more about your parents? Impress Mum with her greyish-blue diamonds and Dad with his fast Porsche cars. Something precious to finally match what they had.*

I was settling scores in my head when an alarming thought crawled out of the dark. It was so twisted, I didn't want to look at it head-on, didn't want to shine a light on it for too long in case it became real. But it could be real.

Couldn't it?

*What if Matt had been the targeted victim?*

I laughed at first. And then I wanted to be sick. The idea seemed so incongruous, so absurd, I had to clutch the edge of the desk for support. Matt, once my fiancé and tormentor—a victim.

All along I'd dismissed his involvement as purely fortuitous, partly owing to lack of information. Now, though, a very different perspective began taking shape. Scissor Sister must have sensed danger when she read their messages. Matt had become a real threat to her plans. Backing this up: the tampering with his car.

But what about Holly? Could it be possible she never was a target? Could her death have been the result of unfortunate circumstances? After all, there'd been no way to predict she would hop back into Matt's car.

I'd always wondered about the link between Scissor Sister and Holly, had always kept her mysterious words in the back of my mind: *Scissor Sister is watching you.* Like two people walking in each other's shadow.

*Two people* . . .

The idea took root, grew into something that felt right. One by one the pieces of the puzzle began to shift together and turned into a picture: the real face of Scissor Sister.

My throat closed up, and all of a sudden the room was plunged into darkness. The front metal door slammed shut. Slow footsteps echoing on the hard floor. A shadow on the wall, a figure.

'Gordon?' My voice wobbly and high.

The footsteps stopped. An immediate, deliberate halt. Silence stretched into black, agonising seconds, and now all I could hear was the sound of my heart thudding hard in my chest. I tried to slow down my breathing, let my eyes begin to adjust to the darkness. Then, very slowly, I groped my way between the sewing tables, aiming for the door.

But there came the footsteps again, sure and steady. I broke into a run, and the footsteps behind me ran too. Faster, louder, closer.

Flinging me backwards.

I went down with a cry, hard on concrete, bright, dizzy stars flashing in front of my eyes.

She loomed over me with a sinister smile—'What am I going to do with you, Chloe?'

# SCISSOR SISTER

I've always been a good mother.

I've always put my daughter's needs before my own.

Feeding. Changing. Soothing. Tending.

Once I took her to ballet classes (she refused to try).

Once I took her to the toddler swim school (she began to scream).

On a hot, sticky August afternoon in 1997, I took her to the garment factory. Long, lazy days spent working on a near empty floor, a sign of things to come. I sat her on my lap and guided her tiny hands over a square piece of silk, then let the needle dart through it. I've never seen her eyes shine so bright. Like two stars twinkling in the night sky.

Holly was only five years old.


Two months later, the factory shut.

Four years of hardship. An ugly divorce . . .

On her tenth birthday I managed to save enough to buy her first sewing machine: a cute, Pink Sorbet Janome, with built-in stitches and a four-step buttonhole.

I taught her how to sew her first pillowcase skirt.

I taught her how to sew her first Belladone dress.

I taught her everything I knew about pattern-making.

When Holly turned eighteen, I bled myself dry to enrol her in fashion school. She studied hard, but she also had a lot of spare time.

That's when she started her blog.

Holly reinvented herself as Scissor Sister.

. . .

'*We could make a little money,*' she suggested one day.

I'd nodded and smiled.

Soon we started designing our own dress patterns, all professionally drawn. It was I who came up with the Scissor Sister logo.

But Holly didn't have a good head for business. She never grasped why her social media following didn't translate into sales.

'*We'll create something better next time,*' she said with a sigh, as if the problem lay with the quality of our work.

But deep inside, I knew I could make it happen.

There was a door out there, a quiet creak.

A dark path waiting to be explored . . .


Holly was horrified when my Union Jack dress went viral.

'*That's revolting, Mum. Please delete that retweet from the far right.*'

'*Don't be so prudish, Holly. Look at the sales!*'

'*I'm just not having it, period.*'

I was crushed with disappointment. Did it ever cross her mind to say thank you to her mother? No, of course it didn't.

She started to mistrust me after that. Then she started to neglect Scissor Sister. Maybe she was having relationship trouble with Daniel. Or was she just too busy with her new job? It wasn't clear. So I took over the blog and became more daring with the writing.

I don't think Holly ever noticed.


The Cleora dress turned out to be a stupendous stroke of luck. Holly found it stuffed on a wobbly bargain rail when she crossed a village near the Scottish border. Some very clueless owner, I suspect.

It was I who came up with the idea that fashion is a multi-billion-pound business. The potential for expansion is huge.

Why five thousand followers when we could have millions?

Why empathy when we could promote fear?

We could seize a large share of the market. We could finally make a real profit.

But Holly wasn't interested. She refused to listen to me. Worse, she told me to never interfere again with Scissor Sister.

My own daughter was discarding me like a vulgar toy.

After everything I'd done for her, all the hardships and sacrifices . . .

So I took control away from her.

She was livid the day she realised. She turned up at my door, screaming, 'How could you, Mum? You stole it from me!'

It! As if Scissor Sister was never real.

Stole! As if Scissor Sister was never truly mine.

Her scorn had left a mark she could never erase.

Holly had failed me miserably.

I knew she was up to no good when I sneaked a look at her phone: Matthew Thorne. I'd met him once—an obnoxious, arrogant twat.

He was in her bedroom hours later, his voice booming through the closed door. 'The dress . . . The dress . . .'

I could hear her resolve wavering.

I knew I had to act fast.

So I slipped out of the store and slid under his car.

But I don't know what came over my daughter. I never expected her to go with him.

I chased after them, the rain pouring thick and the thunder cracking loud in the sky. I drove faster and faster, panic flooding through my veins, horn blaring as I reached the passenger's side. I zipped my window open.

'*Pull over*,' I'd shouted at her. '*Pull over*.'

And then . . .

And . . . then . . .

I stared in horror at the bruises on her face, the cuts, the blood.

Then, the dress—one quick visual sweep: silk flecked with glistening glass shards, but the teal-blue fabric still unblemished.

Unspoiled. Pristine . . .

I screeched my car into a U-turn, slammed my foot hard on the accelerator. Hot tears stung my eyes as I spared Holly one last thought.

*I really, truly wish you had listened to your mother.*

# 35

Suzanne dragged me across the floor until I bumped into something solid—a chair. The screech of metal legs on concrete.

'Sit down,' she ordered, yanking my arm.

I couldn't move. My head was throbbing and my chest felt tight, as though someone was squeezing against my lungs. I tried to draw in a big gulp of air.

'You don't have to do this,' I said, my voice a faint croak.

'Spare me the moral lesson,' she snarled, then hooked her hands under my arms and shoved me onto the chair.

A ripping sound: duct tape, torn off twice, which she wrapped around my wrists, binding them to the tubular armrests. One of my ankles she secured to the chair leg—with my free foot I tried to kick her, a pitiful attempt she blocked effortlessly.

'Play nice, Chloe. Don't make it harder for yourself.'

'I know why you did away with Matt,' I said, my voice stronger now.

'Good girl.' With a mirthless laugh, she strapped the last strip of tape around my other ankle. 'I knew you just couldn't resist looking at my laptop.'

'All part of the plan, I'm sure.'

'Everything I do is the result of careful and precise planning.'

'But your plan did go wrong, Suzanne. I hope your daughter's death will weigh on your conscience for a very long time.'

She froze, raised her hand, and I thought she was going to slap me, but then she took a breath and held my chin in place, bored her eyes into mine—'Holly was weak. She was nothing without me. Now it's your turn to die.'

Suzanne released her hand off me, dropped the roll of duct tape on the table beside her, and frowned. 'It's going to be tricky, sadly. I can't have your death spoil my front page news. I shall have to be a little more . . . ingenious.' She began pacing the floor a few feet away from me, lost in her gruesome thoughts.

Down by my side, my bag dangled open from my shoulder. Suzanne hadn't bothered to remove it. With a jerk, I swung it over onto my legs, spilling out its contents: keys, mints, phone . . . I arched on the balls of my feet, ground my teeth as the tape tugged at my ankles. My thumb was poised over the screen now.

'Tell me, Suzanne,' I said, 'why did you turn Scissor Sister into a brand promoting far-right propaganda?'

Suzanne's footfalls stopped; I saw her shrug. 'Sign of the times. Anyone with business acumen would do the same. Besides, I only give the people what they want.'

She started pacing again, clearly wanting more time to debate my fate. I needed to keep her distracted, make her talk. I tried again —'What did you make of that note against Holly? I mean, her being called a slut.'

A vein in Suzanne's forehead twitched. 'It was unexpected, but the timing couldn't have been more perfect.'

'Why's that?'

'When the news of her infidelity spread through town, I decided to exploit the situation to my advantage. It was me who wrote that anonymous letter to the committee.'

'I don't understand. Why would you sabotage your own store?'

She shrugged. 'The store was nothing more than a façade. I needed Denise Drummond to make me persona non grata, to use some petty moral grounds against me. That way I could focus all my attention on the factory.'

'A real stroke of genius.'

My sarcasm completely passed over her. 'Thank you, but I like the dismissal part better. Or, should I say, when I faked being dismissed by Scissor Sister.' She laughed. 'You should have seen the look on these women's faces—*Poor, poor Suzanne.*'

'My mother never thought that of you.'

'Your mother behaved like a right cow,' she snapped. 'But I'm glad you offered your services to redo my store. Nice job, Chloe! I'll consider it family payback.'

I suddenly felt very sorry for Colin, wishing I had never involved him in all this.

'But why did you kill Cordelia?'

Suzanne flapped a hand in the air and sighed, as though the question was tedious to the extreme. 'I had to get rid of her,' she said, matter of fact. 'She knew too much. Shame I didn't make it look like a suicide.'

I shook my head. 'It's too late, Suzanne. The whole town knows her death wasn't an accident. In fact, the police will be here any minute now. I spoke to the chief inspector yesterday, and—'

She started to laugh, a horrible, high-pitched laugh that made the hairs on my arms stand on end.

'How naïve you are. Did it even occur to you why the police never launched a formal investigation? Why Matthew and Holly's deaths were recorded as accidents? You couldn't even see that Gordon and I had been working together all along.'

I folded forward in my chair, suddenly spent. The realisation was like a punch to the stomach.

No one knew I was here.

No one could help me.

'What is he getting out of this?' I asked in a whisper.

'Oh, just a ten percent share of all Scissor Sister's profits,' she smirked. 'Enough to make sure your little friend Josh Stanmore rots in jail for a long time.'

'You won't get away with this, Suzanne.'

Her eyes were filled with pity. 'I already did.' Then, staring down at the phone on my legs, she snatched it, amused. 'What were you planning to do with it? Call a friend?'

She clunked it down on a sewing table, out of my grasp, then moved towards the filing cabinet and unlocked the top drawer. She began sifting through it—suddenly plucking a pair of surgical gloves from within and put them on, the tight rubber snapping into place. Then, something gleamed in her hands: a long pair of silver scissors.

I could feel a hollow form in the pit of my stomach.

'These are my favourites,' she said, running a finger along one of the blades. 'People often underestimate how versatile sharp scissors can be. Tyres are a little unpredictable, but then I had to deal with a moving target.' A slow smile spread across her face as she turned to me. 'That won't be the case this time.'

My head buzzed with panic. I pulled at the tape on my wrists, but it barely budged.

Suzanne tutted. 'Don't be like this, Chloe. I promise to make it as painless as I can.'

She looked at the set of steel pigeonholes next to her. Her hand paused over the row of blue names, her index finger pointing—a silent game of Eeny, Meeny, Miny, Moe—and then settled on one of them.

'Tsvetana!' she exclaimed. 'She fled Bulgaria to seek refuge in England with her two little boys. Nice girl, sad story. God knows what the poor thing would be doing without me. Probably prostitution.'

I swallowed past the dryness in my throat. 'What are you going to do with me, Suzanne?'

She dropped her scissors back in the drawer and crouched by my side. 'Let me explain. You became horribly jealous when you found out I was manning the factory. So you came all the way up here to kill me. You broke through the door, left your fingerprints— everywhere— and threatened Tsvetana, who was working on her own. She panicked and killed you in an act of self-defence. A pair of scissors plunged straight through your heart.'

I stared at her. 'No one will believe this. Tsvetana isn't even here.'

Suzanne shrugged. 'Doesn't matter. I'll bribe her.'

'You're sick,' I spat.

'Oh, come on, Chloe. Imagine the publicity stunt! Everyone will be dying to put their grubby little hands on our story.' Her gaze was distant for a moment, her smile nauseatingly blissful. 'Nothing sells like tragedy.'

'Suzanne, you don't have to—'

'It's time to say goodbye.'

She stood up and marched back towards the drawer. My stomach was churning. My head was spinning with fear, a sickening sense of panic.

Suddenly, a noise outside, something rhythmic: the sound of running boots. The front metal door banged. Someone jiggled the handle forcefully.

'Police! Open up right now.'

Suzanne froze. It wasn't Gordon's voice, and for a second she seemed unsure what to do. She yanked off her gloves, dropped them along with the scissors inside the drawer, and locked it.

With a crash, the front door flew open . . .

'Police!' a man shouted. 'Hands in the air!'

I couldn't put my hands in the air but Suzanne slowly raised hers, her chin held high in defiance. Two more men in dark uniforms and helmets burst through the door, quickly followed by a senior officer with a dusting of salt-and-pepper stubble on his face. And then, right behind him, Josh.

I felt my heart surge when he rushed to my side.

'Chloe,' he whispered and gently unpeeled the tape off my ankles and wrists; I watched it fall to the ground into long, sticky black curls.

'This man is an impostor,' Suzanne said angrily. 'Why did you release him?' She dropped her hands and turned to the senior officer, who introduced himself as Detective Inspector Townsend.

'We're aware of that fact, Mrs Paige. What's not clear to us, however, is the clandestine nature of your activities.'

Suzanne stared at him in shock. Then she sighed and looked down modestly. 'I'm almost ashamed to admit it, but it's true, Detective Inspector. I've decided to make use of the defunct factory again. I can assure you my sole concern was to bring jobs back to the community.'

'When did you reopen?'

'Three weeks ago.'

*Lie.*

'And what is this young lady,' he said, pointing at me, 'doing strapped to a chair?'

Suzanne glared at me. 'Her name is Chloe Westfield. She came to see me last week and offered her help to redo my store. I should never have trusted her—I should have known she had an ulterior motive. The truth is, she resented my success, Detective Inspector. She quietly sneaked in to kill me, but I got the better of her.' Suzanne paused, raised a shaky hand to her face. 'I'm so glad you're here now. I can hardly believe my own luck.'

'Liar,' snapped Josh. 'Chloe is innocent. You're the murderer.'

Suzanne's hand flew to her chest in outraged shock. 'Me? How dare you! I never in my whole life—'

Detective Inspector Townsend gave an awkward cough. 'Please, both of you. Perhaps we should ask the young lady—Miss Westfield, I believe—about her version of events.'

I could feel the floor lurching beneath my feet, blood rushing to my brain. I tried to settle my gaze on the detective inspector.

*Pause. Breathe.*

I opened my mouth to speak, but the words were fluttering through my head like wild, untamed butterflies.

'Please take your time, Miss Westfield.' He nodded in sympathy.

I was suddenly conscious of the beating of my heart—slow, slow, slow. Always one beat slower. Even Suzanne's words came to me in slow motion: 'See, Detective Inspector. She can't even deny it.'

A pair of blue eyes searching mine, anxious and pleading. 'Chloe?' Josh's voice. Distant. Alarmed.

He said something else to me, his mouth shaping the words, but the sound was distorted, his voice garbled as if heard through water. I smiled at him, but I was drowning. Slipping away.

She came to my rescue then.

Gliding through the group of policemen, she appeared before me more luminous than ever: not a nebulous grey shape, no teal-blue silk floating around her. She was translucent yet whole.

'You must go back, Chloe.'

I squeezed my eyes closed for a moment. My legs and arms were feeling strangely leaden and featherlike at the same time; two distinct sensations and yet the same one—as though I was still bound to the chair and somehow floating above it. Heavy yet unburdened, like teetering on the edge between two worlds.

'You must go back, Chloe.'

I wanted to tell her I couldn't go back, that I just didn't have enough strength left in me. That life was seeping out of my starved body like sand through an hourglass. But she simply smiled—that beautiful luminous smile again—as though she already knew. A blazing white light pulsed around her as she reached out, her hand in mine almost solid, a searing energy shooting through my body like an electric shock.

My breath hissed as air filled my lungs.

And then I remembered . . .

The policemen stepped back to let me pass as I walked between the rows of sewing machines, where I found my phone on a far table. The screen showed an audio file, almost twenty minutes long. I pressed the red button to stop the recording, slid my thumb across the solid white bar to rewind to about halfway through. It was worth a try.

Then I turned the volume up.

Suzanne's voice crackled through the speaker: '*I had to get rid of her. She knew too much. Shame I didn't make it look like a suicide.*'

Behind me the silence gave way to commotion and noise. I caught sight of Holly floating out the open door, where she rose over the treetops among the birds flying free in the sky.

# EPILOGUE

The next morning many headlines trumpeted praise for Scissor Sister. Tabloids, in particular, were quick to churn out their nationalistic rhetoric:

**SCISSOR SISTER: TAKE BACK OUR COUNTRY AND FASHION INDUSTRY.**

**STOP MIGRANT FLOOD. BUY SCISSOR SISTER NOW!**

There were more, of course. Some were a little more subdued, others too sickening to mention. By midday, a cybercrime unit had broken into the SS intranet and reported a huge spike in online orders.

One final blaze of glory.

By evening, they'd pulled the plug.

The police searched every cranny of the factory, but only when they broke into the old workers' homes did they find the stockpiles of dresses: 3,248 Cleora clones in total. All sheathed with plastic covers and lined up on wheeled racks. Almost twice that number had already been shipped abroad.

As for the original Cleora, I found it hung on a padded velvet hanger in Suzanne's closet. When I ran my fingers along the silk, I smiled. No spark. No light. Peaceful and *un*cold.

After talking to Graham Holmes's eighty-year-old sister on the phone, I packed up the dress and walked to the post office, the sky above town cloudless.

· · ·

On Tuesday, Tina dropped in to announce she'd fortuitously bumped into the factory girls, including Martika ('That sweetie's got a right old dirty mind!').

I'd worried about those whose blue names had been in a row: Aniah, Elena, Magda, and mother of two Tsvetana, who had just lost their jobs.

And then out of the blue, Tina said, 'The committee gave us the thumbs up to reopen.'

'The factory?' I asked.

But Tina winked and refused to say more.

One thing she did confess was that she'd babbled about Patsy's affair to Mrs Foster. It turned out Mrs Foster was a close friend of Suzanne's.

On Thursday, Detective Inspector Townsend asked me to the police station to *tie up some loose ends.* He had set up temporary headquarters in Heavendale for the week, right in the office where I'd first met the chief inspector.

Josh had suspected an inside job all along, and had his contact at the Met do a background check on Gordon. He discovered that Gordon and Suzanne happened to be the same age and had attended the same secondary school in Carlisle. Gordon also had a strong background in IT, which explained why the SS intranet was so impervious to hacking. By the time of Josh's arrest, the matter had quickly escalated to the higher ranks.

Gordon Smith eventually confessed to deleting 'unwanted' police records. One of them involving the mention of strangulation marks on Cordelia's neck.

'Please sit down, Miss Westfield,' Townsend said when I entered.

As I expected, he had taken time to dissect my audio recording. He asked me a few questions (seemed relieved I'd recovered the power of speech), and supplied the obligatory frown at the part when Josh and I broke into Cordelia's home, though I didn't think he really minded. The detective inspector struck me as the kind of man for whom results trumped a certain lack of orthodoxy.

He sighed when he flipped back through his file. 'Have you heard of Francis Loncar?'

The name was familiar, thanks to a high-profile murder trial last year. A damning case, but Francis Loncar had completely turned it on its head. He was known as the 'Last- Ditch Guy,' the guy guilty people called in. Rich people.

'He's a famous attorney, right?'

Townsend nodded. 'He's now representing Suzanne Paige.'

I stared at him in shock. 'How can she afford him?'

'The money isn't coming from her. To be perfectly frank with you, we can't trace the source.'

'You mean . . .'

Townsend sighed again, shut his file. 'Someone is interested in replicating her frightening business model, Miss Westfield. A high-tech giant, a supermarket chain, or an insurance company—God knows. Of course, I'm speculating here. Mrs Paige may very well have a rich friend.'

I tried not to shiver at the thought of Suzanne walking out of court unscathed. *Could Scissor Sister exist under a different name? Could this really happen all over again?*

Downstairs, Josh waited patiently for me. He must have seen the anxiety on my face, because he rose from his chair and laced his fingers between mine.

I had scheduled an appointment with Doctor Andrews that afternoon, to start my treatment. Josh had insisted on being there too.

'Are you okay?' he asked.

I hope there will be a time when I can say I'm finally okay. That I am better, or maybe even healed. That the past will stop eating me from within. But for now, all I could do was nod at him and try.

'I'm so proud of you, Chloe.'

My heart fluttered a little as, hand in hand, we made our way to the door.

Across the road, my mother waved to me with a tentative smile.

# DID YOU ENJOY THIS BOOK?

## You can help make a difference for the author by showing your support!

Reviews are the most powerful tool in an author's arsenal when it comes to getting attention for their books. Honest reviews help bring the attention of other readers and spread the word so more people can enjoy the stories authors have to tell.

If you enjoyed this book, please consider taking a minute or two to leave a review on any of your sites.

## We appreciate your support!

## ACKNOWLEDGMENTS

Much thanks to my publisher, Meaghan Hurn, who walked me enthusiastically through this first-book thing, and to Rae Eckman, who helped me whittle this story into shape by giving invaluable feedback.

Gratitude also to my very first editor: Caroline Kaiser in Canada, who believed in this book so passionately that she spurred me on to query publishers and agents. Without you, *Cold Dresses* would most likely have gathered dust in the bottom drawer. I am eternally grateful.

Many thanks to my great circle of friends, particularly those who offered repeated advice, support, and good cheer while I was writing: Carolin Hollingsworth for your unwavering belief in me (*my dear, dear friend, where would I be without you?*), Paulo Andrade (*you too are a gem!*), and also Nadia Bennouna, Jason Swan, Barry Thomas, Giles Leslie, Maryrose D'Angelo, Bill & Anne Cooper, and my little brother, Alexandre, who always cheers me on. I'm sure I'm also indebted to a great many people who, at any point during this journey, provided kind words at crucial points, like when I was about to burn the damn thing.

Lastly, I'd like to thank my beloved husband, Lee Thomas, who knows just how long this journey has been and witnessed the highs and the lows. I wouldn't be here without you. Thanks for putting up with me and for loving me back.

# READ ON

- About the Author
- Book Club Questions
- Interview with the Author
- And Much More!

# ABOUT THE AUTHOR

David Pelletier was born in France of an Irish-Catalan mother and a French dad with Canadian roots. Now living in Watford with his British partner, he sometimes sees himself as an "international bastard".

A keen runner and sewing enthusiast (Yep, he sewed that plaid shirt), he dabbled in various career paths before devoting his energy to his true passion.

*Cold Dresses* is his debut novel.

Connect with David:

http://davidpelletierauthor.com/

On Instagram: @ davidp_author

# BOOK CLUB QUESTIONS

1. What was your initial reaction to the book? Did it hook you immediately or did it take time to develop and bring you in?
2. Do you think the story was plot-based or character driven?
3. What was your favorite quote/passage?
4. What made the setting unique or important? Could the story have taken place anywhere?
5. Did you pick out any themes throughout the book?
6. How credible/believable did you find the narrator? Do you feel like you got the true story?
7. How did the characters change throughout the story? Did your opinion of them change?
8. How did the structure of the book effect the story?
9. Which character did you relate to the most, and what was it about them that you connected with?
10. How did you feel about the ending? What did you like, what did you not like, and what do you wish had been different?
11. Did the book change your opinion or perspective on anything? Do you feel different now than you did before you read it?
12. The book is being adapted into a movie, who would you want to see play what parts?
13. What is your impression of the author?
14. Who is your favorite character and why?
15. If you could meet one of the characters right now, what would you say to them?

# INTERVIEW WITH THE AUTHOR

**Can you give us a few autobiographical words?**
I was born in France of an Irish-Catalan mother and a French dad with Canadian roots. In the late 1990's, I emigrated to Great Britain where I now live in Watford with my British husband.

**Do you have any formal education, credentials or honors you'd like to share? We love giving authors an opportunity to show off.**
I have a postgraduate degree in Interior Design & Architecture, although the only practice I've ever done was for friends or within the comfort of my home. It's fair to say I've forgotten most of it by now.

**Speaking of showing off, do you have bragging rights on anything that you'd like to share?**
I speak three languages and a half (I didn't stay long enough with my then Italian boyfriend to learn the other half).

**Why do you I write. Is there a philosophy behind the words?**
I tend to only write what's truly meaningful to me. Writing is a cathartic and healing process through which I speak my own truth. Although *Cold Dresses* is by no means autobiographical, it's based on themes that played an important part at one point or another in my life.

**Can you share with our readers what your favorite books are and why they're on your list?**
I tend to read more psychological thrillers than mysteries. My favourite author is Gillian Flynn. *Sharp Objects* is definitely a

favourite of mine! More recently, I've really enjoyed *Goodnight Beautiful* by Aimee Molloy.

## Can you tell us a little about your writing style?

I don't particularly like florid language. I wouldn't say my writing is sparse but I tend to avoid long, unnecessary descriptions. I strive for sincerity and authenticity when describing my characters' journey.

## What's your writing process like?

I'm a slow writer going through bouts of procrastination and struggling to stick to a daily word count. Saying that, I constantly think of ways to improve the story until I reach a place that feels 'true' to me. That's when the words start to flow, but I usually have to peel off a lot of layers before I reach that very special place.

## Do you have any Professional & Literary Affiliations?

I subscribed to Jericho Writers last October.

## What are you working to accomplish?

It's a difficult question to answer. The fact I'm soon to become a traditionally published writer is a dream come true for me. Healing is an important part of the process. Ultimately you hope your writing can entertain people as much as it can touch them. And make them think too!

## Do you have any works in-progress?

I'm currently working on my second novel. It's not a complete departure from *Cold Dresses* but it certainly has a different flavour. All I can say is that it's shaping up as a psychological thriller rather than a mystery.

**What are some fun facts about Cold Dresses?**

I initially named the first draft *A Pattern to Die For*, which was rather humorous at the time but with zero tension throughout. The whole thing was an absolute mess!

**Anything else you'd like to let our readers know about you?**

There's a quote by Confucius that I try to live by whenever life gets hard: *Our greatest glory is not in never falling, but in rising every time we fall.* Oh, and thank you for buying my book!

## ABOUT THE EDITOR

**A New Look On Books**
**Raven Eckman, Editor**

Raven is a freelance editor by night and fangirl at every other available opportunity.

She always knew books were her passion, well after her grandmother's challenge to read a book a day and obtained her B.A. in English with a concentration in Creative Writing from Arcadia University.

Currently, she is drowning in her TBR list, revising her second WIP, and expanding her freelancing business-all while looking for more bookish things to get involved with.

She is active on Twitter, Instagram and sometimes Facebook when she remembers.

**Editor Links:**

**Website:** https://anewlookonbooks.com/

**Twitter:** @rceckman

**Instagram:** @anewlookonbooks

## ABOUT THE BOOK DESIGNER

**Triumph Book Covers**
**Diana TC, Designer**

Diana Toledo Calçado, better known as Diana TC, was born in 1996 and grew up in Azores, Portugal.

She has been heavily influenced by her artistic family and has studied multiple forms of art while growing up, from metal embossing to traditional ceramic tile painting.

She now freelances full-time creating book covers, specializing in the genres of Fantasy, Paranormal, Romance, and Suspense. She also works on original illustrations, fine art, and writes her own novels during her free time.

**Designer Links:**
   **Website: www.triumphbookcovers.com**
   **Facebook:** @triumphcovers

## ABOUT THE PUBLISHER

Hurn Publications is the proud publisher of great writers and gifted storytellers, beloved books and eminent works.
We believe that literature can fuel the imagination and guide the soul.
There is a book on our shelves for every reader, and we relish the opportunity to publish across every category and interest with the utmost care, attention to diverse inclusion and enthusiasm.

**Find your next great read: www.hurnpublications.com**

**HP Newsletter Signup**

Signing up for our newsletter gets you **Book Reviews, Books On Tour, Cover Reveals, Giveaways** and **Book Sales** delivered right to your inbox.
Stay up to date in the Indie Publishing world!

Link: https://www.subscribepage.com/hurnpublications

# COPYRIGHTS PAGE

Paperback: 978-1-7347634-2-3
eBook: 978-1-7364509-2-5
Hardback: 978-1-7364509-8-7
Library of Congress Control Number: 2021930749

First Edition: July 2021
Edited by: Raven Eckman of A New Look On Books
Book Cover Designer: Diana TC, www.triumphcovers.com
Hurn Publications | Temple, TX www.hurnpublications.com

CPSIA information can be obtained
at www.ICGtesting.com
Printed in the USA
FSHW011806170621
82473FS